SANCTUM

A DARK BRATVA ARRANGED MARRIAGE ROMANCE

WICKED VOWS
BOOK 2

JANE HENRY

Sanctum: A Dark Mafia Arranged Marriage Romance

Copyright © 2024 by Jane Henry

Cover photography by Michelle Lancaster

Cover art by Popkitty

TRIGGER WARNING

Please note: this book contains themes and depictions that may be triggering or distressing to some readers. Please be advised of the following content:

- **Sexual Assault:** There are references to sexual assault and its aftermath throughout the narrative.

Reader discretion is advised, and if this theme is potentially harmful to you, please consider your well-being before proceeding.

Playlist

Scan QR Code to listen to the playlist for
'Sanctum: A Dark Bratva Arranged Marriage
Romance" on Spotify©

SYNOPSIS

When I run, he always chases.

Where I go, he always follows.

Primal, Powerful, Possessive.

Aleksandr Romanov is my nemesis...

And my new husband.

He thinks I'm the spoiled mafia princess.

That I have the world at my fingertips.

I may be his new wife,

But he doesn't know the real me.

No one does.

But when Aleksandr touches me,

He cuts me wide open,

As if trying to see the secrets I hide.

Every touch becomes foreplay,

Every look stokes our passion.

Our hatred turns to obsession.

But when he unearths the secrets I've kept well hidden from the world...

I have nowhere left to hide.

No one to save me from the truth,

No one to save me from my enemies...

No one to save me from the only man I've ever loved.

CHAPTER ONE

Aleksandr

"I'LL DO whatever it takes, Mikhail. Whatever our family fucking needs." When I close my eyes, I can still see my brother Lev, his face beaten to a bloody pulp. Unrecognizable. It was a threat, a thinly veiled warning meant to send a message to my brothers: *we're watching.*

Jumped after a late-night gym session, it was five against one. Lev is a formidable opponent, but his pair of fists didn't stand a chance against the pack of five masked men wielding broken bottles, a length of pipe, and a goddamn baseball bat.

We'll find who did this and when we do, they'll wish they were never fucking born. But until then, we have to plan our next move strategically.

My older brother Mikhail paces in front of me, his hands shoved into his pockets. The blue light from our computer monitors casts shadows on the floor of his dimly lit office.

We've been at this all damn night. Empty pizza boxes are piled haphazardly in a corner of the room, the emergency stash of vodka long gone. The entire atmosphere of the room is charged, the weight of our decision impacting all of us.

We haven't been able to find out who beat him. Not yet. But we got the message. The death of our enemy Fyodor Volkov was only the beginning.

I pinch the bridge of my nose, my eyes stinging from staring at the computer screen for way too long.

Mikhail blows out a breath. "I know. That's the problem, Aleks. I want to be sure bringing the Bianchis in through marriage is the best next move."

I push away from the desk and stretch, my muscles aching from lifting earlier and sitting too damn long. On instinct, I glance at my phone to check the security details of our family. I'm always on hyperalert, but ever since Lev took a beating, I'm damn near glued to the screen.

I glance through the list of everyone who isn't present. My mother and Polina are both at home, Viktor and Nikko in their homes, our younger brother Ollie in Moscow. Lev is still in the hospital. I can fit my entire world in the palm of my hand.

The security cameras show nothing out of place, including the two men we have in holding we transported back here to America from Russia.

I sit back down while Mikhail continues to pace.

"Mikhail, it's probably best we don't make decisions when we've been up all night." Kolya leans back in his chair and strokes his beard threaded with silver. The group master-mind, my late father's war buddy, Kolya's taken on the position of father figure of the group even though he's only half a generation older than we are and younger than my father was.

While Mikhail and I have changed into tees and jeans, Kolya's still more formally attired in a dress shirt and neatly pressed pants. He's well-meaning but ought to know by now you don't talk me or Mikhail into letting anything go when the security of our family's at stake.

Still, Kolya tries. "Go to bed. Go home to Aria."

"Home to Aria?" Mikhail's wife Aria appears in the doorway, wearing Mikhail's tee and sweats, the only clothes that apparently fit her when she's stuck in the office nine months pregnant. Her hair's in a messy bun, her glasses perched on the edge of her nose. She has a laptop in one hand and a large plastic cup filled with something vibrantly pink, in the other. "I've been here working in between naps the whole time, I just didn't want anything to do with the vodka shots for obvious reasons."

Before Aria came, I was the group cybersecurity expert...at least ostensibly. We all knew the real job I got paid the big bucks for doing was hacking — until Aria showed me she was better. I've gotten over it, though, mostly because she isn't just better than *I* am. She's better than anyone in the goddamn world.

Aria isn't well-versed in Bratva business, though, which is why she sticks to some jobs, and I do others.

"C'mere." Mikhail sits in his office chair and gestures for her to come to him. She sidles onto his lap and plunks her computer on the desk. The real reason she's here is because Mikhail doesn't let her out of his sight. Not that I blame him. If I cared for anyone half as much as he does her, I wouldn't let them out of my sight either.

"I've been listening to everything you said, I just needed to do so in a comfortable position." She nestles in against my brother. "Though if I knew you were *this* comfortable..."

He kisses her temple and wraps his arms around her, whispering something I can't hear in her ear.

I look back at my computer, a headache brewing behind my eyes.

"Aria, what's your take?" I ask. If there's anything I love about my sister-in-law, it's that she is absolutely Mensa-level brilliant, likely the smartest person I've ever met. Just for fun, she learned *Russian* in a few short months. She can out-code anyone in the goddamn world. In the digital age, having the world's best hacker on our team puts us at a decided advantage.

But even Aria hasn't been able to identify the perpetrators.

"Alright, I'll fill you boys in on what I'm thinking here." Her fingers fly over the keyboard like she's performing a magic trick. "We have two informants that we can trust, and I think—"

"*Maybe* trust," I interrupt. "I'm not convinced. You know we haven't released them yet, right?"

Mikhail's eyes narrow on me. He doesn't like that I interrupted his wife, but we can deal with that later if he wants to be a dick about it.

"You still don't trust them?" she asks, her eyebrows rising. "Seriously?"

"Of course not."

"What will it take?" she asks, giving me a curious look.

"A decided show of loyalty. Some skin in the game. Talk is cheap." I shrug. "They need to fucking bleed for us before I'll trust them."

"I agree," Mikhail says soberly.

"As do I." Kolya nods in agreement.

"Alright, alright," Aria says, shaking her head. "Simmer down. All I was going to say was that they might be able to point you in the right direction."

I shake my head and Mikhail and I respond in unison. "No."

Aria sighs. "This is driving me batshit crazy."

"You and me both," I mutter. "The masks mean we can't use facial recognition."

She contemplates her laptop screen. "And the quality of the video looks like an iPhone at a rave. I just think your prisoners might have some useful info is all."

Dmitri Petrov and Pavel Kuznetsov turned tail on their former mob after the death of their *pakhan*, Fyodor Volkov. Before he hung himself in prison, Volkov's life mission was to decimate my family. He kept his men at odds and controlled them with intimidation tactics. There were no leaders, a sham of a hierarchy, and in the wake of his death, they've begun to fall apart.

Petrov and Kuznetsov turned themselves in to Mikhail following Volkov's suicide. We've had them in holding now for several months. They haven't had any contact with former associates. I would know because they're under my charge.

"Maybe if you sent *me* in."

Mikhail curses and grips her more tightly. "Are you out of your mind? *Khristos,* Aria. You're not going anywhere near them."

"But if I could ask the right—"

"*Enough.*" Mikhail rarely raises his voice to her but what she's suggesting is unthinkable. For all we know, they could be moles. Patient moles, but moles nonetheless.

With a sigh, Aria logs out and leans back thoughtfully against Mikhail. "Do you guys know about the sequoia tree?"

Jesus. I clench my jaw to keep from snapping. I'm fucking tired and I don't want some fucking science quiz—

"Aleks." My gaze snaps to Mikhail. He doesn't say another word. My name is only a warning. It's uncanny how he can read my mind.

I blow out a breath and shut my laptop. My eyes need a break anyway. "Yes. The sequoia tree is one of the largest in the world. They can grow up to something like three hundred feet in height and they're so big in circumference, some of them have actual tunnels large enough for cars to drive through them. What about them?"

Aria gives me that smug look she sometimes gets when she beats me in a hacking race. She's lucky I love her like a sister.

"And what can you tell me about their roots, Aleksandr?" she asks in a tone a teacher might use when asking a student to recite the alphabet.

I'd tell her to fuck off, but Mikhail's watching and I still value my life.

"Don't know anything about the roots," I admit through gritted teeth.

Aria's eyes glow with triumph. She loves one-upping me.

"One might *think* they have massive roots, right? But no, they don't. Their roots are quite shallow. It isn't the *depth* of their roots that makes them so sturdy but how far they spread."

Kolya's eyes twinkle at her. He slowly nods, and Mikhail gives her a little squeeze.

"You guys are *sequoias*. Kings of the jungle. Volkov *who?* Good riddance. He *thought* he was going to overtake you guys, but no way. And lucky for you, he was so full of himself he practically self-destructed on his way out."

She fires up her laptop again. "So yeah, you're right. This isn't looking good. While you're strong *financially*, our group is comparatively small. While you're strong *physically*, you're still lacking reliable manpower to fortify. And while we're doing our best to grow," she says, patting her ample belly, "it will take time that we really don't have. Mikhail was right when he suggested a marriage with the

Bianchi family, Aleks. We need to consider further unions as well for the other men."

"Yes. We've suffered three physical attacks and two cyberattacks since Volkov's death. We aren't the only ones who want to capitalize on his demise," Kolya says. "We need to solidify our alliances sooner than later. We can't underestimate the potential for ruin if we don't."

My mind whirs. "Right. What does Bianchi bring to the table?"

"Connections," Mikhail says. "I agree with Kolya. We need to secure an alliance that fortifies our defenses. We need a lifeline."

Aria nods. "Right. Also, you guys, we've looked at accounting, and while you are all still richer than God, some of your investments have gone belly-up. While you've all been hard at work establishing yourselves as the premier Bratva group here in The Cove, others have been trying to do the same."

The Cove, nestled in the heart of New York, smack dab between Coney Island and Manhattan, is our stomping ground, the place we own.

I draw in a ragged breath as a chilling clarity cuts through my fuzzy haze of exhaustion. The burden of what happens rests squarely on my shoulders. We don't have the luxury of time anymore. Every second that passes could mean my family's demise.

"There's no more time. My marriage to Harper Bianchi has to happen *now*."

I hold Mikhail's gaze and hide my clenched fists. I can't put into words why the thought of a loveless marriage makes me want to hurl my laptop against the wall of his office. I thought by now I'd have gotten used to the idea. It isn't the first time we've discussed it, but I thought I still had a few more months to warm up to the idea.

It's only a wedding.

For life. To a woman I don't love and haven't even met.

But I owe this to my family.

I swallow the anger that boils inside me at the thought of what I have to do.

Mikhail's still holding my gaze.

"Your loyalty to the brotherhood is admirable, Aleksandr," he says softly.

I despise what I have to do to prove it.

I loved once, and once is enough for a lifetime. I know I'll never love again. The least I can do is bring peace to my family.

I owe this to my brothers. To my family. If someone ever got to my sister Polina, or my mother, or, God forbid, Mikhail and Aria's innocent baby... I'd never forgive myself.

I won't make the same mistake twice.

My phone buzzes with a text. Mikhail nods, silent permission to check it.

I stare at the screen. "Speak of the fucking devil."

CHAPTER TWO

Harper

"LIFT YOUR CHIN UP. And for Christ's sake, Harper, stop scowling."

Ironically, my mother scowling at me for scowling doesn't make me want to plaster on a grin. Still, I don't want to listen to her criticism, so I lift my chin and force the smallest of smiles. The truth is, I'm not even *scowling*. I'm tired, and I don't feel like being used for the hundredth time. I also don't want to have to contend with her rage, so I deal. It's a "pick your battles" kind of situation.

"There, that's better," she says, lifting my chin. I blink under the harsh glare of overhead lighting. "Harper, have you been eating dairy again? What did I tell you it does to your complexion? There's only so much foundation and primer one can use, you know."

I sigh and clamp my lips tight to prevent the powder she's dabbing on my nose from going in my mouth, but there's the added benefit of not having to respond. Internally I tell her that the occasional tiny, barely perceptible pink dots on my chin probably have more to do with stress than an ice cream cone, but whatever.

I close my eyes. I learned a trick when I was a little girl that if I close my eyes when she's primping me, I can pretend I'm getting ready for the big screen. *Pretend it's your team preparing you for the set.*

"Good. Hold still. Your eyebrows are coming in again. Jesus, I thought we just plucked them."

I open one eye. While she's normally high-strung and irritable, this is heading to an advanced level even for her. I flinch when she ruthlessly tweezes a few eyebrow hairs as if they personally offended her.

"Not too much," I protest. "It will make the skin all red and red's harder to cover up."

Pursing her lips in a thin line, she stands back and admires her handiwork. She scrutinizes my brows, my hair, my makeup, then gives me a nod. "You look beautiful," she says coldly, without a hint of warmth or actual appreciation. She's only being pragmatic and admiring the work she did.

There was a time when I could've said the same for her, but the years of covering up my father's backhands have taken their toll.

It's only when I see her lower lip tremble that I really begin to think that something's *really* off.

I look around the room.

"Where's the ring light?" I ask. By now, she should have gotten the ring light, the camera, and everything set to record and film my next splash on social media.

"Mom?" My heart begins to beat faster. "What's going on here?"

Biting her lip, she doesn't respond. Her eyes are shimmering with...*tears?*

What the hell? I can't remember ever seeing my mother cry.

"Mom," I say in a whisper, silently begging her to tell me something, anything, to let me know she's half-human and I'm more to her than a pawn sliding across a chessboard.

A sharp knock sounds at the door.

"Time to go." It's my brother Saul.

Go...where?

She straightens her shoulders and presses her lips into a thin line.

"What's going on?" I ask, my voice hardening. When she doesn't answer, I turn and yank open the bedroom door.

Saul stands in the hallway, a mini, slimmer version of my dad, his brows knit together. "Jesus fucking Christ," he mutters. "Took you long enough."

"If I'd known you were waiting, I'd have taken longer."

Unruffled, he looks past me to Mom. "You didn't tell her shit, did you?"

My stomach drops. What games are they playing with me now? "Tell me *what?*"

That's when I notice Saul's dressed in a *suit*. The only times I've ever seen him wear a suit was to funerals. This can't be good.

He shakes his head and takes a step toward me so he can grip me by the arm. "You'll see. And I'm telling you now, Harper, don't you even *think* about running."

My pulse spikes. I'm dizzy. I know exactly what my family's capable of.

If he's telling me not to run – then he's planning something that's going to make me want to. Are they making me fly to Italy again? Oh, God. *No.* I can't leave, not again. I *have* to stay here. I'm needed here.

They like to give me shit for running but none of them know the real reason.

Saul curses under his breath as he marches me downstairs, his hand still tight on my arm. "Will you let go of me? I'm not going anywhere."

He holds me tight. "She should've told you. Why did you think she made you get changed into something nice?"

My heart beats so fast I'm dizzy.

"Because we were doing a photo shoot. So I could post online, obviously." I throw his own words back at him. "It's my job, remember? How I earn my keep? It's what I'm supposed to do."

"*Did*," he says with a sigh. "I didn't want to be the one to tell you, and I wasn't gonna tell you before it was time, but now you need to know."

Ice courses through my veins. I swallow, trying to quell my rising nerves but it doesn't seem to satisfy the unease.

He's walking me down the length of the hallway to the stairs, our steps noiseless on the thick carpet. This house is enormous. What most people don't know is that three quarters of the rooms are vacant.

"So are you going to tell me or what?" I ask, my voice betraying me. The relentless quaking won't stop.

He clenches his teeth. Stops marching me for a minute. Finally shakes his head and says in a rush of words, "Your future husband's here."

Before I can recover from the blow of what he just said, he grips my arm so hard I wince in pain. "No. Fucking. Running. I swear to God, I'll kill you if you run. We're here to discuss the details and if you fuck this up, there'll be hell to pay."

My mind is still stuck on... Future. *Husband.*

Of course I knew the chances of me being married off to someone were pretty high, but you think about it the same way you think about death. It's there, it will come, but why worry about that now when it's eons away?

I'm twenty years old. I haven't even graduated college yet.

I think back to the look my mother had and the sinking feeling her obvious distress gave me. She loves to parade me around and cash in the clicks, and they love to take every penny I get, but this... this is different.

I try to yank my arm out of my brother's grip, but it's too tight. His fingers are digging into me so hard it'll bruise.

We start walking again, this time at a faster pace and his grip has tightened.

"I won't run," I say tightly. "You're hurting me."

"I don't trust you." The impeccable carpet flies under our feet, the scent of lavender cleanser hitting my nose. My mother's prepared for our guest, probably all day. How could I have missed this?

I try to get a grip as my mind reels. I try to coach my way through it.

I've been through way worse than this. I can handle whatever this is.

And he didn't say I'm getting married today.

I can go play nice, pretend I'm docile... then find my way out. I've done it many times over the years. They've always found me, and there have always been repercussions, but I can do it. I know I can.

Do I hear a voice? I try not to imagine which one of the assholes my father hangs out with thinks he's going to take me home.

Will it be the bald guy with the gold tooth? The one that's always telling me I'm so pretty, and patting me on the head or copping a feel when he gets a chance? Will it be one of my brother's many friends, reeking of pot and whiskey? Or some no-name don from Italy who wants a trophy wife?

It doesn't matter who it is because I know how all of these men operate. I've spent my entire life as the daughter of a mobster.

They'll take you and doll you up for a little while. Then they'll placate you with house cleaners, extravagant vacations, and credit cards so you'll overlook the way they reek of another woman's perfume when they come to bed at night. Some demand order with the back of their hands. But none of them, not one, is ever loyal or faithful. If I'm lucky, he'll be the type that will let me do what I want as long as I don't scream at him when he decides to fuck some pretty little thing.

I won't go, though.

I can't.

The door opens. I lose the ability to speak when I hear the sound of a deep, accented voice, cold as ice and harsh as stone.

My knees shake, knocking into each other.

I thought by now I would've gotten braver, but I haven't. I'm as terrified as ever, just like that night...

No, I can't think of that now. I can't think of anything except going along with whatever happens so I can get through this before I plan my escape.

I've been stashing away some money from tutoring. It's not a lot, but it's enough to buy me time to get a cheap hotel and food when I'm on the run.

And I *will* be on the run. It's complicated, though. So fucking complicated.

Saul and I stand at the closed doorway of the living room. "Smile big and watch your mouth. None of your fucking bullshit, Harper, or I swear to God..."

"What? You gonna pull this in front of my future husband? He's cool with that?" At least my brother won't be able to smack me around while he hands me over to someone who'll probably fill his shoes.

"Harper," he grits through his teeth.

Asshole.

I thought I missed him when he enlisted. There were a handful of times when I was younger that he actually saved my ass. Once I even thought we were a team. He went to bat for me, risking my father's wrath, even when my mother wouldn't. But something shifted when he came back. He was a changed man and no longer my ally.

Saul opens the door. I feel like I'm going to be sick.

"There she is." My father's booming voice makes me jump. I hate that I'm so skittish.

I remind myself of the only person who ever smiles when she sees me. The only person who loves me for who I am, no more, no less. And it's for her sake that I'll put on the brave face I've been taught to wear just to get through this.

I straighten my shoulders, the stranger still hidden behind the doorway. My father's wearing his fake smile, the one that stretches his lips but doesn't warm his eyes. Beads of sweat stand out on his receding hairline, his usual ruddy complexion even redder than normal after a few drinks.

"Harper, sweetheart. Come in and meet our guest."

A chill skates between my shoulder blades. He's pouring it on thick.

"*Go*," Saul hisses. He gives me a merciless tug so hard I lose my footing. My heel catches on the doorframe and I tumble into the room, my hands fly in front of me to grab onto something to right myself... and land on the warm, unyielding, hard-as-hell frame of my future husband.

Sometimes in Hallmark movies, it's cute how a woman stumbles, and her would-be suitor catches her, all gallant and charming. He might help stack the books that tumbled out of her arms after a wholesome trip to the library, or heroically offer to buy her another cup of coffee. Their eyes meet, their breath catches, Cupid twangs his arrow—and the rest is history.

There's a reason that's fiction.

My suitor catches my arms and pins me in place like I'm an errant bird that needs to be put back in her cage. He holds me in front of him, his glacial blue eyes glaring at me.

This one definitely doesn't look old and sleezy... not with that hard jaw made more angular with his scowl, and short-cropped black hair that somehow makes his blue eyes look like they're chiseled from ice. There's no greasy hair or yellowed teeth, no stench of cigars or scent of stale alcohol. No. His well-tailored suit hugs his strong frame, the breadth of his shoulders alone casting me in shadow. He's calm and collected, not leering or swaggering. In short, he's the opposite of the men I've known, and the effect momentarily shocks me.

Or is he?

His rugged handsomeness exudes confidence and power... but something tells me to beware.

He carries an air of authority and a hint of power that exudes alpha male. King of the forest. Everything about him commands obedience, as if he rules my house even though he has no such claims on my family. It's disarming, because a man like him doesn't belong in the presence of my father and brother. He's a king among jesters, and he's staring at me with a derisive curl of his lips. I feel about two feet tall and as awkward as a child learning how to walk.

"Your daughter's clumsy, Bianchi," he says with a downturn of his brows. He's the complete opposite of anything I've imagined.

"You should watch your step," he snaps, in a voice tinged with that accent again.

Lovely. He's a stunningly gorgeous *jerk*.

Experience tells me that the best way to avoid being punished is simply by not talking. I mentally wire my jaw shut even though I'm seething. My brother practically pushed me and even if I *had* tripped—

His large, strong hands are still on my arms. His grip on me feels charged, as if electric pulses are vibrating through his palms. I feel out of sorts and don't know what to do with myself. When he catches my gaze, he releases me.

"Sit," he orders, pointing wordlessly to a vacant couch. "Your father and I have business to discuss."

I narrow my eyes at him to let him know I won't be rolling over and playing fetch for him. But I acquiesce this time since it's only our first meeting and maybe we'll have further chaperoned meetings to look forward to.

Yay.

The men all take seats, Saul next to me.

"My name is Aleksandr Romanov," he says to my brother. He's barely even looking at me. "You know my brother Mikhail."

"I do," Saul says, appearing too earnest, too eager, like a kid hoping to get some attention from the hero he worships. "I got him out of the big house, and he promised to marry off my sister before it's too late." He barks out a mirthless laugh. "Harper, meet Aleksandr Romanov." I wait for him to say "your future husband" but he doesn't have the balls.

"Pleased to meet you," I lie with a sickly sweet smile I hope gives him indigestion.

He doesn't return the civility but only stares at me impassively.

"Mr. Romanov has come here today with a request," my father says, his eyes twinkling greedily. My stomach drops when the sound of my mother clearing her throat startles me. When did she come in here? I look over at her and she wordlessly pulls her shoulders back, a silent admonition to sit up straighter.

I straighten my posture and look away so she can't boss me around again. My entire life consists of people telling me what to do and it seems this guy who thinks he's actually marrying me is no exception.

"Yes?" I ask, when my father doesn't continue.

My father fidgets and gives a subtle nod to my brother. Why, I have no idea.

"The Romanovs are in need of an alliance sooner than we'd planned," my father continues. "That's good news for you, Harper. Mr. Romanov is prepared to make you his wife. I've agreed to this arrangement. We'll be making final plans by the end of this month."

I stare, keeping my face impassive while I quickly do the math. It's the sixth. That gives me just over three weeks.

Alright, then. Plenty of time to plan my escape.

Aleksandr purses his lips, clearly displeased. "That wasn't what I said."

I blink, surprised at his boldness. No one talks back to my father. The red splotches on his cheeks tell me he's holding himself back. He wants this suitor. Likely *needs* this arrangement.

If he was kinder to me, I might feel bad for what I'm planning to do.

"Oh?" my father asks tightly. "What do you have in mind, Mr. Romanov?"

"Apologies for any misunderstandings." God, I have literally never met a single other person who lied as well as my father and this man. The fake civilities are sickening. "I'd like to move on our agreement promptly. You know what we have to offer you, Bianchi. The offer's only valid for twenty-four hours."

What on earth is he offering my father? My father's greedy eyes nearly bulge out of his head as he nods, his jowls shaking with enthusiasm.

"How soon are you thinking, sir?"

Aleksandr swivels his gaze to me and pinches his lips together. Instead of answering my father, he questions me. "I'm told you have a penchant for running. Do you like to run, Harper?"

The fact that he's just called me out on the exact plan I have in mind makes me squirm uncomfortably. This is... not good.

I lick my lips and swallow, giving him a casual shrug. "I... used to when I was younger," I say, my voice strangely husky. It's true. As a child, I kept a suitcase packed and ready to go so I could escape. I'd be punished every time, but it was worth it to pretend I wasn't under my mother's thumb for a little while.

"Lying won't be tolerated either," he says in a clipped tone. "I happen to know that the last time you ran was six months ago."

My cheeks burn with indignation. How does he know that about me?

My brother shakes his head. "I already told them the truth and what he can expect. There's a reason we've made a move to make this happen sooner than later."

But there's a reason why I "run," and it has nothing to do with what they think.

I'm not a child. I don't run into oncoming traffic.

I find a way to escape so I can visit in private. And then I always return home, like a bird flying back to her gilded cage.

I turn my head away and don't look at him.

The stranger clucks his tongue. "You've spoiled her, Bianchi."

My brother squeezes my arm. I bite my cheek to keep from snapping back. I'm not like the other Italian princesses. I don't have a penny to my name. No credit cards. No allowance.

"Spoiled?" my father says with a forced laugh. "I like to think she's experienced and maybe a little indulged."

Hardly. Another lie.

"You've arranged a marriage for me with a wife who's rebellious, flighty, and clumsy, her only merit being mediocre good looks. In Russia, she wouldn't hold a candle to most women." He shakes his head. "Do you have any other daughters?"

Oh yeah? Well he can take his high-and-mighty ass *back* to Russia as far as I'm concerned. My nose stings and my cheeks flame as they continue to talk about me as if I'm a mannequin on display.

"Oh, I'm his one and only, and believe you me, I'm not spoiled," I snap. I clamp my lips together so I don't speak again when my mother gasps and my father glares at me. I have to choose my words carefully.

Romanov looks mildly amused if the faintest twinge of his lips are any indication. "Hmm. I have no other choices, and maybe I've misjudged. I never thought I'd be so lucky as to have a future wife who would be so demure."

Add sarcastic to the list. Excellent.

I cross my arms over my chest. "And *I* never thought I'd be so lucky as to have a future husband that was so gentle and kind. I did hope for mildly attractive, but I suppose beggars can't be choosers."

Fire burns in his eyes. "Life is just full of surprises, isn't it?"

"Indeed."

"Right, right," my father says, rubbing his hands together like the greedy asshole he is, ready to stroke the genie bottle and make his wish. "You say the offer is only valid for twenty-four hours, but we have no need. We'd like to move ahead with this arrangement."

Would we, now?

I tell myself to wait until he leaves, *then* make my plan. Bite my tongue. Hold strong.

"Perfect," Aleksandr says, briefly cutting his eyes to me. "We'll leave immediately. Thank you for agreeing."

Wait.

Immediately?

Even my mother looks shocked, her mouth agape and her posture stiffened, she flattens her well-manicured hand against her chest. "We, Mr. Romanov?"

He doesn't bother looking at her when he replies. "Yes. I want to be married by the weekend. I'll have my people draw up papers and send them to you."

My mother blanches, but my brother nods. He knew this. He fucking *knew* this.

I can't let him take me. If he takes me, there's no hope.

"I haven't packed anything. I'm not ready."

I'm grasping for excuses, desperately trying to rationalize why I can't simply *leave*. An overwhelming surge of panic floods me like icy water in my veins as dread as heavy as lead settles in my stomach. *I can't leave.*

"I packed her things," Saul says.

"No need," Aleksandr says, his accent thickening. "She won't need anything from home. She'll start fresh with me. I'll have my driver come around now." He lifts his phone to his ear and snaps something out in Russian.

Start.

Fresh.

I stare as he takes something out of his pocket. A... checkbook? Who uses checks these days?

My father's watery eyes gleam as he stares at the checkbook, like a dragon eying a pile of gold, drawn to it as if his life depended on it. If Romanov thinks he's actually going to get a dowry...

"I'll write you a check for all wedding expenses, under the condition that she comes back with me now."

"I don't know if that works for me," my father says, the lying, greedy bastard. He doesn't care at all about me, he's only trying to wheedle. "My daughter's innocence, Romanov..."

I look away, my throat tightening. He's painting me as a virgin. In the Italian mafia, virginity is practically a requirement for an arranged marriage.

But what about... in the Russian mafia? How does this work?

My father knows I'm not a virgin. It's the very reason he despises me and wants to get rid of me. They're tricking Romanov with damaged goods and when he finds out... and he absolutely *will*...

"Don't play the altruist now, Bianchi," Aleksandr says in a bored voice. "I won't touch her until our wedding. But if I have my way, that will be in two days' time."

I stifle a gasp.

Two days' time.

How am I going to get away? If he takes me now —

"I can't pack anything?" I ask, my voice trembling. I don't care about my clothes, but I do have a few special trinkets that matter to me. The little box with a lock of hair, a folded picture, and a tiny charm that are mine. They *have* to come with me.

"No." He stands. "Do we have a deal or not?"

My father rises with him, his greedy eyes widening.

"Of course we do."

My mother stands with him, paling.

I shake my head when the reality of the situation hits me hard. "I...I can't go with you now. No. I won't go. I don't even know you. I can't just leave everyone and everything behind like that. If you want me to come to you before the wedding—"

"Harper," Mom snaps. My brother watches in stony silence. My father looks apoplectic when he realizes I'm not going easily. I know that look well, his complexion splotchy and red, the thin line of his lips. It's a wonder he hasn't broken a blood vessel.

I shake my head, a strange memory from high school coming to me. My high school poetry teacher, standing in front of the class, his hand on his heart as he recited a poem.

A poem about death and going gently and fighting against it all, that I loved so much I went home and memorized it.

Though wise men at their end know dark is right,

Because their words had forked no lightning they

Do not go gentle into that good night...

Rage, rage against the dying of the light.

"Harper. Go with Mr. Romanov," my mother urges fervently, as if she wishes she could talk me into doing the impossible. "He will take good care of you."

I'd laugh if I wasn't so scared.

I shake my head. No. I won't go. I *can't*.

My future husband slides out of his suit coat. The taut fabric of his dress shirt stretches tight against his abs, biceps bulging the sleeves. Great, he's strong, too. At least my father's loser friends would've been easier to outrun. He snaps his gaze to my father's. "Do we have a deal or not, Bianchi?"

My heart leaps into my throat. Oh my *God*.

My father nods, fanning himself with the folded check.

"Yes. We have a deal." His cold eyes narrow at me and swipes the check in my general direction. "Take her."

I shake my head and step back. "You can't take me," I whisper.

I feel the wall of my brother's body at my back. The ghost of his hands at my arms before Romanov snaps, "Touch her and I'll fucking kill you. She's mine now."

Oh, God. Nausea spirals in my stomach. My hands shake. It's now or never.

Wait. My brother dies if he touches me.

He can't stop me. It's my only chance.

I gather my courage, take a deep breath.

I stomp as hard as I can on my brother's foot. Elbow him. I shove him clumsily toward Romanov and make a break for it.

CHAPTER THREE

Aleksandr

THE LITTLE BRAT'S so fucking predictable.

I didn't know how fast she was, though.

As soon as she escapes her useless brother, she heads for the hallway. I shove him out of the way and march past him, stepping into the hallway after her. She's already ten feet ahead of me, running like a scared little bunny from a hungry wolf into the night.

Run, little girl, run.

I roll up my sleeves as I watch her choose where to go next. Her mother's yelling behind me, something unintelligible in Italian. Her father's cursing and her brother's righting himself and muttering.

Italians. Always dramatic about fucking everything.

I march toward the door when I see a flourish of honey blonde hair exiting. She's a pretty little thing, and she looks a lot more wholesome in person than I'd expect, being a Bianchi. Sun-kissed hair, high cheekbones, a curvy little body dressed impeccably in designer clothing.

Figures she's a runner.

Unfortunately for her, so am I.

I give her a little bit of a lead. Let her think she can win, that she can outrun me. I'll catch her, and when I do, I'll punish her for this.

Win, win.

A wedding gift, tied up in a neat little bow.

I turn the corner of the house and call my driver. Vas answers on the first ring.

"You see her?"

"Coming this way?"

"Yeah."

The second I got one look at the way Bianchi brought her to me, I knew she was the type they've been pushing around. I don't fucking care about someone I don't know, but I won't let the Bianchis pull one over on me either. I knew if I left her even for a day, she'd be out of here.

I won't go home empty-handed.

I scan the estate grounds and at first don't see her. It's dark out but thankfully there's a full moon. In a stream of moonlight I see a flash of pale skin and gorgeous legs.

I'm after her. I'm faster than she is, but she knows the layout, which will give her an advantage in the dark.

We'll play a little game of cat and mouse. I've always loved the thrill of the chase.

I bark out an order to Vas. "Cut her off at the exit."

The car peels away, heads her off, and blocks the only exit from the driveway. She can leap the fence, which will take way too long, or pivot. She turns and runs toward a wooded area on the perimeter.

I pick up my pace. I'm not even winded, for once in my life grateful for Kolya's ruthless training and insistence we keep ourselves in peak physical shape.

I'm almost grateful she decided to make things interesting. What's the fun in having a meek little wife who already knows her place? It's so much more rewarding to bring her to heel if she fights me first.

Branches snap under my feet as I chase her. She thinks she can hide here in the forest, but like any skittish prey on the run, she's practically making a path for me. A thrill surges through me when she stays ahead of me. I'm a hunter enthralled by her cunning, and she's my target. She can run, but there's nowhere else to go.

I scan ahead of us and notice a barbed wire fence ahead. Our game of cat and mouse is coming to a close too soon.

She cries out when a branch snaps against her but quickly rights herself and takes a sharp turn left.

Then she's gone. Evaporated into thin air, as if she found a portal to another dimension.

What the fuck?

I slow my pace.

I can't help but remember what Aria told me before I left.

"There's something that she's hiding. I'm not sure what, but two plus two isn't five, yet every time I try to do the math... that's what I come up with. Something's not right about Harper Bianchi. Just be careful."

I laughed. "She's a hundred pounds soaking wet. Why do you think I can't take her?"

"No, no, it isn't that.... It's that she's hiding something and it's driving me crazy. Whatever it is has been covered up... It's like... like there's a filter in place, you know? At first glance it seems fine, but every once in a while, there's a... shimmer that tells you things aren't what they seem."

So she isn't a saint. That makes two of us. I don't need a woman I'll love. I need a woman to take my name and my ring, and my goddamn dick so she can have my babies.

She only knows this place better than I do, so it'll take a little more time.

I slow my pace and sharpen my senses. Even though I'm determined to catch and punish her, I have to admire her pluck. I'm torn between frustration that she's drawing this out and begrudging respect. Her evasion's a gauntlet thrown into the ring. My need to capture and claim her feels rooted in the primal need to master.

I look around for a sign of her but see nothing.

Where is she? I flip on my phone's flashlight and scan the wooded area. She hasn't gone far. She's right here.

I look for a large rock or tree, a pile of leaves. Somewhere for her to hide. She's a clever little thing. She knew she couldn't outrun me, so she decided to throw me off the chase.

"Come out, come out, wherever you are," I taunt. "You know it's only a matter of when, not if, I find you." I lower my voice, so she hears the threat. "The longer you waste my time, the worse it will be for you."

A glimmer of moonlight falls on a glimmer of pale pink in the dense foliage to my right.

I pretend I don't see it, that I'm heading in the other direction. Each second that passes heightens the tension. There she is, crouched behind the trunk of a large tree. I draw a breath and lunge at her hidden form. *Score.* My fingers latch onto a mane of hair.

She screams and smacks at my hand. I barely feel it. I could reach for her arm or leg, but she could bite me or twist away. I tighten my grip on her hair instead.

"Ow! Let me go!" she screams as I haul her out in front of me. Victory pounds in my chest.

Now that I've got her, I won't let her go.

I tug her hair back, baring her neck. Illuminated in the beam of my flashlight, her eyes are wide in terror, her hands flailing out in front of her. My dick throbs.

"You're done now." I'm not playing anymore. The need to punish her for running claws at my chest.

I consider tossing her over my shoulder or cradling her in my arms and quickly think of the easiest way to get her out of here.

"Come here." If she moves away from me, it'll hurt her. She reluctantly steps in front of me, and the world falls away. The only sound is our rapid breathing in the dense quiet of the forest.

"Please," she whispers. I don't know if she's asking for mercy or freedom, but she'll get neither.

"Please what? Let you go? Or consider easing up on your punishment for running? The answer to both of those questions is no."

I lean in, relishing the sound of her rapid breathing. Even damp with perspiration, she smells like spring, a delicate, sweet, floral scent with a slightly exotic undertone. What *is* that?

She licks her lips and swallows but doesn't look away. Her eyes, as warm as molten honey, fairly glower at me. She clamps her lips together.

"You're clever, aren't you?" Her eyes spark with intelligence and wit even though she's furious with me. "I don't know why you're so angry. You're the one who ran. Tell me." I shake my head. "Did your family never tell you what your future would hold?"

I don't know why I'm talking to her. I don't know why I'm not tossing her over my shoulder or dragging her by the hair back home, or at the very least, punishing her, right here, for putting me to the test and making me chase her.

"Of course I knew they'd marry me off to some high-paying creep," she seethes.

I quirk a corner of my lips. "You'll learn to respect your husband, Princess."

Fire sparks in her eyes. "You are not my husband yet, and I'm *definitely* no princess." She swallows and I wish I could look more clearly into her eyes in the dark. I will, when she's spread beneath me taking my cock. "I promise I'll go with you, I just can't go right now. I have...I have things I *have* to take care of."

I snort. "I'm sure your socials will survive without a selfie refresh for a little while."

That touches a nerve. Her nostrils flare. "Will your ego survive a few seconds of challenge?"

I could overpower her so easily it's laughable. I could bully her or manhandle her, but that's all too easy, too simple. Predictable.

I have other ways to show her who's in charge.

When I reach my hand out to touch her, she flinches.

Taken aback, my hand freezes mid-air. She was ready for a backhand.

I've got no qualms about my palm across her ass if she deserves it, and I can already tell she fucking will. Hell, she might even learn to fucking like it. But only a pussy backhands a woman.

Christ, who did I murder in a past life to warrant literally getting into bed with the fucking Bianchis?

I want her to know she belongs to me, starting now.

I drag my thumb across her lips, smearing pink gloss. I watch her reaction when I part her lips and press my thumb inside her mouth.

I'm unprepared for the sensual feel of her lips wrapped around my finger. My cock aches.

"Something tells me you're teachable," I say thoughtfully. "I'll train you to submit to me."

The fluttering of her eyelashes and rapid breathing tell me she isn't as unaffected by me as she likes to think she is. I remove my thumb and pat her cheek firmly. "You're beautiful for a brat."

It's impossible to read microexpressions in the dark, and she's obviously well-versed in schooling her reactions. But I don't miss her tone of voice. "You're acceptable for a villain."

I touch my hand to my chest. "A *villain*. I've always liked villains so much more than heroes, don't you? Anyone could be a hero. It takes class *and* balls to be a villain." I reach for her hair again and give it another tug. "We're leaving. We can pick up this little chat later." I whisper into the curve of her ear. "Don't try anything stupid, or you'll find yourself bent over the hood of my car with my belt across your ass while I make an example of you. Is that how you want to leave here?"

Still holding her head up high, she doesn't respond.

"Respect, Harper."

"Respect's earned," she seethes.

"And sometimes, respect is demanded and taken. I intend to take what's mine."

My hand still entwined in her hair, I march her toward the

edge of the trees. I imagine her family's watching, hidden in the darkened interior of the house. Fucking pussies.

The air is cool and crisp, the only sounds our footsteps on crunchy leaves and the hum of the car that idles in the driveway, waiting for us.

"Not one toe out of line," I warn, ready to whip her ass if she pulls a move now.

But she doesn't. She grits her teeth and presses her lips in a thin line.

I open the car door. "Get in." After a moment of hesitation, she does.

Her defiance is like a match to tinder. The primal need to master this woman claws at my insides, a raging beast that needs to dominate and control.

But I can be patient and bide my time.

I slide into the seat beside her, my full body pressed up against hers, a silent cue that she can't get away from me if she tries.

I growl at Vas. "Get us the hell out of here. I'll get my coat later." I don't want to step foot in there again, not now.

She turns away from me so I won't see her swiping at her cheeks. There's no way she's crying because I'm taking her away from *this* home. No. There's another reason.

"Where are you taking me?"

I clench my jaw. "Home."

CHAPTER FOUR

Harper

HOME.

He can say that all day long, but it doesn't mean anything and won't. Call a cow a fish, and it's still a damn cow.

His home will be my prison.

I stare out the window, fervently wishing that the trip will be short. At first, it's hard to see where we're going in the dark. After a little while I notice streetlights illuminate large road signs with an arrow pointing toward The Cove.

My heart beats a little faster. For the first time, I feel the faintest glimmer of hope, but hardly dare to think I could've hit a stroke of luck. Are we heading toward The Cove? This could work to my advantage.

I swallow hard and lick my lips, feigning nonchalance so he doesn't know how much hangs in the balance of his answer. "Where do you live?"

"Did they tell you nothing?" he snaps, sitting so close to me our knees practically knock. I sit up straighter because I'd rather not touch him until that isn't a choice anymore.

My belly dips. There *will* come a time when that isn't a choice anymore.

And when he finds out I'm not who he thinks I am...

"If they'd told me where you lived, do you think I'd bother asking you?"

The air between us chills as he narrows his eyes at me. His voice is tinged with a Russian accent when he responds. "We're heading to The Cove. The Romanov family owns most of the property there. We have a residence in Moscow as well, but The Cove is our American residence." A muscle ticks in his jaw. He opens his mouth as if to say more but closes it instead and turns away.

I pretend my heart doesn't leap in my chest at his answer.

The Cove. We're heading for The Cove.

I had no idea the Romanovs owned the large, sprawling "Little Russia" situated between Coney Island and Manhattan.

In The Cove, the shopkeepers speak Russian. There are restaurants, grocery stores, cultural centers, and an Orthodox Church. There's a beach and a boardwalk, popular in the summer. Less crowded in the winter. If his family owns The Cove...

I can't get my hopes up too high, though.

It might not be the reprieve I'm hoping for. Will I be able to do what I need to under the watchful eyes of the

Romanovs? If they own The Cove, they will have eyes everywhere.

The Cove.

I need more information. I decide to chat with him, get him talking. Maybe I'll learn something useful, like if he has any sisters. There's an unwritten law between women — most of us, anyway — that we have each other's backs. I could sneak away, I could lie... or I could find someone who's sympathetic and plead my case.

"And we're getting married in two days?"

"Unless you decide to pull another move on me."

I turn to face him, taken aback by the fire that burns in the blue of his eyes. How can eyes do that?

"And if I do?" I ask with a thrust of my chin before I can censor my words. Before I can stop myself from talking back to him. I know I'm flirting with fire, but he seems to know how to push every one of my buttons.

Our knees knock together when he reaches for me. I don't have time to prepare myself before strong, rough fingers grip my chin and dig into my skin, searing me. I'm frozen in place, captured in his gaze and the latent threat.

"Then we marry tonight."

My mind reels. *Tonight?* I wasn't expecting that. I wanted him to know I won't cow under any type of abuse, and I've experienced every damn type. I wanted him to tell me what he'd do so I could brave it, because I want to prove to myself that I'll survive marriage to this man.

"And if you do decide to defy me, when I get you alone, I show you exactly what happens to a naughty little wife who decides to disobey her husband." He releases my chin.

There it is. There we go.

There's no denying that I'm afraid, but by now I've learned to school the telltale signs so thoroughly, I barely note the shift in my breathing, the increase in my heartbeat, or how my palms grow sweaty.

I lick my lips. "The old-fashioned type, then."

A glint of something like malice but not quite flickers in his gaze. "You have no idea."

That should scare me. I'm not quite sure if it does.

He'll see that I'm not beaten down with words. I've learned to let them glide over me, mere smoke in the wind. I'm impervious to threats and insults, thanks to the generosity of my fucked-up family.

Thinks she's better than everyone.

You disgrace our family name.

Miss High and Mighty.

Filthy piece of trash.

Fucking whore.

Dishonor.

Slut.

I stifle a flinch at the endless barrage of insults that spin in a loop in my brain.

As we drive on in silence, my mind races, a storm of conflict and confusion brewing. His presence, only a hair away from me, unnerves me. The cold stab of his glare sends a shiver down my spine — an indecipherable blend of fear and excitement.

I chide myself for allowing even the slightest hint of unwanted attraction between us.

We stare at each other, something untold hanging in the air between us. The front of the car dips when we hit a rough patch of road, but the car effortlessly glides as if we're riding on a magic carpet, until we hit a bump and lurch forward. Wordlessly, he holds my forearms to steady me. I use the opportunity to do more questioning.

"So you live in The Cove. Like...alone? Or with people?"

His voice, laced with an unmistakable Russian accent, is commanding yet somehow sexy. "I have a staff of seven."

Staff. He has a staff of seven. I'm curious. We've already entered into rare territory.

Seven is a good number, though. At least one might be persuaded to be on my side...

"Why do you need a staff? Can't clean your own toilets?"

A smirk shows a flash of a dimple. "Now you know why I had to get a wife."

I feel my jaw unhinge as a satisfying smirk spreads across his face.

No. He. Did. Not.

"Just make sure you don't ask me to make you a sammich," I say with scorn, shifting back in my seat.

The low sound of his dark chuckle is a bit unnerving, if I'm honest. I know how to handle a backhand or a derisive comment, a shove into a closet or worse. I know what it's like to be treated like an object, ignored, and discarded.

But cold laughter that makes you shiver is another thing. Deceiving in its simplicity, masked to hide the danger he wears like a shroud.

I imagine the look of horror that would be on my mother's face if she were here right now. She'd hiss at me in that shrill voice that drove me mad. *Harper Lee Bianchi!*

She can fuck all the way off. Harper Lee Bianchi's just had her ass dragged out of her home and shoved into a luxury car with a man who has danger leaking out of his pores. I'm not given permission to sweat, much less fight, on a good day, never mind when my entire universe has spun on its axis. I need a minute.

Disgrace.

Disgust.

Whore.

I grit my teeth and look out the window, surprised to find the view a bit blurry. I'm not a crier. Why now?

For a while, he doesn't talk at all. He's on his phone, casually scrolling through with a look of intense concentration. I left my own phone behind, but a part of me's actually relieved I did. There's no more expectation of keeping up the appearance of perfection with every selfie and post if I don't have my phone.

When my mother discovered that social media could be profitable, she made up her mind. They needed money, and I had a pretty face. She researched everything she could, and the next thing I knew, I was a social media sensation.

I hate it. So I'm glad to leave that part of my life behind.

Phones are disposable, like so many other things. Clothes. Feelings. Daughters, apparently.

Do you have any other daughters?

It would actually get under my skin if I didn't guess that's exactly why he said it.

"We're almost home," he says, still holding his phone. "Come here."

The sound of his voice is like the shimmering surface of a lake I swam in as a child. Placid and calm, but beneath the surface, the frigid depths of the water pulled with a current that could sweep you off your feet and drag you under.

I will not be pulled under.

"Come here? We're in the back of a car. How much closer do you want me to come?"

A dangerous glint in his gaze tells me he's not amused. "Do I need to show you exactly how much closer I expect you to come?" Leaning toward me, his voice drops to a low register. "And I *will* expect you to come, Princess."

Oh, God.

I know this game. I know these maneuvers. He wants to rattle me so he can make his move.

I'm not easy to manipulate regardless of what he thinks. I have *years* of experience.

Holding my gaze, he slowly pats his knee, a silent beckoning. "Hands here, please."

He wants my ... hands... on his lap? What kind of weird kink is that?

Bemused, I obey, my fingers pressed against his pants. The muscles of his sturdy thigh are hard beneath my hands as I arch my back.

There's a click of metal and something cold on my wrists. I look down to see he *handcuffed* me. Just pulled out a pair of handcuffs like a magician.

"That's how much closer you'll come," he says with an air of cold finality. He yanks me by the wrists so my whole body slams against his chest. "Just like that."

The car has come to a stop and the door opens. A flash of moonlight shows he wasn't lying — the glint of silver and light show the Manhattan skyline on full display against the inky sky, as far as the eye can see.

He gets out first then reaches for me. I'm awkward, stumbling with my wrists cuffed, but he has too tight a grip on me for me to fall. The harsh sound of Russian fills the night as his men speak in low voices to one another, a show of deference when they talk to him.

I wonder where he ranks. I only know my family's hierarchy but I'm almost completely unfamiliar with the Russians'.

"Welcome home, sir." The rest all speak in Russian, so I assume the change is for my benefit. I've lifted my head to see where we are, to see where I might plan my escape, when silky fabric goes over my face and my world is plunged into darkness. *He blindfolded me.*

I stumble when I can't see where I'm going. My belly dips and I gasp, trying to brace myself for a fall, but my hands are restrained. Then strong arms wrap around me, and I'm hoisted in the air.

"Watch your step," he snaps, as my belly hits what must be his shoulder. I can't see, of course, but it feels like I'm high in the air and this is extremely uncomfortable.

"With a blindfold on? Sure, that makes total sense. Maybe next time you'll ask me to sing with a gag in, or—"

I gasp when his palm slaps against my ass, hard. I press my lips together. So he just did that, and I have a feeling that won't be the last time.

"I told you to watch your mouth."

I scissor my legs because it's the only movement I can make, and I want to make this harder for him. "Five-star double standards in this house. Well done."

I expect that will earn me another smack, but he doesn't respond. Our pace quickens, though. I can feel the rush of cold air as he walks faster, barking out orders in harsh Russian.

While we move, though, something has me uneasy. I can only guess he's blindfolding me because he doesn't want me to see where we are, so I won't know how to leave. He's done his research about my history of running.

God, I have to, though. But if he finds out...

Doors close. Footsteps click. Sounds begin to fade, except for his footsteps which quickly become muffled. Carpet, then? Observing while blindfolded is not my strong suit. How big is this place? It feels like we've been walking for fifteen minutes, but maybe everything seems to go in slow motion when your heart is beating a million times a minute.

Finally, his steps slow. My body shifts as he adjusts me over his shoulder. There's the unmistakable sound of a lock clicking open, but no sound of a key, so I'm guessing the lock was digital or something. A door opens. I lay still over his shoulder, hoping that if I behave myself and we have come to the end here, now's the time I can get off his damn shoulder and take a look around.

"I told you not to run, Harper. And you decided to defy me right out of the gate. You aren't my wife yet, but you're in my possession, so it's time you learn there are consequences for your actions."

My cheeks feel flushed. My heart's beating so fast I feel sick. Was that first smack to the ass the prelude to —

I scream when I'm suddenly falling, flailing — my body lands softly on a bed. I reach out, grasping for purchase, when his strong, rough fingers grab my cuffed wrists. Panic sweeps through me like a tidal wave, knocking all sense of reason and logic aside. "What are you—*unngh.*" Soft fabric glides against my mouth and chin.

"I liked your suggestion of the gag. You're here in my home and eventually, after I feel you've learned your lesson, I'll let you have some freedom. But after today's stunt we'll start nice and slow. Nod if you understand."

My pulse races so quickly I feel nauseous, but I nod, nonetheless.

"Good. I'll be back soon. You're safe and comfortable enough for now. Behave until I get back. I have to make arrangements."

Arrangements. When did my wedding become a funeral?

The room feels suddenly colder. The door shuts with a final *click* and the number pad outside it beeps.

He's left me alone in here. Bound like a captive so I don't run.

How long will he hold me prisoner? If we're getting married this weekend, there's no way he'll leave me bound and gagged while the minister drags me through the *I do's,* right? I mean, I need to be able to verbally agree.

But after that... after we've said our vows... he'll consider me his property. He hasn't even bothered to hide that.

Then what? When there's no one to stop him from hurting me?

CHAPTER FIVE

Harper

I WAKE to the sound of a door opening. At first, I'm completely disoriented and panic sweeps through me when I realize I don't have full control over my body. My wrists are bound, I'm gagged, and I'm wearing a blindfold.

What in the —

"Oh my *God*." Before I can gather myself together, I hear a female voice. I try to settle my nerves and remember what happened.

I'm being married to Aleksandr Romanov — a beautiful, arrogant prick who thinks he's the boss of me.

My parents gave me away like I was property to be bartered and traded.

My future husband bound and locked me in a room?

What an absolute *dick*.

"My God is right. I thought *Mikhail* was a jerk when I was in this position." A second voice sighs. "We still have time to influence the others."

The door clicks shut. No more voices, so maybe two women. One of them has a higher voice, the second's a bit lower and pragmatic.

"We're here to help you," the one with the higher voice says. "Please don't try to fight us."

Fighting makes no sense when I'm outnumbered. I nod, then realize the blindfold's damp. Am I crying? One tiny little show of sympathy from someone and I'm crying? I have to get my shit together.

Even though I expect them to touch me, I jerk when I feel hands on me. In seconds, the gag and blindfold are gone.

I blink and stare, my eyes getting used to the light. One of them is a tall, willowy blonde with pale blue eyes and fair, ivory skin. The other's shorter, with a huge mane of wavy dark hair in a messy bun, glasses perched on the tip of her nose, and she's obviously very, very pregnant. She looks at my wrists and shakes her head at the blonde. "Handcuffs. He *handcuffed* her. Honestly, have we not made a single dent in their thick skulls? *God.* I have keys in my bag if these are the basic universal handcuffs."

The blonde wrinkles her nose. "Okay, I do not need to know why you have keys for handcuffs in your bag."

The pregnant one rolls her eyes. "Oh, please, handcuffs are so basic they're practically vanilla." She turns to me. "I'm Aria, by the way. Mikhail's wife. Mikhail's Aleksandr's older brother."

I heard his name before. Mikhail knew Saul, and Mikhail is married to the pregnant one.

The blonde nods. "And I'm Polina, Aleksandr and Mikhail's sister." She shakes her head and rolls her eyes. "Unfortunately. Jesus, why couldn't my brothers be teachers or librarians or something? I really need to stop making a habit out of meeting my sisters like this."

Okay, so there's a story there. My heart beats a little faster.

Meeting my sisters?

My voice is husky and faint when I speak. "I'm Harper."

"Harper Lee Bianchi. Who's the literary one in your family?"

I swallow. "My mother."

"Harper, we're going to get you fixed up," Aria says. "Polina's pretty much the only one, other than her mom, that these men will actually listen to, so you're in good hands. Though I'll admit, it's taken a while but I'm getting good at persuading them." She heads toward the door. "I'll be back, just going to grab those keys."

Polina sits on the side of the bed.

"How can I help you? Water? Food?"

My eyes are scratchy from a fitful night of sleep. I was up most of the night trying to plot various ways I could escape, when I wasn't trying to plot my future husband's murder.

"Water and food sound great, but I need to use the bathroom. That'll probably be easier when the cuffs are off. Does he know you're here?"

She nods. "Mhm. I think telling me and Aria to come in was his attempt at being half human."

I'm not sure if that's supposed to comfort me or what. He's sent her here to help but didn't even bother to hide the fact that I'm here against my will, and she doesn't seem terribly surprised to find me this way.

"Once Aria comes back, we'll uncuff you and you can use the bathroom." Her eyes light up. "I've looked through your socials and made notes of all your favorite products. I've got everything you need in there."

I blink. My socials. She's looked through my facade of a life and formed an opinion about me based on that? She's seen the reams of posts of me with my luxury skincare products, the selfies with the shallow captions, my fake friends and promotion of unattainable beauty standards. *Gag me.* I wish I could tell her it's all a lie, that she doesn't have to believe it. That's not who I am.

Maybe I can.

Has Aleksandr seen them, too?

God. Of course he has.

Thanks, Mom.

"That's very kind of you," I say. "Thank you."

"Of course. And for breakfast you usually eat Greek yogurt with berries? The nonfat, sugar-free kind, right? I had staff pick up some of that—"

I shake my head. "No, I hate yogurt."

Her eyes widen slightly, registering mild surprise.

"I'm sorry, I just mean that — no thank you. I don't like yogurt. I'll eat pretty much anything else, though." My cheeks heat.

The door opens and my heart leaps into my throat at the thought it could be Aleks. Even though she said he knows she's here...

"Okay. Found a set. Let's see if they work."

Phew. It's Aria.

I hold my hands out in front of me. Aria's tongue sticks out while she fiddles with the lock. Finally, she turns the key, and the cuffs loosen. My wrists swing free. I stretch my arms out and wriggle my fingers, then lightly massage the skin where the cuffs laid.

"God, that feels good."

Aria screws up her face. "That looks painful."

"What?"

She gestures to where the skin at my wrists is chaffed and reddened.

"I'm fine," I say, shrugging. I am. I've experienced a lot worse than that.

"He'd better make it up to you," she growls. "I could fuck him *up*."

I look at her in surprise. Aleks is so much bigger than she is it's funny to think about her fucking him up.

Polina nods, her eyes wide. "Aria's the queen of hackers. She *totally* could."

"Good to know."

"Okay, off to the bathroom with you," Polina says. "And tell me if there's anything else you need, because I'm calling down for some breakfast."

I nod. "Thank you. I really was starting to worry this whole thing would be under Aleksandr's lock and key." I laugh, but the two of them exchange concerned glances.

Great. That's not troubling at all.

In my family, we don't order breakfast. We used to have staff ages ago, but we don't have them anymore. My mother cooked for a while, but my father was spoiled by our house-keeper and didn't like it.

Here, Polina says she's ordering food. Suffice it to say, I think the Romanovs are quite different from us.

It feels good to take a shower, but I don't spend long because I'm afraid if I do, Aria and Polina will be gone, and I have questions. I quickly wash, then towel dry. I find a fluffy robe on the back of the door. If this wasn't an obvious case of being held against my will, it would almost be like a stay in a luxury hotel.

When my hand's on the doorknob, I hear a deep male voice. I don't move. I wait until I hear the door click shut again.

When I come back into the room, it's just Polina and Aria.

"Did I hear someone else?"

Polina nods. "Aleks stopped by to fill us in on the wedding arrangements."

"Ah, okay."

"Feel better?"

I nod. "I do feel better, thank you." I notice a glass of water on a side table. "Is that mine?"

"Of course, have at it."

I lift the glass and drain it. When I'm done, I sigh. "That was so good."

"Look what this asshole has done. She's practically dancing a jig after a shower and a glass of water," Polina says. "Why did he cuff you, though? That was a bit much, even for him."

Even for him.

"Because he knew I was going to try to get away."

Polina tips her head to the side. "Would you? I mean besides the obvious fact that you've been demoralized as a woman and treated like property," she says with clear disdain, "is there another reason?"

Can I tell her? Can I trust her? Maybe some day.

I don't reply, and I hope my silence is answer enough for now.

Yes...I think I might be able to trust her.

"Do you want to tell me?" she asks in a small voice. Oh, God, I do, so badly it makes me want to cry, but if I tell her and she has any obligation to tell Aleks, he could call everything off. Then I'd have nowhere to go. I hate that my family has put me in this position, but at this point my only choice is to marry him.

"I...I can't. Not now, anyway."

She and Aria exchange a look. They're clever women and at the very least, will have likely surmised that if I'm waiting to share my personal information, I may be trying to keep this wedding going.

Polina fiddles with a delicate gold necklace around her neck. "My family is in jeopardy, Harper. It has been, for some time. My brothers need to solidify the family with alliances and connections. It's the way we survive."

I nod. I know I'm only a puppet on strings, at least in the eyes of the Bratva. "I know how these things work," I say wearily. "I get it."

We sit in silence for a moment. All of us are tangled in this web in one way or another.

"Alright then," Polina says. "Let's get going. You have to get ready for breakfast downstairs." She smiles sheepishly. "That was sort of the argument between us just now. Aleks thinks you should be eating downstairs with everyone."

Everyone? I swallow. "Who's everyone?"

Aria and Polina share another look. Polina sighs. "Welllll. There's a lot of us. Mikhail's the oldest, then there are my other brothers, six in total although one of them is out of the country right now, and then my mother…"

"You have six brothers?" Yikes. Even though Aleks is the one I'm supposedly marrying, the thought of being outnumbered by more of him is a little scary.

"Tell me about it. So let's get you dressed and downstairs."

I'm starving and I want breakfast. I have to face them all eventually. "Alright."

"I picked out a few outfits. You'll find them in the closet."

"Thank you."

She probably picked out clothes the same way she picked out my makeup, but at this point, I don't care. The most important thing I can do right now is make friends with these two so I can survive this. So I can do what I have to.

Allies. I need allies.

I look through the clothes quickly. "Casual?"

"Just something you'd wear to breakfast."

I don't eat breakfast and would probably drink coffee dressed in my jammies, but I get her point. The small stack of neatly folded clothes and the dresses on hangers in the closet are stark reminders that I wasn't allowed to bring anything with me.

Nothing.

I can't think of that now.

I choose a soft pair of leggings and a long sweater suitable for this cool weather, then quickly step into the bathroom to get ready. I swipe on some makeup.

Aria sighs. "I could spend an hour getting ready and still look like a little kid playing in her big sister's makeup."

I give her a wry smile. "I could maybe help with that."

Her eyes light up. "I would *love* that."

I like her.

I get a good view of the house when we walk downstairs for breakfast. I'm not surprised that when I glance through large windows, I find we're nestled in a secure location behind dense rows of trees. I'd bet my last penny the security systems that surround this home are top-notch. He knows every bird that lands on his property, every car that drives by.

The home is modern and almost minimalist, built with sleek, clean lines, not a speck of dust or anything out of place. Thick carpet beneath my feet, framed prints of contemporary art. I note a few things that are a bit out of the ordinary — a control panel for the light fixtures that looks like someone lifted it straight out of a spaceship, a thermostat on the wall with an impressive display screen.

"I'm a tech girl," Aria says when she sees me taking everything in. We walk down a small set of stairs toward the smell of bacon and coffee. "And let me tell you, I *drool* when I come here."

A huge, framed print is mounted over the fireplace in the living room. Takes me a minute to realize it's the TV, though it's framed like a picture and currently displaying artwork. We walk past that doorway and into the dining room.

My stomach clenches as the sound of talking dies down. There is indeed an entire group of men sitting at the dining room table, but no Aleksandr.

A man who looks to be in his thirties stands and walks over to me. Deep-set dark brown eyes beneath heavy brows, golden, tanned skin, and dark brown hair tinged with flecks of gold make him look almost godlike. I find myself mentally comparing him to Aleksandr's darker, rugged good looks, and immediately give myself a mental shake. *Stop.* This man's arrestingly masculine and undeniably attractive but a bit more civilized than Aleks.

He stretches his hand out to me. "Mikhail Romanov, Aleksandr's older brother and head of the Romanov family. Welcome." I nod mutely, unsure what the proper thing to do is in this circumstance.

"I'm Harper." My cheeks flush. Obviously, they know who I am. Everyone's staring at me. Fortunately, I don't have to think on it for long, because Mikhail goes straight to Aria and puts his hand on her lower back.

"Are you alright? How are you feeling?"

"About the same as I was when I saw you fifteen minutes ago," she says, her eyes twinkling. A stab of jealousy hits me. I woke up in bed bound and captive.

I don't deserve tenderness like that.

I don't deserve to be loved.

Disgrace.

Disgust.

Whore.

"Come, sit. My mother will be joining us later. She's getting things ready for tomorrow night."

I blink. Tomorrow night. My wedding.

I nod, still mute, then notice a shadow looming from behind me. I shiver when the temperature in the room drops.

My fiancé has arrived.

While everyone else is dressed in business-casual, Aleksandr's wearing gym shorts and a white tee. His hair's still damp as if from a shower, the masculine scent of his body-wash lingering in the air. I'd bet good money he just worked out. His muscles are evident under his T-shirt, a physique born of hard work and heavy labor.

He nods coolly to me and pulls out a chair for me to sit down. It's almost an intimate gesture but feels so fake, so rehearsed, that it doesn't give me the warm glow I got from watching Mikhail with Aria.

"Not all of my family's here," he begins, as I sit down. Is he just on his best behavior for his family? "But I'll introduce you to who is. You'll meet most of them at the wedding."

I nod.

"Ollie's in Moscow, but you'll eventually meet him. My other brothers." He jerks his head toward the other side of the table, where a few of his brothers sit.

To his right sits a dangerous-looking man, heavily tattooed with a rugged, primal appeal to him. His large frame and menacing scowl make me want to hide. "Nikko, and next to him, Viktor."

Viktor, a hulking, muscular man with a shaved head and a scar running down one cheek, lifts a hand. His strong, scarred features are a bit terrifying.

Polina said she had six brothers, though. Including Aleksandr, I've only met four and one is in Moscow.

"Our youngest brother was recently injured... he's spent some time in the hospital but should be well enough to attend the wedding."

"Oh, I'm sorry," I say, but my words are quickly drowned out by the swishing of doors and the footsteps of staff bringing in large trays of food. I note standard American foods like sausage, bacon, and scrambled eggs alongside a platter of open-faced sandwiches topped with a variety of ingredients. I'm intrigued by the large tray of little pancakes served with sides of sour cream, jam, and honey.

I usually completely skip breakfast even though my socials paint me as the high-protein yogurt lover. Today, though, I'm going to feast.

Aleksandr sits beside me and pours a glass of orange juice and a cup of coffee, placing them both next to my plate.

I look at him curiously, wondering if he had a personality transplant somewhere down in the gym. I mean, I didn't imagine waking up handcuffed and gagged, did I? And now he's the gentleman, serving me juice?

"Smile, you two!" Polina says, holding her phone up to take a picture.

I flash a radiant smile for the camera on cue. I do it without conscious thought. I feel the warmth and weight of his arm across my shoulders and freeze. It's too familiar. Too gentlemanly. Too inconsistent with the way he's treated me.

"Aleks," Polina says. "It's okay to smile for a picture."

Out of the corner of my eye, he flips her the bird.

Maybe we *will* get along.

"Aren't you cold?" Polina asks him, as she walks past us and takes a seat on my other side.

He shrugs. "This is nothing. It's warm here compared to Russian winters."

"Not just the winters," I mutter under my breath. Polina snickers but Aleks only moves a little closer to me.

He leans across me to grab a platter of the little pancake things. His warmth makes my skin glow, and his undeniable masculine scent makes every one of my nerves snap to attention. Aleks radiates testosterone, and my body's taking note.

Dammit.

"What are those little pancake things?"

"Syrniki. Fried cottage cheese pancakes traditionally eaten with sour cream or something sweet like jam or honey. The sandwiches are also a Russian tradition — buterbrody. Here, try them."

"Not sure what I like but I'll try anything once," I say.

He freezes, his fork halfway to piercing one of the small, plump pancakes. "Anything?" he whispers in my ear. "I'll keep that in mind."

I ignore the flush in my cheeks. I hate how easily he undoes me. I have to get back on solid footing.

"Is frowning at your food a Romanov tradition, or are you improvising?" I ask sweetly, before I take a large bite of the pancake. It's rich and sweet and delicious.

"Is unbridled sarcasm a Bianchi trait, or are you perfecting the art?"

"Oh, that's just for you."

A corner of his lips quirks up, but he doesn't look amused. "You wear your defenses like a second skin, Princess."

My heart beats faster. "And you wear your arrogance like a crown, Your Majesty."

Polina chuckles beside me. "I like you, Harper. Oh, I like you very much."

Aleksandr scowls at her. "Stay out of this."

"Not on your life," she answers sweetly, batting her eyelashes at him.

"Behave yourself," he says in a low voice in my ear. He may have no control over his sister, but apparently needs to exercise control over *me*. My skin heats, the small hairs on the back of my neck standing up.

"Or what? You'll break off the engagement?" I whisper back. I lean toward him, so I'm pressed against his bare arm, my breasts flush up against him. I lay my hand delicately on his chest. "I don't seem to remember you having a readily available lineup of women ready to marry you, do you?"

Aria gasps. I look over to see her hand on her belly.

Mikhail leaps out of his chair so quickly he upends it.

Polina grins. "You okay?"

"Was that a contraction?" Aria whispers, her eyes wide.

"You'll have to wait and see," Polina says, ever the calm one. She looks over at Mikhail, who's on his feet and white as a sheet. "Relax, Mikhail, it's her first. You have *plenty* of time."

"You have a crystal ball?" he snaps, his eyes flashing at her.

She waves her hand at him. "Aria, let's make sure you have everything in your bag if you need it. It's good to walk if you're in early labor anyway."

I remember the flash of pain, the trickle of water. The tearing of flesh and the fresh wail.

I close my eyes as a stab of pain hits my chest. I only give myself a few seconds before I open them and reach for a glass of water. They're leaving. I don't want them to leave.

My hand trembles and I nearly knock over the pitcher. Wordlessly, Aleks reaches for the pitcher and pours me a glass.

"Thank you," I whisper, trying to soothe my racing heart with sips of the icy cold water.

Miss High and Mighty.

Filthy piece of trash.

Fucking whore.

I sip the water until my chest burns. Pile food on my plate, even though right now it's all tasteless. Gratefully lift the cup of coffee and welcome the scalding burn of it down my throat.

If Aria's in labor, it could be a good distraction... an opportunity.

I could escape here forever. I could maybe escape the inevitable horror of our wedding night.

CHAPTER SIX

Aleksandr

THE SUN SHINES BRIGHTLY on the crowd of guests, stark in winter without the shade of leaves. I lift my hand to shade my eyes and scan the crowd.

Ever vigilant. Ever watchful. Other than the handful of my family members, I don't really and truly ever trust *anyone*. Someone could be here ready to kill. We all know that being engaged to a Romanov is a death sentence. Mikhail's lineup of fiancées could attest to that...if they were still alive.

Something isn't right. I scan the crowd over and over again, looking for a clue, but unlike reading a computer screen, reading a throng of people isn't as cut and dried.

The sun feels too bright, the brisk wind too cold.

Strains of music begin to play, a Russian classic I can't quite identify. Everything seems a bit hazy and disoriented. I'm hyper-focused on a threat in our midst.

"Aleks." I look to my right to see Nikko, dressed in all black. Why is he dressed in all black? It's a wedding, not a funeral.

Is there a difference in my family?

"Someone's gotten past our guards. There's been a breach in security." He continues telling me details, but my brain is buzzing with the first words he said.

We have to warn the girls. Polina and Aria are with Harper. We have to get to them.

I'm walking down the aisle, the eyes of our guests following me when I see her — Harper. Dressed in dreamy white, a veil covering her face. I have to get to her. I have to protect her. Someone's here with the intent to destroy my family, and she's practically got a bullseye on her.

I open my mouth to tell her to go back for cover when someone screams behind me. Deafening gunshots ring out. I reach for my gun when I hear another scream. I can't find the shooter. I can't find who's the enemy.

I've been here once before, unable to protect the people I love, as helpless as a child.

"Aleks! Aleks!" Polina's shrill voice, on the edge of hysteria, brings my gaze swiveling back to hers.

No.

No!

Crimson blood against white fabric. Harper's doubled over, clutching at herself as if she could staunch the blood with her own bare hands. Blood flows and flows, over the lace and pearls, staining the ground, staining her shoes, staining my own hands when I finally get to her.

No.

I cradle her to my chest, the memory of doing this very thing in a past life as vivid as the pain. I failed. I failed to protect her.

I wake from my dream, my heart pounding. I sit up in bed and stare. I can still feel the sticky warmth of her blood on my hands. Still smell the metallic stench of blood. Still feel the heavy weight of the knowledge that I failed again.

I swing my legs over the side of the bed. I have to move.

The faintest tinge of light outside the window tells me it's not quite dawn.

I close my eyes.

It was a dream. Only a dream.

It's my wedding day, and it was only a dream.

No one's screaming or crying. It's blissfully quiet. Peaceful, even.

I step out of bed and stretch, welcoming the pain in my legs and arms from yesterday's ball-busting workout. I school my emotions at the gym and today will be no exception.

I walk to the window and half expect to see white folding chairs stained with my bride's blood.

There's nothing but frosted grass, though. We're not even having any guests outside. The wedding will be inside.

And that was only a dream.

Then why does my heart still race as if it actually happened?

It did once. Years ago. Another time and another place, but it happened once before.

I walk to the bathroom on autopilot and splash water on my face. Stare at my reflection, half expecting to see sunken eyes and pallid skin like I did for months following her death.

But sometimes images don't match reality. I look too fucking healthy for what goes on in my mind.

A fist pounds on the door. It isn't a knock, but a slam. Nikko probably.

"Come in," I yell over my shoulder.

"Jesus, you could tell me you're taking a piss," he says with disgust.

"I just woke up, asshole. What do you need?" I lift the hand I'm not using and flip him off.

"You think I only come to see you when I need something?"

"No," I say with dripping sarcasm. "You came in here to wish me well on my wedding day. Give me some brotherly advice." I finish my business, flush, and wash my hands. I look at his reflection in the mirror. "Give me a warm hug?"

"Okay, now you're taking shit too far. Jesus," Nikko mutters. "First, happy wedding day."

"Yeah, thanks. All look clear?"

"Crystal clear. Too clear. We've got every goddamn one of us on high alert, and nothing's out of place. Doesn't make sense unless they learned their lesson already and know better than to cross us."

I shrug, looking casual, so I don't betray the staccato rhythm of my heartbeat.

They call Mikhail the Siberian Tiger. Viktor the Iron Fist. Nikko the Steel Serpent.

You could say we have a reputation.

"We don't let our guard down for a second," I tell him, putting toothpaste on a toothbrush. "You want to hit the weights with me?"

He scowls and wrinkles his nose. "Fuck no. Think I have a death wish?"

He lifts with Viktor but doesn't like the early morning ass-kicking routine.

"Fine, be a pussy then. You gonna tell me what you need or what?"

He gives me a sheepish grin. "Well, now that I'm here..."

I roll my eyes and spit out the toothpaste.

"So, uh... got a small issue with some footage that might not look too good for us. Can you clean it up? Make it look like we were never there?"

I narrow my eyes at him. "Mikhail know?"

"Fuck no, but it's nothing big. Just keep it between us."

I snort. "I'll see what I can do."

"Thanks, man."

I need to see Harper.

I just want to prove to myself that it was only a dream.

I need to see her now. When I close my eyes, I can still see her wrapped in a blood-soaked wedding dress. I need to purge that image from my mind.

Nikko takes off and I walk to the guest room where she's staying. We Russians have our traditions and so do the Italians. The idea of an Italian princess sharing a bed with her future husband is scandalous. I don't usually care about shit like that, but I hold to traditions. Simplifies shit.

There's a faint clink of dishes in the kitchen, staff preparing for the day ahead, but other than that the house is still cloaked in the pre-dawn quiet. My steps are noiseless as I walk to her room. The guards I have stationed outside her door scatter to the side when I glare at them to move.

I pause outside the door and listen for a sound.

I knock. No response.

I knock again. Nothing.

I can't hear...anything. No rustling of sheets. I can't even hear her breathing. Panic swoops over me and my vision blurs.

I quickly unlock the door and shove it open, rush in and find — her sleeping peacefully in bed.

I feel like I shouldn't be here. It's my home and she'll be my wife, but without her sassy sparring it feels like she's as vulnerable as a small child.

Blood-soaked satin and vacant eyes.

I shake my head and will the nightmare to be purged from my goddamn brain.

I shut the door and feel my entire body slump in relief. I'm mad at myself for getting so worked up, for letting stupid dreams rob me of my peace. If I feel this way about harm coming to her now, how will I ever survive if I develop feelings for her? I can't let myself fall for her. It's too damn dangerous.

I stand beside her and watch her. Her hands are folded under her cheek, her honey-blonde hair askew on her pillow. The blankets and sheets are wrapped around her body.

The early morning hours, before dawn turns into day, somehow feel intimate and sacred. Outside the window, the soft glow of moonlight is nature's nightlight, a full moon casting shadows that dance across the walls and the form of the sleeping beauty. Even the muted sounds of the waning night outside her window feel weighted and sensual.

I move closer to her. She doesn't move.

I shake her shoulder then step back. "Wake up, Harper."

She startles awake and quickly pulls the covers up higher. She seems confused for a moment, as if trying to decipher reality from dreams.

Makes two of us.

"What are you doing in here?"

"You shouldn't be sleeping so hard. What if I was a predator?" I'm angry she let me get this close without realizing I was here.

Narrowing her eyes at me, she pushes right back. Her voice is still raspy with sleep. "If you made it this far as a predator,

I'd say your security team's shit and you need to hire better security."

She has a point.

My heartbeat slows. The warmth that rose in my chest begins to dissipate.

We stare at each other in silence. Her gaze roams down the length of my body. I'm still wearing the boxers I slept in and nothing else. She licks her lips and tucks the covers around herself more tightly.

"What are you wearing?" My voice is husky. Affected. My breathing shallows.

It's quiet in here but I can still hardly hear her voice. "Aleks."

"You'll be my wife in a matter of hours. I want to know what you're wearing."

The air between us feels charged, thick with the weight of unexpected desire and our impending vows.

"Oh, it's nothing," she says, her gaze holding mine as she slowly relaxes her grip on her blankets. "Just a little set of pjs."

Just a *little* set indeed. I bet it barely covers her nipples and ass.

I can't wait to see what she looks like pinned beneath the weight of my body. Her mouth parted or, better yet — filled with my cock.

I can't wait to see her eyes go soft and her body meld to mine when she comes.

I can't wait to see her on her knees. Wearing nothing but my wedding ring.

I may not love this woman, but I'll enjoy every fucking possible second with her tight little body. Schooling those pouty little lips. Making her beg.

"What did you want, Aleks?" Her voice is still barely above a whisper. A flicker of panic flits across her gaze when I draw near.

I don't know what I want. We're too close, the room too intimate as the sky begins to faintly glow.

"Show me."

The panic spreads across her face, as if she's on the verge of a full-blown panic attack.

"Show you what?" she asks in a strangled voice.

"Show me what you're wearing. Or better yet, what you're not."

God, I'm an asshole. I know she's supposed to remain untouched. I know I'm not supposed to see her, even fully clothed, right now, much less dressed in almost nothing. But I want to see her. I want to take a closer look, when it's just the two of us.

For some reason, I want to tell her she's safe, that she can trust me. I'm torn between the need to make her understand who I am and the need to make sure she knows I'm not going to hurt her.

I will, though. It's inevitable.

She hesitates for long seconds then finally, with a trembling hand, begins to push the bedclothes down.

"Just some pjs your sister brought me." She's rallied, delivering those words in that sassy-as-fuck tone of voice.

"Show me," I repeat. My words are a barely civilized half growl.

With a flourish, she tosses the blankets aside.

"*Fuccck.*"

She's wearing nothing but a tiny pair of satin white pj shorts with a little, pale-pink bow centered at her navel, and a dainty, t-shirt with spaghetti straps that covers her but *barely,* clinging to her curves like sin.

"Look," she says in a voice that tells me she knows *exactly* what she's doing. "It even says *Bride* across the ass. Just in case you forget who I am and need a label."

I've had it with the sassy little brat. "Oh yeah? Let's see."

She tips to the side and flashes her ass at me, just in time for me to slap my palm against it. I relish the satisfying tingle in my palm.

"Ow!" she squeals, flipping back over to her back. "Hey!"

I lean onto the bed on the palm of my hand just as she flops down, effectively pinning her in. Her cheeks are flushed, and her lips are parted. If I didn't know any better, I'd think the swat to the ass turned her on.

Fucccck yes.

Oh, I'll have fun with that.

Starting right now.

I cage her in beneath me. "You know we have rules here for wives and husbands, don't you? Do you know what they are?"

Her eyes twinkle mischievously. "Let's see. First, a wife must secure permission from her lord and master — um, I mean *husband,* Your Royal Highness — before engaging in the act of breathing, most especially too loudly. Second. Under the sacred vows of wedlock, no wife shall ever possess more opinions than her all-knowing husband. She must never outshine her husband in any way."

"Your accuracy is astounding. It's like you were raised in the mafia." I lean forward and trace the little spaghetti strap on her shoulder. She shivers but pretends it doesn't affect her.

Christ, she's gorgeous. Her eyes are bright and warm, her skin clear and vibrant with a slight flush to her cheeks. Silky, gently tousled waves of honey brown hair softly frame her face. She's got a girl-next-door, Italian-girlfriend appeal I fucking love.

If I didn't know any better, I'd describe her as... joyful. Friendly, even. Approachable.

In other words, she's my exact opposite in every way.

"Go on."

"Third," she continues, as if she's just warming up. "The husband reigns supreme. The wife must conduct all business and socialization with the express written approval of her lord and master. She must never hold a contrary opinion to her husband, due to his fragile ego and precarious grip on the patriarchy. She must—she must—"

Her voice falters when I slip the spaghetti strap off her shoulder. Jesus, I can't hold myself back anymore. I want to see her perfect breasts, the way her nipples pebble when I drag my tongue across them. I want to taste her, savor her, *consume* her.

"Did I tell you to stop?"

I slip the second strap off and give the top a little tug. It falls just below her nipples. A swirl of arousal licks at me.

"A wife must — must — never be contrary to her husband. She must never quest-question him in an-any way." She falters as I bend and lick the tip of each perfect, dusky nipple. My boxers tighten against my raging erection just as the first glint of daylight appears outside the window. "A wife must o-obey like a humble servant. Should a wife exercise free will, or commit the unforgivable sin of independent thinking, she will cause her husband to be exceedingly disappointed."

She's a clever one. I'm curious how she'll hold onto that vocabulary and wit when I lick her pussy.

I pull her nipple between my teeth and pinch the other. Her back arches and her lips part.

"Go on, Harper. Stop now and I'll have to punish you. You don't want that, do you?"

A sassy glint in her eye tells me she's willing to give it a go.

Game on.

"An obedient wife wears wh-what her husband chooses," she continues.

"Or nothing at all," I correct, framing her sweet, perfect body between my hands and kissing my way down her breasts to her navel. She stifles a whimper.

"A wife should defer to her husband's superior judgment," she says, her eyes half-lidded now. "Since he has the benefit of patriarchal clairvoyance."

"Always."

I make it to the little bow and plant a kiss *right. There.* "Now let's talk about what happens when a wife doesn't obey her husband, how she's subject to his extreme disappointment and firm correction. Aren't you, Princess?"

She lets out a little squeal when I palm the word *Bride* across her ass. "But if you behave, I'll show you a world of rewards and pleasure."

I kiss the sweet vee between her legs and inhale the seductive scent of her arousal.

"Aleks," she whispers, her voice a tremulous whisper.

"Shouldn't that be *My Lord?*"

Her wrists are in my hand, her body teeming with need when I stand. I want her so fucking badly.

"Polina will be here soon to help you get ready, and I have zero interest in my sister seeing me in boxers with a raging hard-on. I'm told the preparations are an all-day affair."

She nods and bites her lip. "Yes."

"I won't see you until we take our vows, then." I release her wrists to lean in and kiss her cheek. "Promise me you'll behave."

"Mmm."

"I'll be watching you."

The sun breaks through the clouds over the horizon. The glimmer of sunrise looks like hope outside the window. Holding my gaze, she smiles. "I'll count on it."

CHAPTER SEVEN

Harper

THE DAY GOES by in a sort of blur. I'm plucked and primped and preened until I feel like I'm ready for the red carpet. It's a small group, though.

"I tried to hire help," Polina says. "I had a hair stylist and a makeup artist and all sorts of specialists coming. I wanted to give you the best possible chance at knocking everyone's socks off. I wanted every rival mafia group in the country to be drooling with jealousy."

I look around the room. It's me, Polina, Aria, one of Polina's staff members, and a sleek little gray cat who happened to make herself known to me this very morning. Apparently, she's Aleks's and only likes him, but she wrapped herself around my legs and purred like we were old pals.

"Oh, she likes you," Polina says. "Hisses at everyone else but she's your buddy."

Something in my chest loosens when she purrs. I've always wanted a cat, but my parents prohibited us from having pets.

"So what happened with the others you tried to hire?" I ask curiously. I'm fine with the smaller group but just curious.

She rolls her eyes and plants her hands on her hips. "Aleks, of course, the control freak. *No one sees my future wife in her undergarments but her sisters,*" she says in a perfect imitation of Aleks's mild accent. *"The more people we have, the greater the risk of a breach of security."*

I smile at her imitation of him, but a little pang of jealousy hits me. Is this what she grew up with? Men who actually cared about her wellbeing? It's so foreign to me. My father would've taken out a loan to hire a team to prepare me so that I looked flawless and perfect, with no concern about what I wanted or my modesty, and my brother did anything my father made him do.

There's a knock at the door. Since Polina's hands are in my hair, she nods to Aria. "Can you get that?"

Aria fairly waddles over to the door. "One of the staff with some refreshments. Thank God, I am *famished.*"

Polina snickers and winks at me. About an hour ago, Aria ate a fruit cup and a bagel laden with cream cheese, then rummaged through her purse for a packet of mixed nuts she downed in seconds because she said she was still starving. When that wasn't enough, she found a bowl of dinner mints and polished off every one of them.

"Someone's getting close to labor, I think," Polina whispers in my ear. "Her body's fueling up with all those practice contractions."

I smile at her. I've barely even met these two but feel like I've known them forever. I'm as excited as they are for the baby's arrival.

"Here," Aria says, bringing the tray of food over. She slides it onto the dresser. "Oh God, this looks so good."

"Help yourself."

She bites her lip but is clearly holding herself back. She looks hopeful.

"But you're the bride, you need to eat!"

"I'm not really hungry."

Her eyes light up and she's reaching for a wrapped sandwich when her phone rings. With a sigh, she puts it down.

"It's Mikhail. Gotta take this. You two need anything?"

"We're good. Go, appease the baby daddy so he doesn't cause any drama on the wedding day," Polina says with a wave of her hand.

"Girls," Aria says, coming back with a look of concern. "Mikhail says something strange has happened with your socials, Harper."

"My socials?" I don't have my old phone, just a new one Aleks got me "for safety" that I haven't even used yet.

"What happened?" I ask, shaking my head.

Aria sighs. "Looks like someone tried to attack you. Hacked into your account and posted a bunch of things. Couldn't have been you, I've already hacked in and checked the IP address of whoever posted, and they were nowhere near here." She frowns. "You wouldn't have posted these things, anyway."

Do I even want to know?

My new phone rings with the newest name I've entered into my contacts.

Aleksandr Romanov.

My heart races. I've replayed this morning in my mind over and over and over again. I have mixed feelings, to say the least.

I can't think of that now. I can't think of what will happen when we're alone.

I try to hide the tremor in my hand when I answer the call. "Hello?"

"Delete your socials. All of them. Someone's trying to get a grip on you by slandering you, and I won't allow it. Do not argue with me, Harper. If you—"

"I will happily delete them. Are you kidding? I hated them."

Polina looks at me in surprise. She shares a look with Aria.

"Do it now, on the phone with me."

I take my new phone and go to each page, one at a time, to delete them. With every deactivated account, I feel a little bit lighter.

"It's done. God, that felt good."

"Good. I'm sorry if that was hard for you."

Wow. A little humanity from him?

"It's fine."

"Are you almost ready?"

"Almost."

"Staff will be up shortly with some food. Try to eat a little something before the wedding."

I shouldn't be touched by his concern, but I can't help it. After a life of neglect, it's nice to have someone who cares about even the most basic things.

"They already did, but I'm not very hungry."

"What do you mean they already did? I'm looking at it now."

"It must've been the caterers or something, then."

"Oh my God! Aleks, your stupid cat!" Polina shoos it off the tray of food and sighs. "You'll have to send that tray up anyway, your damn cat just traipsed all over this one and nibbled at it. Gross."

"Be nice to my cat or I cut your allowance," he says, and I can't tell if he's joking or serious.

She flips the bird at the phone.

"I saw that, Polina." She gives me a sheepish grin. Is he bluffing, or did he really? We may never know.

I hang up the phone and am in the middle of the finishing touches when there's a knock at the door. My heart beats faster. I've been distracted getting ready for the wedding. I've been apart from Aleks since this morning and haven't had a real chance to think about much, much less fear anything.

But now... now that we're about to get married, every fear I ever had about being alone with him comes to the surface. He'll have me alone. He'll want...sex.

I close my eyes when a flutter of fear makes my heart leap into my throat.

I have feelings about that. Reservations. Dread.

This morning, though... this morning there was a glimmer of hope. A flicker of something like humanity in his eyes. A fleeting thought that maybe, just maybe...

"Are you okay?" I look up, ready to answer Polina, but realize she's not looking at me but at Aria. Aria's gone pale, her hand on her belly.

"I will not have a baby on your wedding day," she says, as if willing her body to stop. "I will not have a baby on your wedding day!"

I smile. "Aria, I met Aleks like two days ago. It's hardly a culmination of years of falling in love. The sooner these guests go home and I can get out of these clothes and into comfy pjs, the better. In other words — go ahead, have a baby on my wedding day."

Polina's musical laughter makes all of us smile. "Oh, I like you, Harper. I like you a lot. Aria, what's going on?"

"Just—contractions," Aria says, shaking her head. "I think they're those fake ones."

"Well, let us know if they get any closer together or intense, okay?" Polina requests, handing Aria a bottle of water.

She turns to me. "I'm studying to be a nurse."

"Ah, got it." That will come in handy.

Another knock at the door. "We're almost ready!"

"The groom's getting impatient. They've played the opening music a few times," one of the guys says.

"Alright, alright, let's go. Don't you know Italian women are never on time for their weddings? It's like a rule," Polina mutters.

I didn't even realize we were that close to needing to go.

It all feels surreal. The sound of the music. The formality of well-dressed guests waiting downstairs, mostly all unfamiliar to me except for the small cluster of my own family I won't make eye contact with.

Polina goes ahead of me, carrying a bouquet of flowers. I don't even know where they came from. I look down at my own hands and realize I'm holding a bouquet of my own. It all feels weirdly dream-like, as I prepare to walk toward my future husband.

When I see him, my heart does a little leap in my chest. I remember the look of desire in his eyes this morning. The way his finger on my shoulder made every nerve in my body come alive.

I remember a whirlwind of intense emotions. The way my voice faltered as he started to undress me. The way my need to be touched by him grew with every second that passed, the way arousal and apprehension warred with each other, whipping my body into a state of incandescence.

The way his assertion of dominance and pushing my boundaries both exhilarated and terrified me.

The feel of his mouth on my skin, the waves of pleasure he sent through my whole body, the effect his commanding words had on my body and mind...

The anticipation of what our vows would signify.

I swallow hard and blink, trying to bring myself back to the present.

There's a priest holding a book. A woman with an elegant silver up-do nearby. His mother? His brothers that I met yesterday and a younger man beside them with his arm in a sling and a bandage on his face. That must be the one I haven't met yet.

I move toward Aleks as if propelled forward by an invisible force. I stand in front of him, my heart beating so fast it feels like the flutter of a hummingbird's wings in my chest. He leans toward me, a hint of a smile on his lips, as he reaches for my hand.

Is he going to be nice to me, then?

"You could look a little less like you're heading to a funeral," he whispers.

That would be a no.

I give him a forced smile back. "Honestly, my thong is up my ass, so don't take it personally. I like to think it's... symbolic."

He stifles a snort as the priest begins the ceremony.

"Why are you staring at me?" I whisper. "Are you really afraid I'll run now?"

"I have to ensure you don't get a case of cold feet. But I promise you, Princess. If you were to run now, I'd derive immense satisfaction in the chase."

I swallow. "Why chase? Do you want me that badly?"

He leans closer. To anyone else, it would look like an intimate whisper of words between two lovers.

We know better.

"Every game has its end, Harper. And I *always* play for keeps."

The priest drones on and on, but I don't hear a word until it comes time for my vows. I nod and agree and so does Aleks. There's nothing the least bit romantic in taking vows to a man you don't know, much less love.

But when he takes my hand and slides a ring on my finger, something in me softens.

When the priest tells us we can kiss, I lift my face to his.

It starts almost tentatively, like two people stepping foot onto a frozen pond, unsure if it can hold their weight. Under the gaze of strangers and enemies and the expectant eyes of those around us, the soft meeting of his lips and mine carries the weight of what lies between us.

Like every interaction between us, it's charged with an electric pulse. His fingers on my chin burn my skin. There's a reverence and tenderness to the way he touches me I didn't even know he was capable of.

For a moment, I forget that anyone but the two of us is here. This isn't just a kiss, but maybe a silent truce, a new path forged by each of our pasts and our future. A whisper of something so much more.

As our lips part amid the hoots and hollers and cheers of the crowd around us, I stand a bit stunned. But I don't have time to reflect on any of this as he takes me by the hand and marches me down the makeshift aisle in the middle of his — our? — living room and toward the dining room.

My family appears out of nowhere, my mother's disapproving frown beside my father's cruel smile. He thinks he won.

"You look beautiful," my mother says. "But remember your loyalty."

Aleks's gaze darkens. "She'll remember who she's loyal to."

The coloring of my father's face tells me he got that message loud and clear.

"Look at you, all dolled up like royalty. You play the part of a blushing bride well."

My cheeks heat. I can't believe he just said that out loud.

Aleks's hand on my back reassures me. It shouldn't — he's not my ally and hasn't been. But now that we're married, now that I'm his wife, maybe things will change.

"Let's go," he says in a low voice. "Ignore them. If they speak to you again, I'll deal with them personally."

We walk past them. They hold their heads high, almost haughtily. My mother gives me the glimmer of a smile. I smile back, not to be friendly but because I want her to know that while this wasn't my choice, I'm going to be just *fine*.

More than fine. I'm going to thrive.

The formal dining room's large and spacious, filled with huge vases of blooming flowers. The waitstaff mills about in formal attire, holding large silver platters of appetizers. Aleks leads me to a table set for two.

I sit down, grateful for the glass of water and flute of champagne to calm my fraught nerves. We'll have dinner, for now.

Then we'll be alone. Just the two of us.

I think back to this morning.

I reach for the champagne and down it.

"I think we're supposed to wait for the toast," Aleks says, leaning closer to me.

"Oh, right. Rules and traditions and such."

"Are you a rule breaker, Harper?" he asks, as he traces his finger down the stem of my glass. Something like lust flickers in his eyes. "Do you like to do things on your own terms?"

Why can't I help but imagine those fingers trailing along my naked skin? Remember what he vowed to do to me if I defied him?

Not *if*, really — *when*.

"I think that you—"

"Aleks." Polina stands in front of the two of us, breathless, as if she's just run here. Her voice is barely above a whisper, her eyes wide and panicked.

I place the flute down and set my hands in my lap to steady the trembling, but Aleks is as placid as can be.

"What is it?" he asks in a low voice.

"It's Misty."

Misty? Who's Misty — *oh*. His cat. Misty's his cat. Did something happen to her?

"She's sick. I thought it was just a normal thing like she had a furball or something clogged in her throat, but it's way more than that. I think she's been poisoned. But that's not the worst of it."

Aleks's eyes are dark and dangerous. Lethal. "Tell me."

"Do you remember?" Polina whispers. "She ate off the tray of food meant for Harper."

CHAPTER EIGHT

Harper

IT TAKES a few seconds for the truth to register before an icy mask of decision falls over Aleks's face.

"Lock this room down. *Now.*"

It all happens so quickly. Guests are vetted and escorted out, staff is questioned. I sit, flanked on either side by two of the bodyguards who were stationed outside my room this morning.

I suddenly remember. "Aleks, earlier today you said you had a tray of food for me, and I told you we already had one?"

"Right. Who brought the tray in?"

"Aria."

Aria says one of the staff members gave it to her and points out a pale, thin woman with blonde hair.

"I'm so sorry, sir," she says, her eyes wide at the look on Aleks's face. "I was instructed to bring it up. That's all I know. I came in late for a shift and one of the headwaiters said you asked for it to be sent up."

The poor girl quakes under his furious look. "Which waiter?"

On and on the questioning goes until Aleks has interrogated everyone on staff. Mikhail oversees the questioning with concern, his brow knitted, but he mostly appears like he's trying to prevent Aleks from singlehandedly murdering everyone.

"Aria could've eaten from that tray," I say in a whisper. "She had the food in her hand but got distracted."

The thought of Aria being poisoned...

Now Mikhail joins Aleks with the murderous looks.

"I want every one of the staff dismissed," Aleks says to Mikhail. "Fired. No one but my wife stays here."

My heart stalls at those words, two words that are foreign to my ears.

My wife.

Within an hour, his cat's been sent to an emergency vet and declared poisoned but fine, and now there's no one but the two of us left in the house. Not a single member of staff. Not one bodyguard.

I have no doubt Mikhail and his men are doing whatever Bratva men do about a potential threat against their loved ones.

Aleks sits brooding, a bottle of beer in front of him. His tie's long gone, his hair a little tousled. He's broody as fuck, and no help for it.

I try to think of him as *my husband* but somehow the vision of him in front of me and the words don't quite jive together.

I nurse a glass of wine and try to make the dots connect.

"We were all adopted, you know," he says thoughtfully, running his thumb along the rim of the beer bottle.

"Oh? I didn't know. I mean, I know hardly anything about you."

"Each of us, in turn, came from nothing. My uncle told me it was a favorite strategy of his father's. My grandfather's."

I take another sip of wine, welcoming the slightly fruity tang and burn. "What strategy?"

"To start fresh. Start anew. He said whenever he took over a business, the first thing he did was fire everyone so he could handpick who worked for him. It was his method of ensuring loyalty." He talks in a low, dangerous growl that makes me shiver. "Burn it all to the ground and start fresh."

"An interesting strategy."

Does that apply to me?

Oooooh.

"You told me to bring nothing with me," I say in a little voice as it dawns on me. "You wanted to start fresh with *me.*"

He nods. "It's how my father established his family. One by one, he chose us. He ensured our loyalty by providing for our needs, taking care of us, fathering us. By giving us a mother that took care of us."

"I see."

He takes another sip from the bottle. I watch his Adam's apple bob up and down while he swallows.

"Did you fire everyone?"

"Yeah."

I polish off the glass of wine and reach for the bottle. He watches me as if mesmerized but doesn't stop me. I try to keep my tone upbeat to quell my rising nerves. "I'm amazed they left so readily, given your cheerful nature and infectious joy for life. You're like sunshine in human form."

He narrows his eyes at me. "Are you baiting me?"

My hand shakes a little as I pour another glass. "Nah."

Of course I'm baiting him. If I can get him focused on sparring with me, it takes his mind off things like murder, bloodshed, and the darker cravings that haunt him. I want to see the man he is beneath the scars and shadowed masks he wears.

And if I'm honest? I want to distract him from the inevitable next step we take alone as a married couple.

"Try again," he says, turning to face me. He finishes the beer and tosses the bottle to the table. I jump at the clang of glass and expect it to shatter, but it only rolls away.

"Maybe it's your magnetic appeal and charisma," I say, taking another generous sip of wine. My thoughts get a little muddled and the view in front of me blurs a little, like the room's been etched in oil pastels. "Your genteel nature and lighthearted sense of humor?"

"Getting there," he says, and I swear his eyes on me feel like he's mentally undressing me. "*Khristos,* Princess. You're fucking gorgeous. How much wine have you had?"

I finish my glass and eye the bottle. "Not enough," I whisper, my words slurred. I reach for the bottle.

"No, Harper."

A chill skates down my back at the utter command in his tone. I pause, my hand on the bottle, and lift my eyes to his. "What?"

"No more wine." Warmth spreads through me from the top of my head to the tips of my toes. "I want you to remember tonight in vivid detail."

Oh, God.

I stand on shaky feet and take a few steps to the vacant, makeshift bar that flanks a wall, abandoned bottles still lined up like soldiers. I reach across and grab a little shot of whiskey. I don't ever drink that much. I don't even know how to. But I do know two things: I don't want to remember this night, and I don't want him to think he can boss me around.

I twist the top off a shot of something amber and don't even read the label. I tip my head back and down it in one gulp, sputtering when I come up for air.

I squeal when the full length of his warm body presses me against the white table. How did he get there? I wasn't even aware of him moving.

"Disobeying me already? We've barely taken vows."

"I'm not. You told me no more wine." I hold up the empty shot. "This isn't wine."

"So that's how we're going to play it," he says in a lazy drawl as he arranges my hands flat across the top of the table.

"Play what?" My voice sounds too high, too loud.

"The way you earn your first spanking."

My cheeks instantly color and my vision momentarily becomes clearer. "Aleks!"

His palm slams across my ass, but I hardly feel it. I'm surrounded by layers and layers of fabric. I can't help it — I'm so tipsy and so wound up I snort.

"Are you mocking me, Princess?"

I am so mocking him, but I shake my head.

"Me? Never. Aleks!"

In one swift motion, I'm up in the air and over his shoulder, my legs scissoring and hands flailing in front of me.

"These layers of clothes need to go."

I'm shaking and want to fight but have no choice.

I don't care how he was this morning. I don't care how my body responded. I don't care that it's our duty, that I have to bear his children, that we're married now, and the expectations placed on us are as clear as road signs.

I'm scared.

By the time we get to our bedroom and he stands me in front of him, my cheeks are damp with tears. I taste the salt and will myself to stop, but I can't. I swipe at them angrily. I feel like such a coward.

I barely register the size of the bed or vases of flowers, the muted neutral colors and simple design of the room, the scent of jasmine and rose and the pile of wrapped gifts and cards on a small table. It's our wedding night, and the only thing that matters to me at this point is what we have to do next.

He unhurriedly undoes the pearl buttons at the back of my neck and kisses the bare skin revealed when each one falls open.

"Why are you crying?" he asks as he slips another button loose and kisses me again. "You're crying, Harper."

I shake my head. "I'm—I'm not," I stutter, but it's no use. I totally am.

When a few more buttons come undone, he slides a sleeve off my shoulder so one full side of me is bared to him.

"You are, and I want to know why. Do you think I'll hurt you?"

He continues the deliberate disrobing until I'm wearing nothing but my white satin wedding bra and matching thong. He lays me back on the bed and sits on the edge beside me.

"N-no," I say, my voice tremulous. "But I don't know for

sure. I don't know who you are, and I don't know what you're capable of."

I tuck myself into the pile of pillows at the head of the bed and watch him. Earlier tonight, when he realized that there was an attempt at poisoning me, the look on his face terrified me. Now, though... now there's a different sort of look that makes me more curious than anything.

"You're brave, Harper. Resilient. This is unlike you."

Goddamn, why is he so perceptive?

I swallow and lick my lips, looking away, but he doesn't allow it. With his fingers on my chin, he brings my face back to his.

"Tell me," he says, in the same voice he used tonight to clear the room, a tone that brooks no argument. I know then that there's no hiding from Aleksandr Romanov. He sees right through me. With his fingers on my chin, he holds my gaze. "Who did this to you?"

A stranger in a crowded room.

Wrinkled sheets and muted screams.

Blood and pain and the knowledge I'd been used and discarded.

"Did — did what?" I whisper, hoping that if I stall, I don't have to face this. Face *him.*

I'm lying on the bed, half naked. He's fully clothed sitting next to me. I'm trying to hide the fact that I'm crying under a mask of bravado, and he's trying to keep his temper reined in.

I'm tired of masks and lies and illusions.

So, so tired.

"You're fucking terrified of being alone with me. Look at you. You're practically curled into a fetal position, and I've barely touched you."

A part of me *wants* him to touch me. Wants him to make me forget.

His brow furrowed he tries to guess. "Did your mother tell you to fear your wedding night? Are you afraid of what the first time will be like?"

I shake my head. It won't be my first time.

"No," I whisper.

What will he do when he finds out I'm not a virgin?

A muscle twitches in his jaw. He's losing patience. "Someone hurt you."

I lick my lips. "Yes."

Leaning forward, he covers my hand with his big palm. "I'll ask you one more time. Who did this to you? Why are you afraid of me?"

I stare at him. We're married now. We share a name, and we'll share children. I can't tell him all of my secrets, not yet, but I'll tell him the rest soon.

"I was at a party," I say in a whisper. "Someone slipped something in my drink. I only remember bits and pieces."

"You were assaulted," he says in a voice I can't quite decipher, but I'm reminded of a lion with velveted paws.

My mouth is dry, my voice hoarse. "Yes."

He doesn't speak for long minutes. Is he going to hurt me? I made a mistake telling him, I know I did. I know the consequences a mafia woman faces for losing her virginity. She's damaged goods.

Miss High and Mighty.

Filthy piece of trash.

Fucking whore.

I've just revealed to Aleks that he was hoodwinked. He was tricked into marrying me, not knowing who I am or what I've done.

"I'm sorry," I whisper. "I thought I could hide it. I didn't want to tell you. If my mother knew I told you—"

He holds his hand up for me to stop. The words die on my lips.

"In your world, a woman's virginity is her pride and joy. It isn't the same for us. And even if it was an expectation in my family, I wouldn't fault you for being assaulted. But I do have questions." I'm shaking, unable to stop it. Wordlessly, he closes his hand around mine. The shaking stills. "Tell me. When your father found out, what was the blowback to your family for the justice he served? I need to know who our enemies are."

I don't quite understand the question at first. He thinks my father avenged me?

"Justice he served?"

Aleks's lips are in a tight line. His eyes have gone black. "When he murdered the man who assaulted you, what happened?"

"He blamed me, Aleks. He never even looked for the man that assaulted me. We didn't know who he was, and my father didn't care." I shake my head. "You don't know how shallow my family can be. They didn't care about me. They cared that one of their biggest bargaining chips was worthless." I shrug. "My brother wanted to get rid of me. He made a deal with your brother, and here I am."

You aren't worthless.

It isn't your fault.

Aleks looks momentarily shocked. It's the first time I've seen a look like that on his face, but I've heard shock is one of the expressions nearly impossible to hide. "Even your brother didn't seek justice?"

I shake my head. "No."

His brows snap together and his voice is as low as the underbelly of a snake when he responds. "I'll fucking kill them."

I shiver because it isn't a figure of speech. He will.

"Who?" I whisper.

"All of them. Your father should've known better. Your brother should've burned the world down to defend your honor. Your mother should've hired someone to find out who assaulted you and made it her life's mission to make them pay."

He really, really doesn't know my family.

"You can't make up fear like this," he says in a lower voice, when the first thunderous rage begins to ebb away. "You're afraid of me because you were assaulted."

He pushes himself off the bed and stalks away, pacing beside the bed before he finally shakes his head. "What to do with your family and our enemy will wait for another day. Tonight is about us." He gives me a curious look. "Do you want me to leave for a little while? Do you need some time?"

How much time would he give me? There are rules in our families.

Who is this and what has he done with the grumpy Russian? I swallow. Think. Do I want him to leave me?

I shake my head. I remember this morning. The hope that flickered like the catch of fire. "No. I'm...willing to try. If you'll listen if I say stop."

"Of course I will. I'm not a monster."

I nod. For the first time in my adult life, I feel like the choice is *mine*. And that's *everything*.

Bending forward, Aleks touches his lips to mine. The kiss is so gentle it's almost chaste.

"Keep the rest on, Harper. I want *you* to control this."

He says that, but he's the one giving the commands. I swallow the lump in my throat and nod. I can do it. I know I can.

I don't want to be naked in front of him, though. I have the same fearful thoughts every day.

"Who else is in this house with us?" he asks.

I lick my lips. "No one."

"That's right. It's just us. You, my wife. And me, your husband. I will not hurt you. And there's no one telling us where and when to do anything. I married you and that's all that matters right now."

A small part of me wonders why I thought he hated me before. Are things different now that I'm his wife?

My hands come to rest on my thighs. I watch as Aleks stands up beside me and slowly strips out of his own clothing, his brow furrowed as if in concentration. I saw him this morning in hardly anything at all, and I haven't been able to get the thought of his golden skin, his muscled abs and toned biceps, the perfect planes of his shoulders, out of my mind.

Soon, we're sitting before each other dressed like we were in the early quiet of morning. This morning, there were only the two of us. The two of us and a long day ahead. He barely touched me. Now, it's the same, only this time we have nowhere to go and not even the semblance of waiting until after the wedding to prevent us from doing anything.

Wordlessly, he leans toward me and kisses my bare shoulder. A shiver trickles down my spine, but I don't move. Another kiss follows the first, as he makes his way down the length of my arm and back again.

A tremor runs through me.

For so long, I've felt like I was only an object to the people I knew, the people I loved. I didn't feel I mattered to anyone beyond what I could do for them. Now, however... I shouldn't let myself believe that I matter to him, but it's hard to think otherwise when he's looking at me that way.

Am I just romanticizing this? Romanticizing *him?* He chased me, forced me into the back of his car, and cuffed me.

But then we took vows. And maybe in this family...that means something's changed.

"You're beautiful," he says in a low voice, as he makes his way to my other shoulder and kisses down the length of that arm, too. "Put your hands in your lap and don't move them until I tell you."

I couldn't disobey a thing he said now if I tried. I'm putty in his hands, helpless to resist the pull of attraction between us. I'm floating somewhere in the atmosphere without the grounding force of gravity anymore.

So I do what he says. I lay my hands in my lap as he continues to worship me. A tentative kiss to the top of one breast. We're like two long-lost lovers trying to remember the way toward each other.

"Lie down," he whispers in my ear. "I want to taste you."

With a shuddering breath, I obey. Wordlessly, he holds my wrists and pins them above my head. "Don't move those hands."

I keep them in place, but when he makes his way down the length of my body, I feel sick with nerves. When he kisses the vee at the top of my sex, my hips convulse but a sudden need to run flashes through me.

"No," I whisper. "Don't. Please, no."

I've never had anyone do that for me before but it's too intimate, too close, and we hardly know each other.

"Don't what?"

"Don't...do that. I'm not ready. Please, Aleks. I'm not comfortable with any of this." As soon as I say it, I regret it. What's he going to do? He's my husband, and by all of the rules in both of our worlds, I belong to him now.

He looks thoughtful for a moment. "If you let me try, it will help prepare you. It'll make it easier."

"There must be like...other things we can do?"

"Yes, but we do have to consummate this marriage. You know that, and so do I. It's the rule for my family and for yours. We can wait, though."

I nod and swallow. He stands and walks over to the dresser. For the first time, I see a small plate of chocolate-covered strawberries, and some champagne. He opens the bottle quietly, with none of the pomp and circumstance of a fizz and pop.

He pours champagne into a flute, and then pours one for himself. I let out a breath.

"Hungry?"

I nod. I'm starving. I barely ate dinner.

"Let's start with these."

He brings the tray of strawberries over, and I reach for one, but he gives me a playful slap of the hand.

"Hey!"

"You can have one," he says. "But only if I'm the one to feed it to you."

Oh, boy. I have such strange, warring sensations inside me. A part of me wants him to touch me. I want to completely forget the assault that I experienced. I want to lose myself in pleasure, and I know it's right there... right out of reach. If only...

And then a part of me wants to move over and go to sleep and pretend this never happened.

"We have no choice, Harper. But we can make this fun."

I know he's right. We don't. Our union was a solidification of two families, a calculated move.

He hands me the flute of champagne. I've already had so much wine, I start to feel a little uninhibited when I finish it.

I lean back in the bed, curious what he'll do next. Even though he's the one I'm watching and he's the one supposedly in charge, I'm the one that's said no. I feel empowered.

"Open."

I hold his gaze while he pushes the chocolate-covered point of a strawberry past my lips. I bite, holding his gaze, and an explosion of flavors fills my mouth. I swallow and lick my lips. Mmm.

"Do you smoke?"

I shake my head, bemused.

I watch as he walks to a corner of the room and opens a desk drawer. Takes something out. Holds it between his fingers, puts it to his lips, and lights it.

The sweet smell of smoke fills the room.

Oh.

He opens a window and I openly stare at him. It's strange, me wearing my underwear, him wearing his.

He's so fucking hot. His legs are chiseled, his ass perfection. His back is stunning. He has tattoos in various places, loops and lines, words and swirls, but nothing I can really distinguish right now.

"Take it easy if you haven't had it before. Do you smoke?"

I shake my head. I might not be a virgin, but I'm woefully inexperienced.

He puts the joint between my fingers. With a shaking hand, I bring it to my lips and take a tiny drag. I sputter a little, but he talks me through it. Soon, a deliciously floaty sensation comes over me.

A corner of his lips quirks up. "You're gonna fall asleep for days after this."

"Sounds delightful. Just make sure you shave me so I don't become the female version of Rip van Winkle."

Aleks's eyes darken. "Shave you? I can arrange that."

A giggle bubbles up. I take the joint back and take another drag.

"Easy," he says. "Now, keep your hands in your lap."

He lifts another one of the chocolate-covered strawberries and puts the smallest tip in my mouth. The flavor of creamy chocolate and tangy, cold fruit hits my tongue. I lick my lips. "Yum."

I watch him polish off three. "Yum, but we need some real food. Let's take a walk."

"I'm high as a kite and almost naked."

"Sounds perfect."

It's strange, walking down to the kitchen wearing next to nothing, but he makes it seem normal. A king in his domain, rummaging around the fridge and coming up with some cheese and crackers, cured meats and olives. We put together a makeshift charcuterie board, pair it with the champagne, and bring it all back to the bedroom. It's delicious.

Emboldened with my stomach full, I ask him a question. "Why did you marry me?" A handsome man like him could've gotten anybody, I would think. "Why *me*?"

He shrugs. "I'm not one for dating. I had a girlfriend a long, long time ago. And I lost her. I haven't wanted to date anyone since then. But you know the rules. You know the expectations. So when Mikhail made a deal with your brother, I agreed."

He had someone before me? She isn't here anymore, but I'm still jealous.

I put a small wedge of Parmesan on a round wheat cracker and take a bite. "And what happens now that we're married?"

"There have been many who were bidding for power in The Cove in the wake of our enemy's death. Now that we're married, it gives us the first stronghold we need. Next step, children." My heart leaps.

"And then world domination," I say with forced cheerfulness.

"Exactly. My mother likes to say that man should not be alone."

"Does she really quote the Bible to you? Does she know who you are?"

"I think it's *because* she knows who we are that she's always quoting the Bible to us. Hoping to save our souls or something."

That makes me laugh. I go to reach for another strawberry, remember his admonition, and very politely put my hand back in my lap.

"Good girl," he says approvingly.

I love it when he praises me. I love it when he looks at me like he's starving and he wants to eat me up. I love a lot of things about the two of us and that's probably dangerous as hell.

He's sitting in a chair across from the bed, spread in that casual manly way with his knees parted and his elbows resting on his thighs. "I want to look at you. Stand in front of me, Harper."

CHAPTER NINE

Harper

I'M *SUPER* DRUNK, or high, or whatever you call the combination of both of those things. And I had no idea this could happen, but I swear every nerve ending in my body's been lit on fire.

I flinch when he reaches for me but have no chance to do anything more before he tugs me onto his lap. The feel of his hardness pressing into my ass tells me he likes what he sees. Pride swells in my chest.

That feels nice, not scary like I'd imagined it would.

"How are you feeling now?" he asks. I hold my breath when he leans forward and slides his mouth over the hollow of my neck. His hair tickles my chin.

"Less inhibited, you could say." My voice sounds distant. "What are you doing?"

His shoulders rise when he inhales. "You smell so good."

"You wanted to smell me?"

"Mmm."

"That's an interesting take on foreplay."

"It's all foreplay, Harper. All of it. You running. The chase. Me catching you. Your sass and wit. Seeing you in that dress. Knowing what was beneath it."

Flames of arousal lick at me. His grip tightens.

"When I was younger, I knew a man who was in college." It's funny to think of Aleksandr as a teen. Younger, innocent, less chiseled. Maybe his beard was scant. Maybe his eyes weren't so hardened.

"He was kind of like another big brother. I was a virgin, and he was giving me some advice."

Oh, boy.

I swallow. Do I want to hear this?

"You know how he told me to make sure a woman was ready for sex?"

"Um. Ask her?"

He smiles and shakes his head, his accent thicker with arousal. "He said to touch her *everywhere* and let her know how much I appreciated what I saw. And then kiss every inch of her body until she was so wet, she couldn't stand it anymore."

Well, damn. "I mean you could maybe do that."

He brushes his lips across my cheek, my jaw, my neck. Moves to my shoulder and the top of each breast before he weighs each in his hands.

"Are you sure?"

"I'm...being persuaded."

I'm nearing boneless when he bends me backward so he can kiss his way down the length of my body, from the valley between my breasts to my navel. The room is thick with anticipation, the warmth of the alcohol loosening my taut nerves, my restraint.

With every second that passes as he continues to kiss me, I sink deeper and deeper into a world where only the two of us dwell.

The magnetic pull between us grows, the connection undeniable. I've been hurt, yes.

But so has he.

I've lost my innocence.

So has he.

It gives me hope that when he finds out my secret, when he finds out everything about me, he'll forgive me.

I almost feel like I can trust him. I almost feel like I could be honest. But right now, I can only focus on what has to happen tonight.

The air, as always, is charged between us. Electric. He kisses his way back up to my breasts, and my nipples pebble in anticipation. When he draws one of them between his lips and sucks, my hips rise of their own accord.

Waves of pleasure rock me when he plies the flat of his tongue against my nipples, one after the other. When I freeze, he stops long enough to issue an order. "Let *go*. Stop fighting me."

I want to protest, to tell him to stop telling me what to do, but with every kiss, every lick and nibble and touch, my resolve begins to crumble. I can't remember the thoughts that held me back before.

His touch is both gentle and firm, confident but unhurried. When his lips find mine, the last vestiges of the world around me cease to exist. A floating sensation overwhelms me.

And then I'm actually floating. We're standing and he's carrying me to the bed. With deliberate moves, he lays me on my back in the middle of the mattress and kneels beside me. We were here once before, and I asked him to stop. I can't remember now why.

My panties are around my ankles, then on the floor. He parts my legs and settles himself between them with confident ease. The heat of his breath on my inner thighs is a promise of pleasure. I start to shake when I realize what he's going to do, but this time, I'm ready.

He smooths his fingers between my legs, easily gliding through my slick folds. "*Khristos*. You're so damn wet."

"Mmm," I say on a choked breath. "I guess that was good advice you got."

His eyes meet mine. He holds my gaze when he drags his tongue upward, right over my clit. I cry out at the sudden spasm of pleasure that seems to take over my whole lower body.

"*Fuuccck,*" he groans. "God, you taste better than I imagined."

He loses himself in worshipping me. A lazy stroke of his warm tongue to my clit, followed by a pulse of his fingers in my core. I'm ramping up toward ecstasy with every second that passes. Over and over again he tongues me, stifling his own groans. My eyes flutter closed. I'm drowning in perfection, my body responding of its own accord.

Everything becomes centered on the smallest connection between us. Every thought and feeling, every hope and dream could fit on the head of a pin. My entire world is right here, anticipating the next perfect swipe of his tongue.

"Are you close?" he asks.

I nod. I don't think I could stop myself now if I tried.

"Come on my tongue," he commands with another lazy lap of his tongue. "Come, Princess."

The sensation overwhelms me and then — I'm stunned by a crescendo of ecstasy. I can't breathe or speak as my body gives way to utter bliss. Spasms overtake me and I lose myself completely to him in total surrender. As the climax overpowers me, the wave of pleasure is tinged with a yawning need for something more, something deeper, a *bond.*

"I want you inside me," I say while still riding through pleasure. "Please, Aleks."

I can't believe I'm *asking* him.

"If you're ready," he says in a whisper. "Are you sure you're ready?"

I nod, a little shocked that I actually think I am. Still, I'm shaking when he gives a final kiss to my clit then slides up my body, his skin so warm against me. When he enters me, I don't ask about protection because I know the family rules as well as he does. Staring into my eyes, he pauses, letting us both savor the moment before gently gliding out then back in, building a rhythm that thrills me.

The depth of our connection is undeniable. A flutter of anticipation weaves itself through my limbs. Every thrust of his hips sends frissons of exquisite awareness to every nerve ending in my body.

We move together in a perfect rhythm, as if this is what we were created for. I find myself on the edge of something deeper, something *more*. I can hardly contain the emotions and waves of pleasure spiraling through me now. What would it be like if I actually cared for him? What would it be like knowing he actually cared for me?

I reach another peak then my mind goes blissfully quiet, our breaths mingling in the cold stillness of the room. For once, I don't have any expectations or fears. It's just me and ... Aleks.

My husband.

More thrusts of his hips have me on the edge of perfection again. He slows his movements until I'm begging for more.

My arms encircle his neck, and my legs wrap around him as he thrusts over and over again. My head sinks deeper into the pillow as ecstasy wraps around me a third time, this time more intense and so much more satisfying, so much sweeter than the first two.

This. Is. *Everything*.

When I finally come down from the high and sprawl out on the bed, he groans and lays his heavy head on my shoulder. It seems he's as boneless and wrecked as I am.

"Passable," I tease in a whisper, reaching for him. "Thank you."

I didn't know a man like him could be so gentle.

"Passable? Goddamn. Well, practice, they say, makes perfect." He nuzzles his head into my chest. "I aim to please."

"Oh?" Caressing the nape of his neck, I lay my other arm over my head as I try to steady my rapid breathing. "You did good."

"That was only the first time, you know. Next time it's your turn."

"Oh, really?" I shrug. "I suppose I could try."

I squeak when, with a rough tug, he rolls over and yanks me onto his chest. Gives me a fierce kiss to the forehead.

"Go to sleep," he growls. "We have work to do tomorrow."

Yes, we do have work to do tomorrow, no doubt. And I have to find a way to get him to trust me. To give me space and room so I'm not held prisoner here.

It's only a matter of time before he discovers my secret. But it has to be on my terms.

I need him to trust me first, or all might be lost.

CHAPTER TEN

Aleks

I GIVE Harper shit about how she velveted my paws and needed kid gloves. But she takes it all in stride and gives me shit right back.

I have work to catch up on and my sister and Aria — still hugely pregnant and due in a matter of days, which has had Mikhail hovering— have been coming by to visit. It helps that Mikhail and Aria don't live far away. Harper isn't alone all the time.

Three days after the wedding, Harper gets a phone call from her mother.

"Speakerphone," I tell her, as I work at my desk on the list of things Mikhail has given me to do. Harper's in the middle of a late afternoon yoga routine in the office, her legs crossed in front of her. It's distracting as fuck, seeing her in a yoga outfit with those skintight leggings and that half-bra thing she wears.

She taps her phone. "Hello?"

"Harper. We decided we'd honor your marriage to your new husband by giving you time to... honeymoon, or whatever it is you decided."

I close the browser and narrow my eyes.

"Mhm," Harper says, rolling her eyes at me as she stands and does this thing where she lifts one leg straight in the air while steadying herself on the other. "And? Now that we've finished our honeymoon you have something to say."

As if we had a honeymoon. Men in my line of work rarely do.

"What happened to your accounts?"

Harper grits her teeth and brings her leg back down. She mutes the phone. "I cannot do a yoga routine while listening to her. It is *not* namaste." She puts the speaker back on.

"My accounts?" she asks, as if she doesn't know exactly what her mother's talking about.

"Your social media accounts. The ones you spent years cultivating! They're gone."

"The ones *you* spent years cultivating," she says, her voice a tremulous whisper. "I hated them, and you knew I did. I wanted no part of the lies."

"Harper," her mother says reproachfully. She releases a belabored sigh. "You know why we had you do that."

"I know exactly why. But you decided you needed me to be married more than anything, so you pawned me off on a

Romanov." I can see the teasing glint in her eye. She's baiting me.

I shake my head at her, but my lips tug at the edges. She's
earning herself a trip over my knee, but she's been pushing
me now for a few days, so I'm guessing that's her intent.

"Harper, you know we didn't pawn you off—"

"That's exactly what you did." She walks over to me, the
phone still on speakerphone. "And you have no idea how he
treats me." With that, she sidles her way onto my lap. I push
away from the desk. Someone's a needy little girl who wants
my full attention, and I'm here for it. "So the answer is, my
new husband, the one who you wed me to having no idea
who he was or how he'd treat me? He made me delete them.
And I won't be doing them again."

The phone clicks off. I'm not sure who hung up — her
mother or her—but the phone sits muted on the desk.

"I'm still going to kill them," I tell her pointedly.

"Is that a promise? And do you mean *all* of them?"

"Your father and brother will pay, Harper."

She swallows. "I know."

She bites her lip and looks away. I'm not sure why.

"Aleks, I—" She opens her mouth as if to tell me something
then shuts it again. My phone rings. I look down to see
Aria's calling.

Harper stays on my lap and lays her head on my chest.
"Always the phone. Why do you get so many calls? Go
ahead, take it," she murmurs. "You have to, don't you?"

I nod, answering, "It's Aria," and put the phone up to my ear.

"Aleks, we need to talk. It's... it's very important."

"Are you alright?"

"Yes, I'm fine. I just found some information that you need to be aware of, alright?"

"I'll call you back in ten. Does that work?"

"Yes. But Aleks? When you call... make sure you're alone, please."

A strange request, but that's fair enough. We have to be discreet.

I hang up the phone and kiss Harper. Her skin's warm from the yoga session, her hair a little damp and tousled. I run my fingers through it.

"You were disrespectful just now, weren't you?"

"How so?"

"You were testing the boundaries. Being disrespectful talking about your husband, as if being married to a Romanov isn't an honor."

She nods and bites her lip, her eyes alight as I silently gesture for her to stand then bend over my knee. I shake my head.

"You should talk about your husband with respect. Did you already forget the rules we went over before we got married?"

"Oh, right," she says with a teasing lilt in her voice. The fabric of her workout outfit whispers against her perfect skin as I pull her leggings down to expose her tight ass, barely covered with a teeny wisp of a thong.

When I place my palm on her skin, she shivers. I caress first one cheek, then the other, taking my time. I know how she is. I know how to make her wet for me.

I palm her ass firmly, building the anticipation while I lecture her.

"When you talk to others about your husband, don't you think the right thing to do is to be respectful? Tell me."

"Yes, of course," she says, nodding. Her cheeks are flushed from her anticipation and her head-down position over my lap. "I was only teasing."

The first slap lands and she hisses in a breath. She fucking loves this. "Good. I'm glad to hear that," I tell her, right before I deliver a second smack, then a third. "You should behave yourself," I warn. "I've given you time to get used to things."

"What is that supposed to mean?"

I give her another slap. "Watch that tone."

I spank her until her skin is bright pink and red hot to the touch. "Have you learned your lesson?"

"Have I?" she whispers, parting her legs as if to welcome me.

"Jesus, how am I supposed to get any work done under these conditions? I want to be sure you're going to behave yourself."

"Of course I am."

"Are you going to obey me?"

"Mmmm."

"Good. Then stay over my lap."

"Aleks!" There's so much I want to do to her, but I've treaded lightly. Our first night together indicated to me how afraid she was of being touched. I won't use her or abuse her in any way.

"Are you ready to make it up to me?" I ask.

"Of course."

"Good girl." I massage her reddened skin. I slap her inner thigh. "Open."

I'm hard as fuck when I finger her pussy. I relish the way she moans over my lap. I slick my fingers in her wetness and drag the tips across her swollen clit. "You liked your spanking, didn't you?"

She squirms and moans in response. I've got a raging hard-on as I finger her pretty pussy until she arches her back and comes.

Fuck, she's gorgeous.

I give her perfect ass a parting slap. "Go get ready. I'm ordering lunch. You'll eat in here with me."

She leans in, her cheeks flushed and her eyes bright, and gives me a kiss.

I kiss her back until she melts against me. I send her to get a shower while I walk to the kitchen and start to think about what dinner could be.

Once I've taken stock of what we have on hand, I pause to call Mikhail. He tells me Aria's on the phone with her midwife.

"Why? Everything okay? Any news?"

"Any day now." He's so high-strung and worried, but they'll be fine.

Half an hour later, Harper's perched on a stool in the kitchen, nursing a glass of wine. "You're going to make me an alcoholic," she says with a laugh.

"Doesn't look like you need much assistance."

"Hey!"

I shrug. "You walked right into that one."

I pause in front of the open fridge, a package of steak in one hand. "What are you *wearing*?"

She looks down at her clothes as if to remind herself. Tiny ivory shorts and a matching top.

"This is a *lounge* outfit."

"Looks easy to take off, which is all I care about."

"Of course that's all you care about." She rolls her eyes, but I can tell she's pleased. Slowly, we're getting a bit more used to each other, though we still have a ways to go.

She takes another sip before setting her wineglass down. Even though we're married, it feels like we're dating. We're still testing the waters.

"I'm curious."

"Mmm?"

"What's on the roof?"

I put the steak back in the fridge and shut the door. I've never taken anyone up on the roof before. It's my secret place.

"You want to see?"

It's finally warmed up a bit though it's still not exactly balmy out.

"I do. I've wanted to, so badly, ever since I heard one of your guards talking to another one about it the day I came here."

Everyone's jealous of my roof.

"Come on."

I open the door in the kitchen that leads to the pantry, then show her where a trap door's hidden in the wall. "This is how you access the roof."

When the panel opens under my palm, she lets out an audible gasp. "*No way*. It's like a secret compartment or something."

"Yeah."

We walk up the stairs.

The early evening chill when we reach the roof makes her shiver. I shrug off my sweatshirt and drape it over her shoulders, but I think she hardly notices.

"Oh my *God*. Aleks— this is... How did I not know this was here?"

I shrug. "Because I don't tell a lot of people. In my family, we don't have a lot of privacy. This is mine."

"So no one can track you up here? No one knows where you are?"

"They'd know I'm at my house but no, no one would know I'm up here. And I don't bring any electronics up here."

I sit back on one of the patio chairs, built large enough for a man like me, and flick on one of the outdoor heaters. In the colder months, the vibrant greenery lies dormant and the roof becomes frost-kissed. I almost like it better this way. A splash of color from evergreens and hardy winter shrubs are nestled amidst padded benches and a trellis. It can be cold without the heaters and it's sometimes dusted with snow, but it's beautiful and quiet.

Harper perches on the end of my chair, hands sinking into the cushion, her legs stretched out in front of her. "This is amazing, you know. Truly amazing. It's a secret garden. *Your* secret garden."

"Now yours," I say softly, reaching for her. I drag her sideways onto my lap, and she nestles in comfortably.

Her eyes reflect the night sky as she marvels at the outdoor furniture and carpet, the oversized plants and small waterfall that trickles over rocks, glimmering under the moonlight. I'm not a romantic guy, but this moment feels like poetry. Her mere presence somehow warms the air around us.

Harper's voice is filled with awe when she whispers, "This is like something out of a fairy tale."

We don't have fairy tales in my world, but she can have hers.

I've always seen this as a place to escape, where I can shrug off responsibilities for a little while and just be *me*.

"I bet you don't feel like yourself up here," she says, as if reading my mind.

"This is my sanctuary from the world below." My only one.

"I understand. I'm the same way. I've always had my little sacred spaces. When we lived in a tiny home, I had a closet I made my own. Cleared a little shelf. I would sit there and doodle and color and shut the door when my parents fought."

I nod. I get that, fully. My parents rarely fought, but my father had a temper, and we weren't immune to it.

"I knew that eventually, one day, my parents would marry me off. And I decided that I'd make sure I always had a place of my own. In one home, it was a huge maple in the backyard with a flat patch of grass in front of it. In another, it was a kitchen nook that no one used. I understand why you'd want to keep this a secret, though. When you let someone in, it isn't just yours anymore."

I nod. She knows I let her in.

"Yeah."

She holds my hand in the quiet. Stars twinkle overhead. The heater hums.

"We'll come back another time. I have to go back down and call Aria."

A shadow passes over Harper's face. "Did she tell you why?"

I shake my head. "Not sure but she said it's urgent, so I have to go."

I shut off the heater and we head downstairs. There's something magical about being up on the roof... something transcendent. When we return indoors, we're only mortal again.

Harper heads to the kitchen to grab some food and I call Aria.

"Aleks. I did some digging. Don't hate me."

"There are no conversations that end well after beginning that way," I tell her. "What?"

"Remember how I said that Harper's family felt... off. There was like a mirage? That it felt like they had a filter in place?"

I don't want to hear it. Whatever she is going to tell me, I don't want to hear it and yet I know that I have to.

I pinch the bridge of my nose and let out a breath.

"Yeah. Did you get past that filter?"

I can hear her swallowing on the other end of the line. "I did, yeah. What do you know about Harper? What has she told you?"

I know that she was used by her parents to make them money. I know that she wasn't allowed to go to college or do anything normal girls her age should do. I know that she was sexually assaulted and that she doesn't know who did it.

"Not much. Spill."

"I was at my checkup today with my OB. We have them weekly now. And you know how my mind works, Aleks. You know how I see codes and numbers and patterns."

"Yeah."

I do, because I'm the same way.

The hair on the back of my neck stands up. I know she's going to tell me something big.

"I noted there were code words for tests they took, and I remembered that I came across a few when I was doing Harper's background check, only I didn't think much of it then because they led to nothing. So I looked harder. Deeper. I spent all damn day because fuck it, I don't want you hoodwinked. I don't trust them."

My voice sounds distant. Hollow. "What did you find?"

She takes in a breath. "Don't kill the messenger."

"Fucking hell, Aria, if you don't—"

"She had a baby, Aleks. Harper's a mother. Those times when she ran away from home? It looks like she was going to her child. Those times when she was accused of stealing money from her parents? I'd bet you anything she gave the money to the caregivers. Foster parents, whatever."

Baby. She has a baby.

"I have to go."

"Aleks, be gentle with her. Please. I'll never forgive myself if I—"

I hang up the call and slam the phone onto my desk. It crashes and skitters across the floor.

Harper has a baby.

What else don't I know about her?

CHAPTER ELEVEN

Harper

I'M MAKING some simple sandwiches for us when I look up to see Aleks standing in the doorway, his arms crossed on his chest.

I blink. Something's wrong. A palpable air of anger rises between us like steam.

"What's happened?"

He pushes himself off the doorframe and stalks over to me, his eyes blazing. "You lied to me."

Oh, God. Does he know? How did he find out?

"What are you talking about?" My voice sounds strangely distant. Detached. My ears begin to ring.

Disgrace.

Whore.

I'm hot and cold all at once. I'm frozen in this horror-stricken moment in time, disgusted with myself for ever thinking I could fall for him. Disgusted with him for pretending he cared. A strange, low buzzing fills my ears, like the swarm of a hundred bees, as he continues his tirade, verbally lashing me.

"This is why you ran, isn't it? You ran because you were hiding from everyone."

What? He's in my space, so close to me I could reach out and touch him. There's nowhere for me to go.

"Aleks," I say, my voice raspy and shaky. I hate myself for it. "I didn't— you can't—"

"You had a *baby* and didn't tell me."

Whore.

Disgrace.

Slut.

I move so instinctively, I don't realize until it's too late. Fury and injustice well in my chest. Anger bubbles beneath the surface of my skin, clawing at me, only momentarily relieved when I push him, hard.

He stumbles, looking as shocked as I feel.

"I fucking hate you," I say, emotions blooming into words that make the tears finally fall.

When he reaches for me, I flinch instinctively, but he only pins my arms. With his iron-like grip, he lifts me in the air and binds me in his arms. I open my mouth to tell him everything. To vindicate myself. But I can't. I'm too angry, too distraught.

I don't know where he's taking me or where we're going, but I was raised in the mafia, and if his family's any indication, I just committed a cardinal sin.

I want to tell him everything, but that would mean putting myself at his mercy. I want to scream and rage and hurt him, but that would only make my own pain worse.

He's lifted me straight up in the air, my arms pinned to my sides, and when he gets to the bed, he tosses me on it. I bounce and quickly scramble to the head of the bed away from him.

"You will never raise a hand to me," he says, shaking with the effort of keeping his temper in check.

"Then stop accusing me," I snap. "Go ahead. Hit me. A big man like you twice my size with more power in your little finger than I have in my whole body. I'm impressed."

Anger glimmers in his eyes.

"I told you the truth. I told you what happened to me. And I was going to tell you about my daughter when the time was right. When *I* was ready. Because no one knows about her, Aleksandr, and if that keeps her safe, I aim to keep it that way. We hardly know each other."

"The truth?" he spits back at me, marching around the bed to a sideboard. He twists off the lid to a decanter and drinks the liquor straight from the bottle. "Let's hear it, Princess."

I clench the bedspread. "I told you I was assaulted. One time. I don't know who it was. I was drugged. I woke up bruised and hurting with only vague memories of screaming *no*. I had nowhere to go. No one I could tell." My voice cracks. "Weeks later, I realized my period was late. I was young and naive and didn't know what to do. I had no friends and didn't trust my family. I hid the pregnancy until I couldn't anymore."

He sits in a chair across from me, the bottle still in his hand, but he doesn't speak.

I clear my throat and continue. "I told you, my father blamed *me* for the assault. If I told him I was pregnant, he'd have killed me. I left. Managed to spend the summer in Italy with friends of my mother's. I don't think she knows anything, but I'm not completely sure. I came back to America to have the baby. I had her here in New York, in a county hospital." My voice shakes. "That was two years ago. She's with a foster family in the northwest corner of The Cove."

I look away and swipe at my eyes. "The only time I ever left home was to see her. To bring her money when I could."

He slumps back into his chair. "Fuck."

That could mean a lot of different things. I exhale. "Yeah."

He shakes his head and doesn't speak for long minutes. "I should've asked you and not jumped to conclusions. God, I'm a dick."

"You said it, not me," I mutter. "How did you find out? Aria? She hacked into medical records, I bet. Have her check my dates. They'll all match. Every last one of them."

I can still see her perfect little swaddled body, lying in my arms while I sat in the hospital bed and wept. My breasts ached, my body was tired from labor, and all I could do was hold her and cry because I had to give her away, and I'll never forgive my family for that.

I relive every damn moment in vivid detail, and I hate him for it.

"I had her after twelve hours of hard labor," I say, my voice hoarse. "I got to hold her once before they took her away. I gave her up voluntarily to foster care under a fake name. Then I went back home to my family, who didn't know, or did an excellent job of pretending like nothing ever happened. But I knew. I followed the family that took her right here to The Cove."

"And your family hid the assault because if anyone else knew, you weren't marriageable. Jesus. I fucking hate your family, Harper."

His voice is softer now, as if he's almost repenting for what he did. What he accused me of. He stands and reaches for me, but I push him away.

"Yeah. As soon as my brother saw an in with your family, he took it. My family doesn't have any money. You'll see soon enough. All you needed was a wife, so I fit that bill."

He scowls and shakes his head. "I'm sorry."

I hang my head low. "So am I. I couldn't tell you right away. What if you didn't want to marry me because of it? What then?"

I shake my head and wipe my eyes again. "I had to get married, it was my only chance."

He sits on the edge of the bed. "I want to kick my own ass for accusing you."

I don't respond because I still half wish he could, too.

We sit in silence for long minutes until finally he speaks, looking weary and repentant.

"We're married now. And I told you what my family needed. Do you remember?"

"You need to strengthen your ties and bonds, yes. Wives, children..."

I pause, my voice trembling.

Children.

I don't know what he's going to do now. If he takes me away from her —

"No one said biological children, did they?" he says in a soft voice. "You've promoted me, Princess."

I shake my head. "What?"

"You had a baby before Aria did. Look at you, one-upping the *pakhan* and his wife."

I don't smile, though, I can't. I'm still too wound up, still too shaky.

"Aleks —"

"Tell me about her. I want to know everything." My heart opens a little. I think I might even forgive him.

I shift on the bed to sit next to him, and take a deep breath. "She's two years old. She has these little pigtails. She looks a lot like me. A mini-me, really. She loves stories and coloring, dogs and cats, and loves to go outside for walks or to the playground. She's sweet and sassy and..." My voice catches.

"She's perfect."

"And your parents don't know about her."

I shake my head. "I've kept her hidden from them and if they suspected anything, they quickly feigned ignorance because it doesn't align with their personal narrative about their family."

His eyebrows rise but he just sits on the bed and shakes his head.

"You know there are ways of finding out the identity of the father," he finally says, his eyes boring into mine. He knows as well as I do that doing so means delving into a history I don't want to relive, but it might be the only way.

"Makes sense you'd find a way."

He nods. "And your family will pay for this, Harper."

I tilt my head. "For hiding the baby?"

"Jesus, for not *supporting you*. For not doing everything they could for you. It's not like you got knocked up by some high school boyfriend in the back of his dad's car, but even if you did, you didn't deserve how they treated you." He hangs his head. "And I'm sorry. I really am."

I get up and march around the room, my heart pounding a crazy beat in my chest. Outside the window, the moon is rising, beams of moonlight glowing on the grass. A shadow crosses his features, and he pats his lap. "Come here."

I walk to him, unsure of what he'll do, but the apology is a good first step.

Psychopaths don't apologize.

Sociopaths don't apologize.

Narcissists don't apologize.

He isn't any of those things. He's a flawed human, like the rest of us.

When I reach him, he pulls me onto his lap. I sit and lay my head on his chest. "I knew you were hiding something, I just didn't know what," he says, as he plays with my hair. I love it when he plays with my hair. He runs his rough fingers through it, combing it out. Silently, he separates it into three sections and gently begins to braid it. "Why didn't you tell me earlier?"

"Hmm. The day I met you, maybe? I don't know, there was something about you stealing me from my home and manhandling me into the back of your car that didn't make me oh-so-eager to divulge my darkest secrets. Or the day after, when I woke up handcuffed and bound in bed? Also not super feeling the trust factor. Let's remember, we haven't known each other for that long. The only reason I don't hate you is because you're really good in bed."

He nuzzles my head and breathes in deep. "Good in bed. That sounds almost like an insult."

"You can't take that as a compliment? That's your problem, then."

His fingers tighten at my scalp and give my hair a little tug. "You slapped me, and I let that go because I deserved it. *This* time. Don't take that to mean you can do whatever you want going forward, woman."

I shiver at the hint of a threat in his voice and half wish he didn't have such a hold on me like that.

"I suppose I can behave myself since you're suitably repentant."

Still, I'm not sure where this leaves us. Leaves *me*. My baby doesn't live far from here, and it would be a full-on scandal to bring her—

"Show me a picture."

My heart races. "You want to see a picture of the baby?"

"And tell me her name."

A lump forms in my throat. I nod and pull out my phone. Log into the secure cloud app where I keep all her photos. Serves me well, now that I don't have access to my old phone anyway.

My eyes grow misty when I open up the folder with her pictures. Bright blue eyes the color of cornflowers, pink-tinged chubby cheeks, her face spread wide with a grin. Messy pigtails with wisps of hair escaping make her look adorably tousled.

"The day I had her, there was ivy outside the hospital window. I didn't want her to have a family name. I wanted something different but not too outlandish, so...her name is Ivy."

"Ivy," he says reverently, pronouncing each syllable in his accent. "I like that. Ivy's resilient and sturdy but delicate all at the same time."

I blink and swallow. "Yeah."

"She's absolutely beautiful," he says, still in awe. "She looks like a little angel."

"Oh, she can have her moments," I say, a little too loudly to cover up the shake in my voice.

"It's a two-year-old's job to act like a terrorist," he says with a shrug. "I have younger siblings and cousins. You should've *seen* Polina when she was younger."

That makes me giggle. "She's fierce now. I can't imagine what she was like when she was younger."

"Tomorrow, Harper. Tomorrow, we get her."

Wait.

I stare at him. I shake my head, not comprehending. He didn't say *visit* her. He said *get* her.

"We...bring her home with us? Are you serious?"

His brow furrows and he nods sternly. "You married into Bratva. She needs protection, and she's your daughter. She isn't safe, Harper."

My heart's beating too fast. I'm dizzy and hot.

"But I—I don't even know how to be a mother."

"It's not that complicated," he responds. "You love her with everything you've got. You show her the way to be a good human. And if there was anything your parents did that was wrong or hurtful...you do the opposite."

I can't help it. I smile.

"That sounds...oddly simple. And what do you know about being a good human?"

He tugs my hair again. "I was talking about how to be a good mother. Being a good father is something entirely different."

Is it, though?

I swallow and lick my lips because the idea of Aleks... holding Ivy and trying to be a good father... I swoon a little.

"What does it mean to you, to be a good father?"

He thinks for a moment before speaking. "In my world, you show your love by being willing and able to burn the world down for the people you love. It means your undying protection, no matter the cost."

A beat passes before I speak. I know in my heart he means every word.

"There must be more to it. Isn't there?"

"I don't know if there is. I'm sure you can doll it all up with things like...morals and shit like that, but in the end, do you really love someone if you're not willing to lay down everything for them? No matter who they are? No matter what they do?"

My parents weren't willing to give up anything for me. Not their pride. Not their time. Nothing. Parents like to lie to their children and tell them they love them, but so many people only like the *idea* of loving. So many want to be adored and loved back, but is that self-serving? Is that really what love is?

How would I know?

I want to know.

"Does it have to be complicated?" he asks. "We don't even know each other but there's chemistry here. Does marriage have to be complicated?"

"Not at all. I obey your every command and you buy me nice things. Sounds simple enough."

He tugs my hair again.

"That sounds like a fair deal."

We sit in silence, the weight of what we've revealed between the two of us demanding reverence for a little while. It wasn't just the revelation that I have a child but so much more. We've both said out loud what probably neither of us has ever had the ability to say to another human being before.

I want to raise children with you.

I can be a good parent.

I can be a good spouse.

I can choose to give what I was never given.

Finally, I lean over and brush my lips across his stubbled jaw. I close my eyes when he returns the kiss with a kiss of his own. Deeper. Darker. Dominant.

And then his hands are in my hair as if anchoring himself to me. I bared a huge part of myself to him tonight. I gave him what I've never given any other human being before.

And he didn't trounce on my truth but cherished it. Took us a while to get here, but that only makes it that much sweeter.

He'll bring my daughter to me.

He said she could come here with us.

I need to thank him in a way words can't.

I caress his face, his jaw, the broad swell of his shoulders. I run my hands along his biceps, appreciating how perfect and strong he is. When his mouth parts, my tongue darts into it. I relish the low, utterly male sound he makes, half groan, half growl, and nip his lip with my teeth.

It's just enough of a show of dominance to poke him, and the next thing I know I'm flat on my back and he's on top of me, his full weight pressing me into the bed.

He doesn't ask me what's come over me or demand a discussion. He only slowly and deliberately strips me until I'm bared to him, the depth of his blue eyes boring into me with the power of a laser.

I fumble with his belt, and he unzips his pants. Shoves his clothes off and drops them to meet mine in a tumbled heap as we rejoin each other, naked and bared. He palms my ass and lifts one of my legs to straddle him before he glides into me. My head hits the pillow when I'm filled by him, a glimmer of perfect brilliance shining in his eyes with the sudden need to claim me.

I ride the waves of sensation brought on by being vulnerable and exposed, in so many more ways than he's done to me physically. There's a silent thanks, a silent plea for mercy, an understanding that passes between us.

My eyes widen in surprise when he holds my gaze and brings his heavy hand to the base of my neck. Thick, rough fingers close around me. I gasp for breath.

"Good girl," he whispers when I don't struggle. My pulse spikes and the first wave of pleasure washes over me, a prelude. The rumble of approval undoes the last knot in my chest. My heart races when another spasm of pleasure ricochets through me. I whimper and toss my head back. He comes on the heels of my own pleasure. "That's my girl," he whispers as we ride the high of our joined ecstasy. His fingers ghost over the skin at my neck, and he glides his hand down the length of my body until he cups my ass.

Another thrust sends the last spasms of pleasure through me.

While I lie there on the bed, his hot seed still leaking from me, his fingers travel upward to grasp my chin. His gaze burns into mine with an intensity that would scorch the earth.

"You're my wife," he says in a low growl. "Your daughter belongs with her mother. Your child will live here with us."

I nod, unsure as to why he needs to state this again. Wordlessly, my arms encircle his neck. The tiniest trickle of sweat drips from his temple down the length of his chiseled jaw.

"And while she's here, we'll protect her. Both of us. I'm going to teach you everything I know, Harper. Because make no mistake. There *will* be vengeance for what's happened to you."

CHAPTER TWELVE

Aleks

I ANSWER the phone on the first ring. Mikhail.

"We're at the hospital."

I sit up in bed and swing my legs over the side, tugging on a pair of pants. "What happened?" There's only one hospital in The Cove, and Mikhail would only go there if our family doctor couldn't handle whatever happened. I remember that night we got the call that Lev was found —

"She's having regular contractions and we're heading in."

I close my eyes and pinch the bridge of my nose.

No one's hurt.

Yet. With Mikhail at the hospital with Aria, there's no telling what he's capable of.

"Everything alright?" Harper rolls to her side next to me,

her eyes still bleary from lack of sleep. She was up a lot last night, likely from nerves.

I cover the phone with my hand. "Aria's maybe in labor."

"Ooooh." She sits up and yawns. "Do they need us?"

"Do you need us?"

"Not yet," Mikhail says tightly. "Stand by." And then hangs up the phone.

"He's so fucking uptight."

Harper squeezes her lips together.

"What?"

"It sort of runs in the family, don't you think?"

I toss the phone onto the bedside table as she scoots out of bed.

"I would not say it runs in the family."

"You and I have a very different definition of uptight then," she says, quickly evading my palm swinging toward her ass, which is barely covered by a white lace thong.

"Don't think for a minute you got away with that!" I'm yelling at an empty room.

She mumbles something unintelligible back to me through the closed door of the adjacent bathroom. Sassy as fuck.

God, I love it.

I scroll through the messages on my phone, alert the others that Aria's in labor, and assign guards to head to the hospital to be with them. This isn't the first time Mikhail's been at the hospital, and I know how he is. In his absence, I step in as lead.

"My mother wants to meet you," I tell Harper when she comes back into the room. "Like, visit. You know how things were pretty crazy at the wedding."

She nods. "Okay. So... when do you want to go see Ivy?"

"See her?" I ask, tossing the covers down and standing up. "We're not going to see her, Harper. We're bringing her home. Today, of course."

It's still dark outside these windows, a blue tinge revealing how early it still is.

Her eyes widen. "Today? You want to go today?" I can't quite read her expression.

"Of course I do." That's her *daughter*. I won't leave her with strangers for another second. "She should be here, with you, under your protection and mine."

"We don't even have a bed for her!"

"Seriously, that's what you're worried about? We'll get what we need. I'll get Auntie Polina on it."

She blinks and looks around the room, as if trying to figure out where to put the bed.

"I...I wasn't really ready for this. I mean, don't get me wrong, I can't wait to have her here with us, it's just—"

Her voice seizes and her lower lip trembles. I walk over to her, concerned. "What is it? Are you alright?"

Her nose wrinkles and she bursts into tears. I reach for her, a bit stunned by the sudden torrent of tears. "I cried like my heart was breaking when I had to leave her. When I couldn't take her home. And every time I ran away to go see her and was caught, my parents would be so furious with me. But I had to. I had to, Aleks."

Khristos, I will kill her parents.

"Of course you did. She's your child. I'd level heaven and earth for my child if I needed to."

"I know," she sobs. "Which is why I'm excited about her coming here with us. I'll figure out the mother thing. And the bed thing."

"And I'll help you. We can do this, alright? We've got this."

She swipes at her eyes and sniffles into a tissue I hand her. "You just might win me over if you keep being so nice."

"Nice?" I blow out a breath and kiss the top of her head before I head for the closet. "It's my job to protect you and her. That's what I do, and I don't care if you like my methods or not. But I hardly think that's nice."

"True. You're still a heartless, cold man bound by duty. Apologies for assuming any less."

"First, you slap my face. And then you—"

"It was earned, and you admitted it!" she says, quickly pulling out clothes.

I tuck my morning wood into my pants with a groan. No time. "Second, you interrupted me. Third, you mouthed off to me."

"What? When!"

"You're doing it now and I never forget."

I tug on a tee and watch as her eyes grow hazy. "And what are you going to do about it?" she asks, standing in front of me in only a bra and jeans, which she ought to know is like lighting a match and letting it hover over the wick of a bomb.

"Punish you, obviously."

Fuck needing time.

I snap my fingers and point to the floor. "Knees."

The way she captures her lower lip between her teeth and sinks to her knees is sexy as hell. I unfasten the belt I just clipped and draw it through the loops, unfasten my jeans, and tug my erection out. "Lose the bra then show me why I shouldn't spank your ass."

With a seductive turn of her lips, she slowly slides her bra off before pouting and drawing me into her mouth. I groan, loop the belt, and snap it across her jean-covered ass.

She moans and takes me deeper, further. My cock hits the back of her throat and her eyes water. "Take it slow," I tell her. "*Fuuccck.*"

My head lolls to the side at the feel of her sultry mouth on me. I grip her hair in my fist and fuck her mouth until I'm on the cusp of coming. She moans when I slide out, fist my cock, and come across her sweet, pretty tits.

I groan and take in the picture she makes. "Look what you made me do," I say, shaking my head. "Come here."

I ball up my tee and swipe it across her chest, cleaning her off. "Touch yourself while I finish getting dressed. Just like that. On your knees. Rub your clit and play with your nipples."

I lazily zip up my jeans. Thread the belt back through the loops. Tug on a shirt and grab a sweatshirt. Her head falls back and her mouth parts.

"Don't you dare fucking come without permission."

"Aleks," she moans on a whimper. "You're mean."

"Mean would be making you wear my come and wait for your climax," I tell her with a shrug.

The gleam in her eyes tells me she's game for both.

Jesus, I'm gonna lose my fucking mind with this woman.

I sit on the edge of the bed and silently beckon her over. She wobbles to me, half drunk on arousal. I strip her out of her jeans and panties then lift her, lay back on the bed, and arrange her over my face.

"Aleks!" she protests. I clap my hand across her ass, hard, when she fights me. She tries to stop me but can't reach my arms. I spank her hard, again and again, until she finally complies and spreads her legs for me. I take her hard little clit between my teeth and scrape it to teach her to behave herself, then swipe my tongue through her seam to reward her obedience.

I suckle and lick, lick and suckle, and soon she comes on my mouth with a scream. I lick her through every spasm of pleasure until she slumps on me, give her ass an affectionate parting slap, and drag her back down on the bed.

"Now behave yourself like I told you to, or we'll be even later than we already are."

Her eyes roll to the back of her head for a few seconds before she releases a heavy sigh.

"We are definitely going to need to stop for coffee on the way."

"We will but we have one more stop before we get to the foster home."

CHAPTER THIRTEEN

Harper

"WHERE ARE WE GOING?" I'm trying to pretend I'm all casual sitting next to him in the SUV, but I'm still as warm and pliable as softened caramel. I wonder if he knows that sex does that to me. It's healing, in its own way, to lose control to him. To let him actually pleasure me.

I don't have many recollections of the night I was assaulted, but the few that I do have fade every time Aleksandr touches me.

"We were supposed to take you to the shooting range this morning. That was my original plan."

"Oooh." My eyes go wide and my heart races a bit faster. "I'm going to learn to shoot?"

"Learn to shoot?" The familiar darkness shadows his face and his grip on the steering wheel tightens. "Fuck yeah, you're gonna learn to shoot. And not just shoot. I'm going to train you in hand-to-hand combat and self-defense. There *will* be justice served, and you'll have your hand in it."

Imagine being empowered. Feeling like I'll be able to defend myself if anyone ever tries to assault me again. Because while I love the thought of Aleks seeking vengeance as well, I don't like having to depend on a man to do it for me.

"Don't get any ideas," he says with a warning cut of his eyes. "You'll never be able to overpower me, Princess."

My heart thumps in my chest.

That's what he thinks.

I mean, I could have fun trying, anyway.

"Aleks, what's the plan here? I mean, we go in and tell them that she'll be coming home with us?"

"Yes. We're stopping first at the police station. Got a friend there who does car seat safety."

Oh my God. Our first stop is to get the baby's car seat installed. I almost laugh out loud.

"What?" he says, as he flicks the directional. "You don't fuck around with that shit, Harper. Needs to be installed safely."

The police station looms ahead.

"You're a *mobster,* that's what."

He curls his lip. "In your world you call those fucking men *mobsters.*" He lifts his chest, his accent thickening. "I'm *Bratva.*" Another cut of his eyes. "We'll have a talk about that later. You'll have to practice saying it correctly."

Another heart somersault. I keep it together. "I don't think we'll have time. We're bringing home a *child*."

"A child who will have a nanny and the endless attention of her Auntie Polina. We'll have plenty of time."

I frown at him. "Not sure I want a nanny."

"You can spend as much time with her as you like, but the nanny's not optional. As my wife, you'll be expected to attend events with me, and we have hours of practice ahead of us."

It's a lot to take in all at once. "What if I want to be the one to soothe her when she cries?"

Why does my voice sound all shaky? Why is it that the only thing I can think of is the way my mother used to send me to bed and lock the door and I would cry myself to sleep?

Am I crying?

I turn my head away so he doesn't see.

"Harper." His voice is the slightest bit softer now. "No one is saying you won't get a chance to mother your child." We pull to a stop outside the police station. The weight of his hand is heavy on my knee, but I don't look around yet. "I wouldn't have planned on bringing her home to you only to deny you that. But devoting every minute of your time to her won't work in our world."

There are many things that won't work in our world.

He parks the car and taps a text out on his phone.

"Telling Anton we're here."

"So you have a friend here."

"Of course. Didn't your father?"

When I left home, all he had left were enemies. I don't answer.

The door to the station opens and a tall, fit man in his early thirties strides out. He nods to Aleks. Aleks pops open the back of the car and takes out an enormous box.

"Wow, did that materialize out of thin air or what?"

"Aleksandr has a way of getting what he wants when he wants it," Anton says, and I can't tell if it's only a statement or a warning.

"Anton, meet Harper." Aleks stands taller. "My wife." I don't miss the surge of pride in his voice when he says *my wife*.

My heart melts a little.

Anton extends his hand to me but one look from Aleks and he pulls it back and gives me a little wave. Ha.

"Now let's get this going, we're on a schedule."

"Not even sunrise yet and you're on a schedule," Anton says with a shake of his head. "Alright, we begin by making sure we're on level ground."

The two of them get all sweaty and breathless anchoring the seat into position. It's one of those fancy ones. Finally, Anton points to a little bubble on the base of the seat like a mini level. "When that's in the center position, you're good to go."

They do some kind of brotherly fist bump thing, and we're on our way.

I wouldn't ever tell him, but it's absolutely adorable that he got a *car seat*.

His phone on the dash has the directions I gave him on it. It says we're only fifteen minutes out. This feels so different from other times. I've been here before, but always surreptitiously, never with the intent of taking Ivy back with me — and never with a dangerous man by my side. Some of his brothers look like they could pass as normal civilians, with some effort. But when Aleks leans slightly to the side to crack his window, the outline of a gun bulges under his tee. There's nothing normal about him.

"I still feel guilty we're taking her. It'll wreck them."

Aleks raises his brows. "This is the right thing to do."

"*So* right, and I get that." A part of me's elated not to leave her again. "But I— they've had her since birth."

"But she's your baby. That's the risk a foster family takes. The goal is usually reuniting the child with the birth mother, isn't it?"

"I don't know about usual but... well, yeah. It's what they sign up for, I guess."

He squeezes my hand. "It is."

There's more than that, though. I have so many fears. And even though I've already talked to him about being a mother and it helped, all of that worries me.

"What do I do if she doesn't sleep in the middle of the night?"

"I think you'd... well, probably, maybe rock her. Give her some milk. Soothe her until she's sleepy."

I nod. Okay, I can do that.

"And what if that doesn't work?"

He scratches his nose. "Hmm. Well, presumably the nanny will know about things like that."

Oh, right.

I guess I'm just in a place I've never been before. Married, to a dangerous man I still hardly know. About to co-parent with him. Guilty I'm taking Ivy away from the only people who've ever loved her.

But love is messy and complicated. Protection wears many hats. And I know there are difficult choices ahead, but the hardest part of all is admitting I've never *had* a safe place to go.

Is this what I'm offering my baby?

Why does the thought of being *safe* terrify the hell out of me?

"You're doing that thing again."

"What thing?" He shouldn't be noticing patterns with me already. It isn't fair.

"That thing where you bite your lip because you're all up in your head. You're thinking about something, and you probably won't tell me what."

I shrug. I guess there's no real point in hiding anything. "I just feel strange with the thought of having a safe place to go for me and the baby, you know?"

He shakes his head. "No. I don't know. What the fuck does that even mean?"

I huff out a mirthless laugh. "It's just so foreign to me, but it makes no sense that it scares me." I don't expect him to respond. I don't even get it myself.

But when he does, he takes me by surprise. "I have a small detour to take you on before we arrive. We're not far now and I want to show you this first."

My heart beats faster. My palms are sweaty. I'm so nervous to get to their house, I could throw up, so I welcome the detour.

The changes around us at first are subtle. We leave the vibrant, bustling streets of the city. The smooth asphalt under our tires becomes a rugged road filled with potholes and litter. Graffiti marks subway signs and the vibrant store-fronts become sparse. Boarded-up windows and stained walls give me an unsettled feeling.

"Are we still in The Cove?" I ask in a whisper.

Aleks's jaw tightens. "Just outside it." I'm relieved he and his brothers don't own this area.

The air itself seems heavier, as if forgotten dreams and broken promises linger behind. The buildings themselves appear tired and worn down, as if their shoulders slump beneath the weight of what they carry.

There's no lush greenery or pretty trees lining the streets here. Nothing but old metal and bare trunks, never mind the weeds that fight their way through cracks in the pavement. Worse than anything, sounds of cars driving by and people chatting have quickly given way to something else entirely.

A dog barks, followed by the shout of a man and the dog's yelp. I wince even though I can't see what happened.

"Why are you bringing me here?" I shiver and look away. I feel sad to see homeless people cowering in doorways, trash littering the ground. If the houses and surrounding buildings are neglected...what about their inhabitants?

"Aleks," I whisper as he brings the car to a stop. This is a place people like us come to for hookers or weed and nothing more.

"Before I was adopted by my father, I lived in that house there." He points to a brick house with steps that were once painted but have now faded. "We came from Russia and had only been here a year or two."

A broken window's stuffed with remnants of newspaper that's yellowed. A sickly-looking cat scowls at us from the stoop.

"I'm sorry." I may not have grown up in a good home, but I didn't grow up...like this.

"Don't be. It's not why I brought you here."

He drapes his arm over the steering wheel and turns to face me.

"When I left here, I was a kid. I barely knew how to tie my shoes or spell my name. And everything in my new home was shiny, pretty, and new. And it made me so fucking uncomfortable. I didn't want scrambled eggs and fried potatoes, like my mother tried to feed me. I wanted the packaged, sugar-coated food I knew. It was what was familiar to me, even though it wasn't what was best for me."

I look back at the house. It's hard to imagine Aleks as a child, but somehow, seeing this place makes it easier to do so.

A door swings open and a young girl with long, wavy hair hanging down her back comes out. Her face is streaked with tears and her eyes are red from crying. My heart twists looking at her. She trots down the steps and runs down the street, her hair waving in the wind behind her.

I've seen poverty and I've seen wealth, and I've seen plenty in between, but this is something very different.

"Harper." I look over at him. "Just because we're used to something being broken doesn't mean it's what's best for us," he says quietly. I nod and swallow my own fear and pride. I lift my chin.

I can be the mother Ivy needs. I know I can.

Aleks starts the car up again. I watch in silence as the girl stops and bends to pick something up in the street. She holds it up to the light and shoves it in her pocket. Her step picks up and she smiles.

I remember being a little girl myself, afraid of my father and scared of my mother. I tried to please them and never learned that I couldn't, that it was never in my control and never would be.

In minutes, we're back on the main road, and not far from little Ivy.

When he takes the turn down the street to her house, he asks me, "Are you ready?"

"Let's go."

CHAPTER FOURTEEN

Aleks

MY GIRLS ARE ASLEEP.

My girls.

I barely knew Harper a few weeks ago and didn't know Ivy existed, and today, I'd do anything to keep them as peaceful as they are now. When I peeked in on them, Harper's lips were softly parted, little Ivy's hand resting in hers. I lifted a blanket and placed it over them so they didn't get cold, and let them rest.

I pace the room, looking out the window. We set Ivy's little toddler bed up in the small room next to the master, which has a connecting door that closes between the two rooms.

She came with us willingly, and her foster parents — Isaac and Abigail Brooks — were brave about it. Isaac, a local minister, shook my hand but said very little. We paid a good sum to keep everything off record, and I pulled some strings to keep our names out of anything official, but I'll make it all up to them.

The Brooks family's home was modest and clean, with one simple car in the driveway and evidence of older children — a bike leaning on a porch rail and a forgotten jump rope nearby.

I feared Ivy would put up more of a fuss leaving, making it harder for Harper, but she didn't. Sometimes, kids know. I have no doubt she'll miss where she was, but she knew Harper was her mother.

I'm relieved, anyway. It's one less battle to fight.

Abigail cried but quietly handed her to Harper.

"I'm sorry," Harper said. "I'm really sorry."

"Don't be. I prayed for this. She's supposed to be with you, but we'll miss her."

It'll take time, but building any new family does. I should know.

My mind reels from everything I've learned and experienced in the past few days.

Tonight, we begin our new lives as a small, nuclear family.

Tomorrow, Polina comes to help while we interview nannies.

My phone beeps with a text.

> Mikhail: Sent us home. Early labor, and she isn't ready yet.

I pity anyone in that hospital that didn't deliver a baby to Mikhail. I pity Aria for dealing with his belligerent ass.

Still, I can't help but gloat.

> tf are you talking about?

> Got a kid, man. I'll fill you in tomorrow.

The phone rings. Of course. He's not gonna wait until tomorrow.

"Yeah?"

"That any way to talk to your *pakhan?* Jesus. Tell me everything."

He's the older brother and head of the family so I have to, in detail.

"And you picked her up today?"

"I did. It was time. She needed to be with her mother."

"Wow. No one can ever say you waste time."

"Of course I didn't." If there's anything I've learned it's how quickly your life can change. If someone in your circle's in need of protection, you drop fucking everything and get it done.

"You did the right thing." I didn't know I needed his praise until I heard it. I stand a little straighter. "How's Harper?"

I look through the doorway and lower my voice. "Sleeping with her as we speak."

"Careful with that."

"With what?"

"Letting them share a bed."

"Your kid's still *in* your wife and you're already giving me parenting advice?" He can fuck off with that.

"I seriously need to kick your ass and teach you manners."

I square my shoulders. "Come on over and try."

He laughs. "Asshole. I'm just saying, the whole bed sharing thing can get out of control."

I snort. "That's your biggest concern?"

"Listen, it happens. Mama sleeps in the bed with the baby, baby gets used to it. Next thing you know, Papa's sleeping on the couch grumpy as fuck because he's not gettin' laid anymore."

He might have a point. I frown. "They can share a bed *tonight*."

Mikhail laughs. Good, let him. See how much he gets over the next few months after that baby arrives.

"We need to fill everyone in tomorrow. Good job, Aleksandr. We're strengthening more and more every day."

I nod. "We are. It'll be your turn, soon enough. Maybe even later tonight. We'll see."

He blows out a breath. "Better get some sleep just in case it is."

"Interviewing nannies tomorrow."

"Smart. Any luck on your research?"

The hunt for the man who assaulted Harper's in full swing, but we have nothing substantial yet. We will.

"Not yet."

He growls. I told him everything and his taste for retribution is as strong as mine. I forgive him for being a know-it-all.

"Good luck tomorrow. I'm gonna get some rest, will fill you in when the baby gets here."

I can't help but needle him one more time. "Hard not being able to control something, eh?"

"Happy to remind you what I *can* control, asshole."

I groan. Touché.

"Good luck to you, too. You'll need it."

He hangs the phone up with a deep sigh. I do like to get the last word in.

I roll my shoulders and yawn. Need to get some rest.

Tomorrow begins Harper's first lesson in how to shoot to kill.

CHAPTER FIFTEEN

Harper

I WAKE BESIDE ALEKS. Blink. And promptly leap out of bed.

Was it a dream?

"Relax," he grumbles, his big hand wrapping around my wrist and dragging me back down. "There's a monitor."

He points to the monitor on the bedside table that shows the sleeping form of my daughter in the other room.

My daughter. *God.* How did this even happen? It feels so strange and hard to grasp.

I fall back on the bed, my heart beating too fast. "Are you sure she's breathing?"

He points back in the monitor's direction. "Yes. See how her little chest goes up and down? She's very happily sleeping. I can set up biometrics if you want." He settles into his pillow and shuts his eyes.

Might seem a little over the top, but...

How did I get here? I think back.

I have a vague recollection of Aleks waking me up and carrying me to bed, then tucking me in. Ivy was already asleep.

"What time is it?" I ask.

He opens one eye, his voice groggy with sleep. He is not amused. "Middle of the fucking night and I'm exhausted. Go back to sleep." He closes it again.

I try, but it's more early morning than middle of the night, and I can't sleep. My mind's racing with everything that's happened in such a short time.

I pace around the room and stare at the monitor. I look at Aleks, bare-chested in a pair of boxers, one arm lazily flung over his eyes, his huge hand on the pillow. I stare at his tattoos, only shimmers in the darkness.

He's definitely asleep.

I don't know what he does when I'm asleep, but he seems to have the sleeping pattern of a cat. Not totally nocturnal, he naps and lounges in small intervals only to wake up ready to go on the prowl and hunt. I, on the other hand, *love* sleep. It was a coping mechanism when I lived with my parents. They wouldn't usually bother me when I was asleep.

I walk back to the monitor and see sweet Ivy. I've heard some kids aren't good sleepers even at her age, but so far so good.

I need to see her. I want to prove to myself that she's here and that she's okay. I never had the privilege of looking after her in the middle of the night when she was a baby. It seems like it's a rite of passage of sorts for a mother.

I might even climb back into bed with her, whether he likes it or not.

I tiptoe over to the door between our rooms. My hand on the knob, I wonder if I'm being overprotective.

I guess that's a mother's prerogative.

It is for some mothers, anyway. A little pang hits my chest. I can't get back what I've lost, but I can control the next stage of my life.

I open the door and enter the room. From the doorway, I can hear the faintest sound of her breathing. See the gentle rise and fall of her chest. Little wisps of white-blonde hair are scattered on the tiny pillowcase. She clutches a little teddy bear in her chubby fist. My nose tingles and my eyes grow misty.

I kneel beside my daughter and gently smooth the wisps of hair away from her face and behind her ears. Bend and kiss her.

"I'm sorry," I whisper. Sorry for leaving her. Sorry for not keeping her the very second she left my body. I know I had no choice, but I don't know how I'll ever fully forgive myself.

How do I learn to be a good mother?

You love her unconditionally. You teach her. And if there was anything your parents did that was wrong or hurtful...you do the opposite.

What had my parents done that I hated?

Used me.

Treated me like an object.

Hit me when I annoyed them and downplayed my fears.

I guess it honestly wouldn't be that hard to do better.

I can do this.

I want brothers and sisters for Ivy, too. A part of me wonders if *he* does.

Aleks isn't like a regular guy you'd meet that might, say, coach Little League or teach them how to drive a car.

The two of us, both me and Ivy, are in a world that's totally new. While Aleks says we've fast-tracked life, we have a lot to make up for. Maybe evolution or God or whatever made the gestation period for human children nine months to give our brains time to adjust to the *concept* of a helpless life-form fully dependent on us. I never let myself mentally prepare, because I knew I wasn't going to be able to keep her.

To be honest, I've hardly gotten used to the concept of having a *husband*.

Ivy rolls over, her cheeks rosy, and sprawls out on the bed. She looks like a little angel.

Soon, we'll interview nannies. Aleks says his family's eager to spend more time with me. Get to know me. I guess my white-knuckled wedding day didn't really count.

I finally pull myself away from Ivy so she can rest and tiptoe noiselessly back into our bedroom. Aleks is still fast asleep.

Outside the window, the winter-swept horizon's filled with bare trees, the branches sparse. When I look closer, though, I can see the tiniest hint of buds on the branches outside this window. The sun is beginning to peek through clouds, as each day we march closer to spring, we get more and more sunlight. It feels like a sign. Hopeful. Still dark and cold but there's promise of life in the air.

I stretch and do some early morning yoga, my face toward the sun, content for now in the knowledge that my husband's here with me and there's hope for him yet, and my daughter's safe in the other room.

I stand and stretch, then notice a small notebook beside Aleks's phone on the bedside table.

Curious, I do a little...investigating, you might say.

Pay off mortgage.

College funds for the other kids.

Anonymous donor.

Isaac and Abigail Brooks.

There's a series of routing and account numbers below their names.

My hand flies up to my mouth to stifle a gasp when I realize what I'm seeing. So many zeroes...

My phone lights up. I look from Aleks to the phone and back again.

"What did you do?" I whisper.

I tap on the phone and my eyes widen when I see a message from Ivy's foster mom, Abigail.

> Harper: I can't thank you enough. I know it's early but I was up at the crack of dawn. We miss Ivy so much. I sat on her little bed for a little while but gave thanks she is with you now. And then I saw the notifications. I know it had to be you. Tears of gratitude. Thank you, thank you. You didn't have to do that. Bless you!

I swipe at my eyes.

> Abigail, it was my new husband, but I'll be sure to thank him. I am so grateful for all you've done for Ivy.

> Please do! And don't be a stranger. We'd love to stay in touch.

I'm not sure Lutheran minister and Bratva mix well, but I guess we'll see.

"Who you texting?" Aleks's sleepy-sexy growl of a voice makes me jump.

I put the phone down. "Abigail."

He pushes up to his elbow, scrubs a hand across his face and cocks an eye at the monitor. "Didn't I tell you to get your ass back in bed?"

"Couldn't sleep."

He grunts and plops back onto the pillow. "Come 'ere."

I crawl into bed next to him after my own peek at the monitor to make sure she's still sleeping soundly.

"Why were you texting Abigail this early? She text you first?"

"Yeah. She wanted to thank me for what we did for them."

He shrugs and closes his eyes, still half asleep.

"Thank you for that."

He grunts. "Talk's cheap, woman. You can thank me with that mouth later."

"Are you trying to use me for sexual favors?"

"Always."

I reach under the blanket and slide my hand along the length of his cock. The utter maleness of his groan makes me instantly wet.

"Harper. *Later*."

I feel his body tense when I stroke him through his boxers. "*Fuck*."

"Mmm?"

I slide under the covers and find his warm length. Pull the covers down so I can breathe a bit more easily. Tug down his boxers so his cock springs free.

My mouth waters. I swallow. I've never wanted a man before Aleks, and even "want" is kind of an understatement.

I bend my mouth toward him and swirl my tongue on the very tip, tasting salty pre-cum. I swallow.

"Still want me to stop?" I ask in a husky whisper.

I stifle a moan when he tangles his fingers in my hair and wraps them around his fist. "Stop now and I'll spank your ass."

I grin, then brace myself so I can fully take him and slide him into my mouth. He helps with firm thrusts of his hips. I suck him in and slide my tongue over the length of his cock.

My thoughts begin to short-circuit as sensations overwhelm me. His hand fisted in my hair, guiding my mouth up and down while I suck and lick. His fingers on my hand, showing me how to cup his balls while I suck him. The guttural sound of his moan edging on my own arousal. His voice, all husky and rough, whispering filthy, perfect words I could play on repeat and never tire of hearing.

"Good girl, that's my perfect little wife. You know just how to please me. Just like that. You're a fucking wet dream come to life, Princess."

I smile and close my eyes, losing myself in the way his rough hands feel in my hair, the coarse hair on his thighs feels beneath my hands, the velveted steel of his cock in my mouth. The sense of absolute *power* that courses through my veins.

"Jesus *fuck*," he says with a groan. "Stop or I'll come in your mouth."

"S'okay," I whisper and go right back to it with another languid suck.

His grip in my hair tightens to painful. "*Stop.*"

I pause reluctantly.

"I want to come inside you," he says with a growl.

As I slide on top of him, I stare into his eyes. "You weren't kidding about one-upping Mikhail, were you?" No condoms, no birth control. We have a two-year-old in the other room and he fully plans on getting me pregnant.

He holds my gaze. "No."

He splits me wide open in one savage, perfect thrust. My head falls back as heat rushes through my body.

"Grab your tits," he says in a rough whisper that makes my nipples harder. I obey, moan, and shift my hips as he makes me ride him. "You come when I tell you to."

"Mmm," I say with a whimper. "God, yes."

I take a peek at the monitor, horrified at the thought of Ivy waking up — he claps a hand to my ass.

"Hey!"

"Eyes on me. She's fine," he says with another hard slap to my ass.

My cheeks bloom with fire as he rolls us over and positions me beneath him. His mouth falls to mine as he kisses me, our tongues entwining and our breathing matched. If I still hated him, I think I'd learn to forgive him simply based on how perfectly he fucks me.

"Beg me before you come."

"I'm already there," I moan, the first powerful spasm of ecstasy rocking me.

"*Beg*." His hand's at my throat. Gripping. My heart beats so fast I'm dizzy. Something dark and deep and primal in me wants to test him, push him, see what he can do.

I hold his gaze, a silent challenge.

The thrusts of his hips slows, and he licks his lips. The fire in his eyes tells me he likes the challenge as much as he likes my submission.

"Harper," he warns.

"Mmm?"

Bending his head to mine, he whispers in my ear. "Polina's coming to watch Ivy today. I'm fully ready to leave Ivy with her and bring you back here to chain you to my desk while I work."

I swallow. "Sounds fun."

What am I doing?

"I'll use your mouth whenever I want it and only let you come when you've behaved yourself."

"Mmm. The anticipation's killing me."

So's the swell of his cock inside me and my growing need to climax, but I won't give him that satisfaction.

"Do you really want to test me?"

My hips rise to meet his. Bringing my nipples to his lips, he licks. A warning. I stifle a whimper and close my eyes.

The lick becomes a bite. My eyes fly open, and I stare at him.

Holding my eyes, he lifts his hips and thrusts harder. My head falls back and I brace myself, so close to release I'm going to snap.

"Fucking beg me."

"Beg you for what?" I say in a breathy whisper.

I nearly weep when he pulls fully out.

"Aleks! *No*. I'm sorry," I amend. "I'll beg. Please. I'm sorry, alright, my *God* you controlling jerk, *pleeeasssee*."

Shaking his head, he bends his mouth to my ear and bites. "You're a brat. I should tie you up and take my belt to your ass before taking your pussy and making you wait for yours."

I glare at him but quickly forget my gripe when he thrusts back into me. *Oh, God, yes, I'll do anything for this, anything for more.*

I reach out and tentatively run my hands along the length of his bare shoulders as he holds my gaze. I clasp my fingers behind his neck and meet every thrust.

"Please," I whisper. "Please, Aleks. *Husband*."

That pleases him. He brushes his lips across mine before he nods. "Come, Princess."

I drown in pleasure, joined with his. Wave after wave courses through me and he hisses out a breath with his own release.

We're finally panting and sated when he drops his forehead to mine and lets me go.

It's then that I realize the voices in my head have been silenced.

There's nothing now but a symphony of color and perfection playing a sad but lovely tune in the background as I gave myself over to pleasure.

"I'm gonna fuck you hard at the range for that."

"For what?"

"Making me lose focus."

I hold back a grin.

"When are we going again?" I ask as if I don't know precisely. I dart a glance to the monitor and my heart stops.

"Aleks!"

"Mmm?" He rolls off me and reaches for his discarded tee from last night.

"Where's Ivy?"

CHAPTER SIXTEEN

Aleks

FUCK.

I yank on sweats as we race into Ivy's room. "Ivy!"

A little head pokes out of the closet. She has a stuffed animal in each hand. "Doggie!"

Harper collapses on the edge of the toddler bed. Her whole body trembles in relief. I'd join her if I wouldn't crush the damn thing.

"My God, we need a better monitor," she says in a shaky breath.

"Jesus. Tell me about it." My heart's still racing. Parenting's gonna fucking kill me.

My phone buzzes with a text. I run a hand through my hair.

"You have to stop distracting me," I whisper to Harper

because I love to give her shit. "I missed four calls from Mikhail and two texts from Polina."

She snorts. "Not on your life."

Shaking my head, I walk to the other side of the room and call Mikhail while Harper listens to Ivy chatter on about what she found in her closet.

"Do you ever have your phone on anymore?"

"I called you right back. And excuse me but I believe when you first married Aria you were unreachable too. Give me a minute."

"No. Answer your fucking phone when I call you or I'll move her into a separate house."

I shake my head. "You'll stoop to that level just to keep me from winning?"

"You have no idea."

"Did you just call to give me shit about not answering the phone?"

"No. I called to tell you that Aria had our baby early this morning."

"Wow, you really couldn't stand it, could you? Congrats! That's awesome. Just one?"

He chuckles. "Just one."

"So we're even?"

"For now."

We hang up and I turn to face Harper. My heart seizes in

my chest at the sight of Ivy on her lap, flipping through a board book.

"We gotta get ready to go, Harper. Let's get her dressed and go meet Polina downstairs. She said she'll help the first week."

"Bear," Ivy says with wide eyes. She points to a picture of a fluffy little bear on the cover. Then she points her tiny finger at Harper. "Mama."

Harper smiles and her eyes water. "That's right, baby." She looks up at me, her voice a little husky. "She's always called me Mama. They were good about that. What was up with Mikhail?"

"Aria had her baby."

She drops the book so quickly Ivy's eyes widen. "What? And you didn't tell me? Honestly, you men!"

"What? You hardly know them."

"But they're family now! And they had a baby!" She looks thoughtful. "No wonder you were so into me this morning."

I roll my eyes at her. "I'll remind you that you were the one that initiated."

She waves me off. "Boy? Girl? How much did the baby weigh? What did they name him or her?"

Shit. I shrug. "I have no idea."

She stares at me as if not comprehending. I guess those are things women ask when they find out there's a new baby. "Listen, we have to go. On second thought, go get changed, Polina will come up and help me get her ready."

She frowns.

"What is it?"

"I want to dress her. I don't want to leave, Aleks."

"We'll come back soon, I promise. You can dress her if you're quick about getting ready yourself."

"I can skip washing my hair! I don't need long." She leaps out of bed and takes Ivy by the hand as if I just told her we were going to Disney World.

I don't know if I'll ever really understand women.

I stand with my arms crossed, just watching them. Harper opens the dresser Polina bought yesterday and picks out two little outfits. "Which one?" she says. "Pink or purple?"

Ivy points to the pink one and Harper nods. "Smart choice. Come here, and let's get you ready to meet your auntie."

After we're dressed, we go downstairs to the kitchen. Polina's practically pacing. "Oh my God, I thought you'd never come down! I've been dying to meet you, Ivy!"

She crouches down and waves to Ivy. "Hey there, sweetie. My name is Auntie Polina."

"Elsa!" Ivy says, her eyes wide.

Elsa?

Harper and Polina burst out laughing.

"Someone wanna fill me in on the joke?" I mutter.

Harper grins. "Elsa's a Disney princess with long, long blonde hair. She's sort of iconic with her big blue eyes and blonde hair and blue dresses."

Okay, that's kinda cute. "Polina, Elsa, whatever, we're starting to interview nannies today. I want them to go through a few rounds of questioning and background checks. Will you help?"

"Of course!" Polina holds out her hand and helps Ivy up to the table. "Would you like some breakfast?"

Ivy nods. Something in me loosens, but I can't determine what it is. It's cozy here in the little kitchen. Domestic, even. My heart surges in my chest knowing that we have the power to make this a better life.

"Do we have to leave?" Harper says, biting her lip. "She's so sweet and I want to eat breakfast with her."

"We do. I had everything set up for us and we have to get this done. I promise, we'll spend plenty of time with her later. We'll even go to one of those little stores at the mall and get a balloon or something."

Harper's lips twitch. "Aleks, the look of actual pain on your face when you said mall—"

Polina slices a banana into little coins and shakes her head. "I'm impressed, brother. Very impressed. But don't forget you promised Mom we'd have lunch."

"Do I ever forget anything?"

Polina thinks it over and finally shakes her head. "Definitely not."

"Great," Harper mutters. I tug a lock of her hair.

"Let's go."

In the dense, shadowed forest behind my house, the air is thick with the smell of damp earth, the carpet of pine needles and leaves muffling Harper's quick footsteps. Her whole presence seems like a contradiction, like a miracle pieced together — delicate in appearance but with an air of unspoken strength. She's excited.

"You have no idea how badly I've wanted to do this," she says, her eyes shining. She's practically vibrating with excitement. "I found one of my father's guns once, and it felt so amazing in my hand, but then he caught me and he beat the shit out of me."

Beat the shit out of me.

I'll remember that.

Not that Kolya didn't beat our asses if we fucked around with any weapons, but that's different.

"You must remember safety is everything when you're using a gun," I tell her while I look over our pistol range. The targets are a series of concentric circles painted on steel plates — simple, but useful. The same type Kolya used with us when we were younger.

"Okay, let's hear the rules," she says, her hands tucked behind her back.

"Are you mocking me?" I ask, all playfulness gone. She must take this seriously.

"Mocking you?" she says with wide eyes. "I hear and obey, Master."

She is absolutely mocking me.

I give her a serious look. "This isn't the time or place for fucking around, Harper. There are nonnegotiable rules about firearm safety."

"Aleks, I'm hardly going to wave a gun around for fun or brush my hair with it," she says, rolling her eyes.

"Roll your eyes at me again, woman. Go ahead, I dare you."

That gets her attention. Swallowing, her cheeks flush pink. "Okay, I'm paying attention."

"Good." My voice is firm, leaving no room for negotiating. This is serious shit. "First. Always, *always* act like your gun is loaded. I don't care if you personally made sure there's no ammunition in it at all, you must train yourself to treat every single fucking weapon as if it's loaded. Got it?"

A curt nod. "Got it."

"Second, when handling a firearm, for example, when loading or unloading it, always make sure you point it in a safe direction."

Another nod.

"Third. Never, *ever* point a gun at anything you aren't willing to destroy. It's not something you use as a warning. When you shoot, you shoot to kill. Only experienced shooters can do anything less."

"Yes. Understood."

She's the perfect model student, so far. Her sober nod seems to mirror my own seriousness.

"Fourth. Keep your finger off the trigger until your sights are on the target and you're ready to shoot. If you're not careful, you could accidentally discharge a round. It happens all the time, even to experienced shooters. All it can take is a loss of focus for a second. Are you getting all of this, Harper?"

"All guns are loaded even when they're not, point it in a safe direction, only point at what you want to obliterate, finger on the trigger when you're going to shoot." She nods. "Got it."

I stifle a growl. "Finally, always be aware of what's in front of, either side of, and especially behind a target. Depending on the type of round you're using, bullets can travel well beyond the target. Always think one step ahead."

"Makes sense. I won't forget." Her voice carries the weight of responsibility. I nod, softening a little as I step back so we can get ready to begin.

I slide the weighty handgun into her hand, expecting to guide her through this slowly. It's my custom 1911 in .45 ACP, the one my father gave to me on my eighteenth birthday. "This gun is incredibly powerful. The bullet it fires is a larger caliber than what most people use in handguns, even those most police use. It's designed to maim and kill. The gun is going to kick back hard when you fire it so brace yourself for the recoil."

I expect her to hold it cautiously, like it's an animal ready to bite. I expect she might shake a little, as she gets used to the weight of it and the responsibility of holding a gun. But that isn't what happens at all.

When the gun hits her palm, her transformation is instantaneous.

The very air around her crackles and shifts as if the metal of the gun has a magnetic pull. The weapon seems to be an actual extension of her. Her stance shifts, and she seems to don an air of certainty. The slight widening of her eyes tells me she feels it, too, the sense of absolute rightness.

It's as if she's shedding a skin, revealing her true persona.

I've never seen anything like it.

Harper was born to hold a gun.

I take a step back.

I planned on framing her from behind to show her how to hold it, how to stand. I planned on reminding her to be careful.

I don't say anything. She *knows*. Somehow, she just knows how to hold it correctly, how to align her sights.

With absolute calm, Harper raises the gun. Her posture is flawless, grace married with lethal precision. There's no hesitation, no fear, only the sound of her breath enveloped in the dense forest around us.

She fires.

The bullet sings through the air and strikes dead center of the target with a force that rings the steel plate like a church bell. Without hesitation, she fires again, and again, every fucking bullet hitting perfect center.

Her aim's so perfect it's almost supernatural. Her instinctive ability to control of the massive recoil is breathtaking to watch.

I stare at her in disbelief. I fired three hundred rounds through this same gun before I felt even remotely competent with it.

I blink. Stare some more. A slow grin spreads across her face.

"Wow," she breathes, turning to me with the gun pointing down. "Oh my God. That felt amazing. It was as easy as breathing. I thought that would be a lot harder."

I shake my head, incredulous. "There's no fucking way that was the first time you've shot a gun. No one shoots like that right out of the gate. Did you lie to me?"

The snap of her brows together warns me that I pushed a button. I haven't forgotten the slap across my cheek. She isn't lying.

"Are you kidding me? When the hell do you think I'd have the chance to shoot a gun? I told you, I touched my father's gun once and he nearly killed me over it." Her brow softens. "It felt like this, though..."

"Like what?"

She swallows. "Like it's an extension of me." She marvels at the gun in her palm. "Like...like I was created to do this."

I watch her with a mix of awe and newfound respect.

All my brothers are skilled with weapons, thanks to our tireless training and years of study. Only one's a natural, though: Nikko. His skill is unparalleled. He's the only person I ever met that talked about his weapons like he'd talk about making love.

"Are you serious?" I ask because I don't know what else to say.

"Deadly serious. Now are we going to stand around here chatting, or can I shoot some more?"

I set up cans for her to hit, target after target. I watch, shaking my head in disbelief, as my wife shoots with the skill of an absolute master. Shot after shot pings. Her gaze never wavers, her skill perfection. I can't help but see her for what she well and truly is: a force to be reckoned with. Her skill and prowess with weapons transcends practicality. It's a fucking art form. She's Mozart with a 1911.

Unparalleled. Breathtaking. I'm hard as fuck simply watching her.

"Drop the gun," I say hoarsely.

She turns to look at me, her cheeks flushed and eyes bright and wide, as if she's just come from a run on the beach. "What?"

"Drop it," I repeat. "Now."

As she walks to me, the gun discarded reluctantly, I place a call.

"Nikko?"

"Yeah?"

"How soon can you get here?"

"Fifteen minutes. I'm at Mikhail's. You okay?"

I swallow. "Yeah. Bring your shit. Everything. I have to show you something."

I hang up the phone and toss it next to her gun. When she reaches me, I stab my fingers into her hair and pull her head back. Her breathy groan makes me even harder. I shift my grip and lift her up, turning so the line of trees gives us privacy. We're alone in the dense cover of the forest.

Wordlessly, I slide her down and bend her over a low-hanging limb. Holding her in place with one hand, I yank down her leggings and panties in one swoop. Spread her legs. Pull my cock free and feel for her wetness with the head of my cock. Satisfied, I thrust into her in one hard motion.

Her head flies back and she braces herself on the limb. I fuck her hard, silently, until her body shudders beneath mine and I spill inside her.

When we're finished, panting and hot, she tips her head to the side and twists her torso, staring up at me over her shoulder. "What the hell was that all about?"

"Watching you with that gun was the sexiest fucking thing I ever saw in my life."

Her grin lights up her whole face. "Really?"

"Really," I say, zipping myself up. "And my brother's coming over because he's better at shooting than I am."

He's better at shooting than anyone.

Actually, we'll see about that.

I fist her hair at the nape of her neck and lift her, giving her a hard kiss. "And when you're with him I want you to remember exactly who you belong to."

Her lower lips sticks out. "Why him? Why can't you teach me?"

I bend and kiss her cheek, then her jaw, then her lips again. "Because you're a better shot than I am, Princess."

A smile tugs at her lips, her eyes alight with the thrill of what's just happened. "I know."

I slap her ass. "Oh yeah?"

"Yeah."

I lean in and whisper in her ear. "He's here. I saw his car pull up. You remember the way my cock felt in you. You're still wet from me. Remember you're *mine*."

When Nikko arrives, his sharp, assessing gaze sweeps over Harper with an intensity that might have intimidated someone else. Harper only smiles at him.

"What do you need?" he asks me.

"You see that target?"

He grunts.

"That was her first try."

He scoffs. "Right."

"I'm serious."

"Oh, really?" he asks, clearly a skeptic. "Let's see, then."

Wordlessly, he goes to the remnants of the target and replaces it with a series of much smaller, far more intricate patterned plates.

"Show me."

Harper nods, her demeanor unflustered, as Nikko explains the tasks that would challenge even the most seasoned marksman. "First, you'll hit the smallest target at the edge." It's a fucking dot from here. "Then, no pausing, you'll switch to the other targets I've set up. These are designed and positioned to mimic unpredictable movements. Real-life targets don't have bullseyes painted on them."

She rolls her eyes which makes him clench his jaw, but she's my wife, not his. He can fuck off.

"If you manage that, I've placed an explosive target at the farthest distance. You hit that and you'll be rewarded with an explosion. And," he says with a reluctant nod, "my respect."

It's a daunting challenge. Fuck knows I'd fail. My heart pounds with pride when she lifts her weapon and simply nods. "Got it."

Got it?

Without hesitation, she shifts. Once again, it's as if her body is fused with the gun, as if they're one. She pulls the trigger. The bullets whiz through the air with a surgeon's precision as she hits every goddamn target.

"Fuck," Nikko mutters under his breath. "*Kak ona eto uznala?*"

How did she learn this?

"*Ona ne uchilas', ona prirozhdennyy talant.*"

She didn't learn it, she's a natural, a savant.

I'm holding my breath when she gets to the explosive target.

It's so far away it seems like a mockery, but her determination is palpable.

She fires, the bullet a streak. There's a moment of silence, then the clearing erupts with the sound of an explosion.

Nikko shakes his head. "Holy shit, Harper. Where did you learn to shoot?"

Her eyes twinkle. "Aleks taught me."

I growl. "Harper," I say, my voice tinged with amusement.

Nikko snorts.

"Can I use a different gun?" she asks. "I want to play around with them."

Nikko gives me a sidelong glance.

I nod to her. "Yeah, baby. Pick your poison."

She chooses another, Nikko's custom Glock 19 with the silver slide and red-dot optic.

She licks her lips. When she takes her stance, Nikko's eyes widen and he curses reverently. He sees what I see.

"Hit the pinecone at the very, very top," I tell her. A lone pinecone hangs from a high branch of a distant white pine.

Nodding, she takes aim and shoots. The pinecone explodes and the pieces fall to the ground.

"Holy shit," Nikko whispers.

"Yeah." I start to laugh, shaking my head. "You're the only one I've ever seen that can shoot like that, brother."

"She's too skilled for fucking target shooting," Nikko says. "Forget that. I need to take her to The Hidden Mark."

The Hidden Mark is a private, discreet place Kolya designed for us to practice.

Buoyed by Nikko's acknowledgement and the thrill of mastering these challenges, it appears Harper's ready to up the ante. Selecting a series of difficult targets, she calls them out. "Top left, purple target."

Bang.

"Center right, target the size of my pinky toe."

Whiz.

Each shot rings out with clarity, her laughter mingling with the sound of bullets finding their marks. She isn't amused but buoyed by the knowledge that she's found her personal super power.

"Look, you know you can't teach someone this shit, right?" Nikko asks. "So don't even entertain the thought that she pulled one over on you. Fuck. This is skill someone's born with, brother."

I nod. "I know." I shake my head and laugh mirthlessly. "Her fucking father beat her for touching his gun and he didn't even know what he had, right at his fucking fingertips."

Nikko growls beside me. "I knew I hated the asshole."

"Tell me about it."

I watch as Harper continues to shoot. She doesn't take a break. It's gorgeous, like watching a skilled pianist's fingers dance over the keys, or a figure skater's seamless gliding on ice.

"Harper," I call out, in both amusement and warning. "Remember the point is precision, not showing off. You're still holding a fucking gun."

But Harper only winks at me, a clear signal she has no intent of slowing down. She lines up a shot so far and so hard to reach, hitting it would be almost miraculous.

"Harper," I say, taking a step toward her. "You're only showing off now."

"Oh, yeah?" she answers playfully. "Gonna do something about that?"

"Woman," I warn. "Do you need me to remind you to be safe?"

She pauses and gives me a quick glance as if the words have finally cut through the thrill of the game. "Is that a promise, Aleks?"

She's still wet with my come but it seems she needs my handprint on her ass to remind her. She fucking loves to defy me, the little brat.

Nikko chuckles beside me. "Oh, brother, you have your work cut out for you, don't you?"

I groan, even as my chest swells. "You have no idea." I give him a sharp look. "Keep this between us, Nikko. Mikhail will have to know soon, but for now, just us."

Nikko nods. "I get it. You'll outfit her?"

I nod. "Absolutely."

CHAPTER SEVENTEEN

Harper

I'VE NEVER FELT anything like this before.

Nikko stands beside me. A big guy covered in tats, he's ruggedly handsome but more boy-next-door-meets-mobster next to Aleks. His large frame and menacing scowl would scare me if I wasn't more experienced by now.

"I've never felt anything like this before," I tell him, shaking my head. "I don't know how to describe it."

"I get it," Aleks says beside me. "This is what I'm like when I'm breaking code. When I'm deep in the weeds, unraveling numbers and letters and breaking through."

"State of flow," Nikko says. "You're in the state of flow. Can take people a long time to get there. We call it natural instincts."

Aleks nods. "You're fully focused. Everything else fades away. Time can slow down or speed up. You have absolute control over everything and know intuitively what will happen next. You can almost envision it."

I stare at him, my eyes wide. How did he know that?

"I've never felt so in control in my life. It's like I'm commanding the sun to set or the moon to rise. It's like... like..."

"Waving a magic wand," Aleks says. "I get it."

"Aleks! Nikko! Harper! Are you guys coming or what?" Polina's a little dot by the front door.

I glance at my phone, shocked to see hours have passed. It's lunchtime, and his family's due to arrive any minute.

"Oh my God, I can't believe it's this late already. I need to change, fix my hair, and see to Ivy."

I spin around, looking for a place to put the gun down when both Nikko and Aleks flinch. "*Harper.*" I wince at the sharp sound of Aleks's voice.

"What?"

"Freeze. Stay right there." He puts his hands out as if he's trying to stop someone from jumping off a bridge.

I look down to see the gun in my hand pointed straight at him.

"Relax, I'm not going to shoot you," I say with a laugh as I drop my arm.

Nikko grimaces and Aleks puts his hands on his hips. "You've already forgotten the gun safety we went over when we started. *That* doesn't come naturally to anyone, woman."

I narrow my eyes at him. "Don't mansplain to me, Aleks."

His gaze snaps to mine, his jaw tight. "Sass me again in front of my brother," he says in a low growl. "See how that works out for you."

A lick of heat curls up my neck and spreads across my chest. I swallow and turn away from him so the gun's pointed at the dense woods when I snap the safety in position and slide the gun back in the metal box it came in.

I feel a sense of loss when I'm not holding it anymore.

"You look like someone just died," he says. When I don't contradict him, his voice gentles and he takes a step closer to me. "I'll get you a holster, baby. Sexiest little fucking thing you've ever seen, I promise. Wait until you see the custom kits you can get."

Nikko folds his arms on his chest. "Need to see how good she is with other weapons, Aleks. Someone this good with a gun, good chance she's skilled with a knife, too. You ever used a knife, Harper?"

"To cut my chicken? Yeah. As a weapon? No."

The guys exchange a look I don't quite understand.

"We'll talk about it over lunch."

My steps feel lighter, my heart soaring as we head back to the house, my sexy husband beside me, my daughter waiting for me, and a newfound skill I never knew I had within me. I can't wait to get back out there again.

My lighthearted steps come to a halt when I get to the front door. Voices — *lots* of voices — drift out from inside the house, and some of them are woefully too familiar.

I swivel my gaze to Aleks. "You didn't tell me my family was coming."

The way his brows snap together in a scowl, he didn't know either. "Who invited her family?"

Polina sits at the kitchen table with my little Ivy. Ivy's swinging her legs and coloring in a little coloring book. Next to her is a huge stuffed teddy bear, a rainbow-colored sippy cup, and a lollipop the size of her head.

"Jesus, Polina." Aleks seems momentarily at a loss for words.

"What? My first niece, I'm going to spoil her, don't you dare try to stop me. And don't ask me, I have no idea who invited them, but it wasn't me."

I stare at Aleks. "I'm not ready for them to see Ivy," I whisper. My stomach is in knots.

Aleks has that look he gets sometimes that scares me a little, the haunted glare that tells me he'd do anything if he felt he was justified.

Anything.

"Someone invited them."

"Invited who?" Aleks's mother walks into the kitchen, her silvery hair in an elegant up-do. She's the picture of class and grace.

"Her family," Aleks says. "This was supposed to be just us."

His mother looks pained. "You said to invite family and I misunderstood."

Aleks sighs. "I did say that. I can see how that might be confusing."

Even though I'm nervous and high-strung, my heart melts a little. My father would've been breaking things by now.

"Harper, I'm so sorry," his mother says. "I feel terrible. Please forgive me."

"Of course."

Ekaterina grasps my hand and speaks in a low voice. "Do they know about Ivy? She's a delight, Harper. I adore her." My heart melts a little.

I shake my head. "No, they don't. But it's fine."

Ivy sings in a little voice, swinging her legs from side to side. I look up at Aleks who finally nods. "Listen, this wasn't part of the plan, but we're not going to hide Ivy or who we are, Harper. Not now, not ever. You get me?"

I swallow and nod. "Of course."

"We'll be out in a minute," he tells his mother. "Maybe serve some wine."

"Of course. I know. Don't worry," she says with a wink. "I've got this."

"Mama," Ivy coos. She waves to me from the table and points to the coloring book.

"It's beautiful," I tell her.

She's trusting me. Hopeful. She doesn't know that there are people in the other room that hate me and won't want anything to do with her. All she knows is that I'm Mama.

Maybe that's all that matters.

I remember how it felt to stand out there with the gun in my hand, knowing with certainty that I'd hit every damn target I aimed at.

I can do this.

They don't have a hold on me anymore. The only two people that do are right here in this room with me, and their holds on me are the type I'm not sure I want to ever let go.

"Let's go," Aleks says. I walk over to the kitchen table and, after admiring Ivy's picture, help her out of her chair and take her hand.

"I wish I had time to freshen up."

His gaze gentles when he looks down at me holding Ivy's hand. "Come here," he whispers, leaning over to run his fingers through my hair. "There. Your hair looks gorgeous, all wavy and sexy." He bends down and kisses my cheek. "And you don't need makeup. I love that natural flush on your cheeks." His mouth comes to my ear. "You know who you belong to, Harper Romanov, don't you? You're my wife. You belong to no one else."

I nod. Take a deep breath. Square my shoulders.

The three of us walk into the dining room hand in hand.

My brother hasn't come, only my parents. My father looks from me to Aleks with a scowl that would've made old me cower. I smile at him instead, a vivid reminder that he can't hold me back anymore.

My mother stares, her mouth slightly parted as she looks from me to Ivy then back again.

"And who is this?" my father asks, his gaze wary as if he suspects.

"So nice to see you again," Aleks says, extending his hand to my father. He acts as if my father didn't ask a question at all.

It feels like Aleks's whole family is here, even though a quick count tells me we're missing at least two of the Romanovs. It's a large family, though, so much bigger than what I grew up with.

Polina sits beside her mother. Ekaterina smiles at everyone, though her mouth is tense. Nikko takes a seat across from a hulking, heavily tattooed man with a rugged charm and black leather jacket: Viktor. Beside him sits a man with graying hair and wise eyes, and next to him, a young man with visible bruising on his chin and his arm in a cast – Lev.

"Ollie couldn't join us, as he's traveling," Ekaterina explains. "And my eldest son Mikhail expresses his regrets, but he and his wife just had a baby. He won't be joining us either. Wine? This is a wedding gift from our friends the Rossis," she says, and I wonder, is it my imagination or is she testing the waters? My family *hates* the Rossis.

"Friends with the Rossis," my father mutters. "No one mentioned that."

Aleksandr pours my father a glass of wine. "No one asked. Our conversation was brief. Do you not get along?"

"Get along?" my father snaps. I know what he's like when that vein throbs in his temple. "They've overtaken all of Tuscany with their wine. And none of them would take me up on my offer of Harper."

I stare. I can't believe he just said that out loud, that he tried to pawn me off on the Rossis and they declined.

A muscle ticks in Aleks's jaw. Ekaterina stares and Polina's cheeks flush pink. Recovering, I lift my own wineglass and give Aleks a grin. "Fill 'er up, husband," I say loud enough for my parents to hear. *Husband. That's right. HUSBAND.* "The truth is, the only reason the Rossis declined was because I was twelve years old at the time, wasn't I? And they've all been married since. Even in Italy, they don't marry *children*, do they?"

Ekaterina's expression grows even more incredulous, if that's possible. "Younger than in America sometimes, but no, they don't."

"You wouldn't have gotten *married* that young," my mother says, her cheeks flushing. "We were only trying to make an arrangement."

"I'm glad that fell through," Aleks says. "My win. I'll have to remind the Rossis about that the next time I visit Boston. Have you met Ivy?"

I nearly spit out my wine.

"Ivy?" My mother asks, paling.

"That's me," Ivy says, reaching for a glass of milk I poured for her.

"Ivy, careful—" I warn, but I'm too late. Her little hand knocks the glass over into the glass of wine beside it, sending the liquid in it soaring straight into my mother's lap. She leaps to her feet with a screech. Aleks has the audacity to snort, but poor Ivy looks like she's about to burst into tears.

"It's alright," I tell her gently. "Accidents happen. You didn't mean to."

I reach for a napkin and mop up the milk.

"Leave it," Aleks says. "Staff will get it. Is she alright?"

Oh God, he's looking at Ivy with concern. If he starts to care for this little one, I'm going to fall head over heels in love with him. I'm already halfway there.

I nod, but he leans in close to her anyway. "It's alright. Mama's right. We don't cry over spilt milk here." He winks at me. "Maybe vodka..."

My father stiffens.

Ekaterina ushers my mother away from the table, promising to help her clean up.

Nikko grins at me. "Roll?" he asks, his eyes twinkling. We have a secret, just between the three of us. I can't fucking *wait* to get back to that gun. If only my father knew.

"This is your daughter?" my father asks, his eyes boring into mine.

"She is," I say proudly, my chin lifted high.

"It's a shame you didn't tell me before negotiations what Harper brought to the table," Aleks says. He takes a platter of sliced chicken and puts a piece on our plates before serving himself, then handing it to his brothers. "The Romanov family is in dire need of expansion. Harper has a child."

"What'd Mikhail say to that?" Viktor asks, passing a large bowl of salad around the table.

"Jealous," Aleks says with a grin. My father shakes his head, confused and obviously furious, but doesn't respond.

Despite my resolve, I feel the weight of my father's disapproving glare. It's been too long. I've been on the receiving end of his vicious temper too many times and need more distance than I've had thus far. The silent indictment of my choices burns me.

"It's a pity," he says, helping himself to another glass of wine. "In our family, we uphold the sanctity of marriage. We discourage those who bring children into the world without a proper family in place."

The table falls silent. I can't believe he dared to bring his hatred and prejudice here and display them, right in front of my husband and his family. My cheeks flush with anger and embarrassment. I look down at Ivy, who's thankfully unaware she's the subject as she happily munches a buttered roll.

Aleks places his fork down and leans on the table. I open my mouth to say something, to protest, but he gives a gentle shake of his head. He's right — anything I say my father will dismiss. Addressing him needs to come from Aleks.

"A proper family," Aleks says calmly, even as his eyes burn with fire, "is not defined by societal approval and most definitely not by you. It's built on love, respect, and the courage to stand by each other no matter what."

My father's eyes narrow on him. "Well said for someone who heads a mongrel family. We all know who you are and how your father piecemealed street orphans together to structure his 'family.'"

Aleksandr's eyes narrow right back at my father. "You'll leave my late father out of this. Harper has shown more strength and integrity than those I've met who hide behind the facade of tradition. She is not alone, and I stand by her and her child unquestioningly."

My father sputters, his cheeks flushed with rage, as Ekaterina and my mother enter the room again. I feel sick to my stomach.

Aleks, however, placidly goes back to his meal and begins to cut his chicken. "Now would be a good time for you to go. The only reason I've given you any leeway at all is because you're an old man." He spears my father with a look. "*No one* talks about my wife that way. Old man or not, if you ever disrespect her again, you'll answer to me."

My heart swells with gratitude, love, and newfound strength. His declaration in the face of my father's judgment means more to me than he can ever know.

"We're leaving," my father sputters, as if it's his idea, and gets to his feet. My mother, dressed in too-tight clothes because she's obviously several sizes larger than Ekaterina, only stares.

I hate her in this moment. I hate her for never standing up for me. I hate her for never defending me or making anything in my life easier. I hate her for staying with my father when he abused me and used me and for her own complicit part in all of this.

My hands shake when I cut up Ivy's chicken. Aleks's hand covers mine.

He speaks in a voice meant only for my ears. "A woman who holds a gun like it was carved into her hand can control the shaking with effort," he says quietly. "Let it go."

I remember the way the gun felt in my hand.

The shaking steadies.

Aleks raises his voice. "Viktor, why don't you escort them out."

CHAPTER EIGHTEEN

Harper

LEANING in to whisper in my ear, Aleks says, "I'll pay a visit to your father tonight. We'll have a talk, man to man."

When I stare with wide eyes, he shakes his head. "I'm not going to hurt him, Harper. But if your brother's there... I make no promises."

I feed Ivy little bites of chicken and praise her for sitting at the table so quietly. "I'm hungry," she says. "Cookies if I eat lunch?"

I nod.

"Well," Ekaterina says, standing. "Wine isn't cutting it here, my loves. I think we need to bring out something stronger, shall we?"

I like her already. She comes back to the table with a bottle of vodka in each hand. "Harper, vodka flows in our blood. It's strong, though. Care for a taste?"

"I care for more than a taste," I reply. "Thank you."

Aleks's eyes shine at me. I had no idea saying yes to his family's favorite drink would tickle him.

Ekaterina hands me a shot. I take it and down it in one gulp before I realize they're all staring at me, still holding their full shot glasses. I stifle the need to sputter, liquid fire burning my throat. "Oh, I'm sorry," I say, my cheeks warming. "Do we all drink together?"

Aleks snorts. "Don't worry, we drink alone, together, in pairs, in groups. You're fine."

Still, he links a finger with mine, holding my gaze while the rest of them hold their drinks.

"To new beginnings!" Ekaterina declares.

"New beginnings."

Lev, the youngest one, pulls up a remote and hits a button. A large white screen descends. "Now that our guests have left, we need to have a meeting. I'm going to patch Mikhail in on a call."

I hardly pay attention to what they're discussing, since none of it pertains to me. I know none of the names or places, though Aleks keeps looking at me. Instead, I'm trying to take in the family.

Most of Polina's attention is on Ivy. When Ivy gets antsy and wants to get down from the table, Polina gestures for her to come over to her. Ivy leaps up on Polina's lap and Polina shows her how to shake the salt and pepper shakers into little piles on her empty plate. My mother would've made me sit with my hands folded and I'd have gotten in big trouble for getting up, but I'm glad the Romanovs seem a bit more at ease, at least when it comes to Ivy.

None of them are surprised that she's here. I wonder if Aleks warned them ahead of time.

At one point, Ivy wriggles down from Polina's lap. I expect her to come to me, but instead she taps Viktor's arm. He'd be the last one whose arm I'd tap, but Ivy is undeterred.

Wordlessly, he reaches down and lifts her up onto his lap. She turns to face him and traces a finger down the side of his face, where stubble meets scars. Then ink on his neck. "Dirty," she whispers, shaking her head. She lifts a napkin and dabs at the tattoo on his neck.

Polina snorts. "Out of the mouths of babes."

Aleks winks at me, and my heart does a little somersault in my chest. I draw in a deep breath.

Lev is speaking animatedly with his hands, like we Italians do. Nikko watches. Unlike the others, he's still eating. He cuts every piece of food with militaristic precision, sets his knife down, then carefully eats each bite. He doesn't seem to be a man that's quick to make decisions but rather is thoughtful and meditative. I was born and raised in the mafia, so I know how this goes. He's skilled with a gun, careful and precise — this guy's the assassin.

I shiver and lift my empty shot glass for another refill. Half an hour later, Ivy's made the rounds and visited with everyone at the table. Lev looked a bit awkward but spoke to her kindly, explaining why he had "boo boos" and "Band-Aids." Nikko poured her a glass of water and made funny little animals with his cloth napkin. When she reached

Kolya, dessert was served. He broke little bites of cookies onto his plate and handed her each one. But when she got to Ekaterina, she reached her arms out to her and laid her head on her chest. When I looked up a few minutes later, Ivy was asleep on her shoulder, Ekaterina stroking her back.

I look over at her, a bit jealous. I want to hold my sleeping daughter, but I'm glad that she has a safe place with Ekaterina.

Thank you, Ekaterina mouths to me. She strokes Ivy's sweet blonde hair and gently rocks her. My heart warms. Ivy has moved from the only family she had and been welcomed with open arms into a new one.

This family is *nothing* like mine.

I'm not sure what to think. My brother and father told stories of the Romanovs. We heard of their exploits and merciless cunning in the streets of The Cove. When I'd first arrived here, I'd wondered how much of that was exaggerated. But I'm on the inside now. I'm one of them. They wouldn't treat me the way they'd treat an enemy.

I remember that Aleks said he'd pay a visit to my father tonight...

"We need to begin to plan the gala," Ekaterina says.

"We have months still," Nikko says, shaking his head.

Polina scoffs. "Spoken like a man," she says, rolling her eyes. "Do you have any idea how far ahead most of our vendors are booking? Of course you don't. You think we snap our fingers, and they just show up?"

Nikko shrugs. "That's how Mikhail does it."

She snaps back at him in Russian, and he responds with a quick retort. I have no idea what they're saying, but after a few minutes of heated discussion, Aleks holds up a hand.

"Enough," he says in that tone he has that demands attention. "Ivy's sleeping. You two behave yourselves. Nikko, unless you're planning on handling the details of the gala yourself, we do need to discuss it. But Polina, understand we don't give a shit about details. We trust you to handle matters."

She purses her lips and nods. "That's fine. All we needed to do was make sure we vet the list of guests. You guys make friends and enemies so quickly, the people we are friends with one day are our archenemies the next, so we don't want to misstep."

Aleks shrugs. "Fair enough."

She starts going down a list of names of people. The only ones I recognize are the Rossis from Boston, and based on the earlier discussion, I'd welcome them myself.

"What's the gala?" I ask.

"Romanov family tradition," Aleks supplies. "Every year, my family hosts a huge gala, a charity event with an elite guest list. We spend months planning the event. Last year's function raised three million dollars for the children's hospital." He shrugs. "It allows us to maintain our front as a legitimate business while skillfully forming alliances and networking."

Ah. "So a charitable front."

"Mhm." He turns to face the rest. "Does anyone else have business to bring up?"

"Viktor," Nikko says, "I heard your little venture recently ran into some...turbulence. It's a shame when people don't see eye to eye. Do you need me to smooth things over?"

Ah. Here we go. The veiled hints at who they really are and what they really do. It's like sitting at a dining table with vampires who seem nice enough, until the hostess pours a glass of blood into a flute.

"I might need your help," Viktor grumbles, his arms crossed on his chest. He doesn't look like he needs *any* help whatsoever, so the fact that he agrees tells me this is a big deal.

Lev speaks up. "Got Mikhail finally."

"Sorry," Mikhail says in a stage whisper as he appears on the screen. "This place has shitty Wi-Fi."

"You mean the hospital?" Lev snorts. "Tell me about it."

"Why didn't you guys tell me? I could've helped you," Aleks says. My master computer hacker. Of course he could.

"Aria said the same, but she's been otherwise occupied," Mikhail says.

"How is she?" I ask.

Mikhail smiles at me. "Harper. Good to see you at the family table. She's amazing. Tired, sore, but says it was all worth it." He pans the iPad over so we can see where Aria's fast asleep beside a little bassinet with a baby rolled up like a baby burrito, all swaddled in blankets.

"Oh my God," Polina says, covering her mouth with her hands. "Tell me they're taking visitors!"

"Soon," he says. "I promise."

"I'm going to buy all the things and do all the things and you have no idea what you guys are in forrrr," she singsongs.

"Maybe it's time you get some kids of your own," Nikko says. I don't know him that well, but there's a teasing glint in his eyes that tells me he's needling her.

She either missed that, or it's a touchy subject, because her cheeks flush pink and she purses her lips. "You can mind your own business, Nikko. I don't see *you* putting a ring on a finger or knocking anybody up, do I?"

"Polina!" Ekaterina hisses so she doesn't wake up Ivy.

She only shrugs. "They're not going to get rid of me that easily."

Something in me squeezes. Tears prick my eyes and I have to look away.

My family got rid of me that easily. God, it *burns*.

A warm hand covers mine. I look up to see Aleks still focused on the family meeting, but he squeezes my hand wordlessly.

I flip my hand under his and squeeze back.

"You remember that judge that gave us shit?" Viktor says, reaching for a cookie.

"The one with the mustache?" Nikko says in a growl. "Yeah, I remember well."

"Let's just say he developed a newfound appreciation for community work. Next week, he'll be joining you for a round of golf, Kolya."

Kolya's eyes twinkle. "Fascinating what a little charity work can do for perspective, isn't it, gentlemen?"

Ahh. Here we go with the mobster — excuse me, *Bratva* discussion. They just have more class than my family.

Kolya turns to Aleks. "Has Stravinsky caught up on those gambling debts?" He shakes his head. "Poor guy. He may need a little financial counseling, Aleksandr. Just to make sure he understands how crucial timely payments are."

A muscle twitches in Aleks's jaw. I shiver. "Last I checked, Stravinsky was vacationing with his trophy wife in Bermuda. So yeah, I think a little financial counseling is in order."

Ekaterina purses her lips and rocks Ivy gently. "Mikhail, I wanted to let you know that I witnessed one of your soldiers spending time with that Anderson boy down at the grave-yard when I put flowers on your father's grave."

The whole room tenses. "Are you serious?" Mikhail asks. I have no idea what they're talking about, but apparently, she just dropped a bomb.

"Oh, yes," she says, gently running her fingers through Ivy's hair. "Maybe it's time we have a bit of a discussion about family values and what we mean by loyalty, hmm?"

My eyes widen when Aleksandr sits up taller. "Viktor, are you free tomorrow night?"

"Of course," Viktor says. There's something about the way he chomps the cookie that reminds me of a tiger.

"You and Nikko have a planned hunting trip then, don't you?"

"We do."

He cuts his eyes to me. "Harper, I think it's time you joined them."

Nikko grins, but Viktor looks bemused. "You want your wife to go with us?" He leans forward. "You *are* talking about the — hunting trip — down by the beach house, aren't you?"

Who goes hunting by a — *ohhh*.

Well, shit.

Aleksandr smiles. "I am. Nikko, we need to tell them what we discovered today."

"I'd rather show them," he says. "May I?"

My skin prickles with awareness and I suddenly feel a little nauseous. What are they going to show? Do I want to know?

Why does the daughter of a mobster still get queasy when it comes to things like this? Right now, as far as I can tell, they're talking about "hunting," which I assume has some sort of assassination vibe, "financial planning" due to someone's poor financial choices, which I can only assume means beating somebody the fuck up, a "discussion" about family values and loyalty, which naturally means someone's in deep shit, and an offer from the family hitman to "smooth things over."

In other words, this family discussion isn't for the faint of heart.

"Can you see, Mikhail?" Nikko asks as he pulls up a second screen on a laptop.

Mikhail sits up on the screen, his eyes alert. "Clearly."

"Excellent."

Nikko hits a few buttons and an image that looks vaguely familiar pops onto the screen. When Aleksandr's grip tightens on mine, I realize I know why it's familiar. It's footage from earlier today, outside.

Oh my God.

I stop breathing when I realize that's...me. Holding a gun.

Those targets weren't... *that* far away, were they?

Everyone watches in silence as I hit the first target, then the second. Audio booms from overhead speakers.

I suddenly remember what else we did out there. "Aleks," I whisper in a strangled voice. "Shooting wasn't the only—"

"Don't worry," he whispers back. "I know exactly where every camera on this estate lies. You're safe." His eyes darken. "Do you think I'd fuck my wife where people could see?"

I shiver. God, he's so damn protective and I love it so much. I swallow. "No."

He kisses my cheek and says softly, "No one sees what's mine, Harper. No one touches what's mine. You're my wife, for me and me alone."

I swallow and nod as the footage continues.

I hit every damn target. It's like having an out-of-body experience. I don't even recognize the woman on the screen. She looks— capable. Confident.

Badass.

Finally, it's as if someone hits a thaw button on the room and everyone springs into action.

Viktor curses reverently. Ekaterina's eyes dance. Polina stares, her jaw unhinged.

Nikko grins. "I've never seen anything like it in my fucking life." He shakes his head. "We're having a contest. You all can place bets."

"My money's on Harper," Lev mutters. He looks at me with newfound respect. "Who taught you?"

I lick my lips. "Um, no one." I shrug. "It's just... it kind of came naturally."

Disbelieving murmurs go up, though no one's bold enough to challenge me in front of Aleks. Kolya, however, chuckles. "I knew one man in the military with such precision. When the military caught wind of his prowess and skill, he became one of *their* most beloved weapons." His eyes cut to Aleks. "Advice, Aleksandr. Please consider keeping your wife's exceptional talents between us alone, and no one else. *No one.*"

Aleksandr's eyes harden. "Absolutely."

"This is stunning, Harper," Mikhail says with obvious admiration. "Would you object to aiding our family if we have need of your skill?"

I'm seriously kind of touched he asked me instead of just assuming. I clear my throat. "This is my family now," I say. "Of course." But do I really know the full extent of what I'm agreeing to?

"Oh my *God*," Polina breathes. "Can you teach me?"

I shake my head. "I'm sorry, I don't have a single clue how to teach someone."

"Which is exactly why you know her skill is natural," Kolya confirms.

I like this guy.

"There's something I'd like you to keep in mind, Harper." I look up to the screen to see Mikhail's serious gaze on me. "Please."

I nod, swallowing, a bit overwhelmed by the sudden intensity of everyone's focus on me. "Yes?"

"There's a big difference in knowing how to shoot and knowing how to kill," he says. The quiet in the room underscores the gravity of what he's telling me. "We could be under attack right this minute and you'd likely be able to shoot to kill and be successful." He leans forward. "It's something entirely different knowing it was your bullet that took someone's life."

My stomach turns. Aleks squeezes my hand. I nod wordlessly.

"Get acquainted with your weapons," Mikhail says. "We'll keep your skills between us. And Harper?"

I nod.

"Welcome to the family."

"Thank you." I clear my throat. "I have something to say."

Mikhail nods. Aleks watches me, his blue eyes on fire.

"There are...situations... that might need something other than a deadly kill, am I right? Like... warning shots or maybe you need someone to disable a weapon, or, or... a camera or something. I could...disarm explosives or something. Incapacitate without causing a fatality."

Aleks nods emphatically. "Absolutely."

"Noted," Mikhail says. Behind him, a baby cries and Aria stirs in bed.

"Aleks, she's more skilled than any of us, but there's a world of information you can still teach her. Are you ready?"

Aleks nods. "I am."

"Excellent," Mikhail says. "And just in time." He sits up straighter. "I just got notification that there's a mysterious drone flying over your house and three unmarked vehicles driving around the perimeter of your estate." He looks at me. "Harper, ready to showcase those non-lethal skills?"

CHAPTER NINETEEN

Harper

EKATERINA STANDS, a faint smile in her eyes as she gives me a wink. She's the very picture of grace, her clothes unwrinkled, not a hair out of place. I'm still wearing the clothes I wore for practice earlier, and I'm in desperate need of a shower. I feel awkward, disheveled, and woefully unprepared.

Polina turns to Ivy and takes her hand. "Come with Auntie, Ivy. We'll have some fun. Mama will be back soon." She reaches out to squeeze my hand. "Show them what you've got."

That didn't put any pressure on me at all.

I realize my hands are shaking and remind myself of what Aleks said earlier. *A woman who holds a gun like it was carved into her hand...*

I steady the trembling and turn to Nikko, who tells me, "This way."

I follow him down a hallway, Aleks close behind us. "Take her to the holding," he says in a low voice, presumably so only we hear.

Nikko nods wordlessly, takes a sharp turn down another hallway, and stops in front of a door. I definitely need to spend more time figuring out the layout of this place. It feels like a labyrinth.

I watch as he punches in a passcode, slides a finger along an identification strip, and opens the door. When we enter, my jaw drops. Meticulously organized in a way that is all Aleks, I'm immediately struck by the harmonious arsenal of weapons.

I take a look around. The walls are gunmetal gray, soft lighting showcasing a glass stand outfitted with handguns and pistols, knives, and other things I can't quite identify but which look lethal at first glance. Items for close combat.

To the right lies a long, sturdy tabletop, disassembled weapons' parts and items for cleaning neatly arranged — a workplace, it seems. I open one of the heavy drawers, my eyes widening at the sight of row upon row of neatly organized ammunition.

At the far end of the room there's a secure door that looks like it's made of solid steel. "What's back there?"

"The big guns."

My eyebrows rise.

"*Literally*," Nikko says with a chuckle.

"It's beautiful," I whisper reverently. I feel as if I've just stepped into an art gallery. Aleks and Nikko share a look.

"You should see Nikko's place."

I hold back a gasp. I can only imagine.

"Should be called the armory," I murmur. "Why the *holding?*"

Frowning, Aleksandr looks back to Nikko. They share a silent understanding. They're wondering how much they can tell me.

Do they trust me?

I haven't known them long enough to really trust them, though marriage and bringing a child into the home, not to mention the tutelage we had outside on the lawn, seem to lend themselves to an almost immediate intimacy.

"Take another look at the table and weapons, Harper," Aleks says quietly.

A shiver runs down my spine.

Beside the workplace table there's a sturdy metal chair bolted to the ground. At second glance, I note the black restraints that hang nearly to the floor. A large black box sits next to the chair.

The secure room doesn't house just weapons, but also various items meant to torture and interrogate.

I remember Aleks's gentle way with Ivy even while I remind myself that I can't ever forget who he truly is. He's been kind to me, but if I ever turned on him. If I ever betrayed his family...

I wouldn't. I'd die before I did that.

They're my family now.

I look up at the two of them, my heart pounding, and point to the box. "May I?"

"Yes, but we don't have a lot of time." Aleks nods toward it. "Go on."

I know what I'm going to find before I open it. I unfasten the latch and stare at the neatly coiled rope, blindfold, pliers, and remote control. Items meant for interrogation.

"If I looked around this room, I'd find more than weapons, wouldn't I?"

Aleks nods. "You would."

"Do I need to?"

He shakes his head. "Not now, no. Let's get you out there and shoot down that fucking drone."

Five minutes later, I exit the room feeling ten feet tall and invincible. The fact that he's made me wear a bulletproof vest probably has something to do with that.

We head to the entrance that takes us to the roof, my gun by my side. Nikko's packing a weapon, too.

"Hey. I thought I was doing this."

"Harper, asking Nikko to go anywhere without a weapon's like asking him to cut his eyes out. Not gonna happen."

"Fine, but this is my turn."

Nikko grins and holds his hands up. "Have at it. Let's see what you've got. Do you see it?"

I look up at the night sky and narrow my eyes. "Yep."

It's hovering at a distance, ducking into the shadows, but even from here I can see the camera lens pointed at our property.

"Not today, boys," I say under my breath. I lift the sniper rifle Nikko chose. Take a minute to aim. Control my breathing. My focus snaps into place like a camera lens framing a focal point.

"Where are you aiming?" Nikko asks in a low voice.

"If I hit the propulsion system, it'll be inoperable."

"Perfect," Aleks says beside me.

There's not a shadow of a doubt in my mind I'll hit it with the first shot.

With a single, well-placed shot, I destroy the propulsion system. The drone stops, spirals downward, and hits the ground in a little *puff* of broken pieces.

"Excellent," Aleksandr says. Warmth spreads through my chest because I know I just did something huge.

"I want to shoot something else," I say with a pout. "That was too easy."

"Go ahead," Aleks says, pulling his phone out of his pocket and checking a text. "But Polina says Ivy wants her mama, so be quick about it."

Ping.

Ping.

Ping.

The drone's smithereens.

"Cars have gone," Nikko says. "Lev's looking at footage."

I sigh and put my gun away. I'm nowhere near satisfied but my girl wants me.

"That was fun."

"Not so fun when you're hitting moving targets trying to kill you, but let's hope it doesn't come to that," Nikko replies.

Aleks's eyes flash at him. "It better not fucking come to that."

He holds his hands up. "Relax, brother."

"Not on your fucking life. You vowed to keep her safe."

"And I will."

Humph. Maybe I don't need a man to keep me safe.

"Now that I obviously know how to use this, I want a weapon of my own." I side-eye Aleks. "Please," I tack on, to be polite. "I don't want to borrow other people's things. It's yucky, like using someone else's lip gloss."

"No jewelry or flowers for you, then?"

I shrug. "I didn't say I *only* wanted weapons..."

We make it downstairs, and I put the gun away with a sigh.

"Soon, Harper. You'll have another chance soon, I promise. Now go, be with Ivy. I have to head out."

We meet Ivy in her bedroom. She shows Aleks and me her princess pajamas and toys and yawns widely.

"Stay in bed with her tonight," Aleks says when we step back into our bedroom.

"Why?"

"Because I told you to," he snaps.

I look up at him. What the hell was that?

Remember who he is.

"Yes, *sir*," I say mockingly as I strip for the shower. I test the water and gasp when I turn to find him right beside me.

"Do you think I'm kidding around, Harper?" His blue eyes have grown stormy, his lips pursed in a straight line.

"No, I think you're fucking uptight," I snap.

"Careful, woman," he says, shaking his head. "If you think —"

"That I'm going to have a mind of my own? Yeah, Aleks, I'll have that whether you like it or not. I just shot a drone that was targeting your family — *our* family — out of the sky. I took a vow to protect you and yours and you showed me the inner workings of your arsenal and holding. I know for a fact you've held prisoners in there and also know you hold them in another place now. So stop pretending I'm some delicate flower that doesn't have half a brain enough to figure shit out and maybe *then* I'll show you some respect."

His eyes flare with something like arousal and the next thing I know, he's pinning me against the doorway. The bathroom fills with steam from the shower as he cages me in, as if reminding me how much bigger he is than I am.

"You'll show me respect now before I whip your pretty little ass," he grates in my ear. "You'll show me respect because you're my wife and because I demand it."

"That's not how it works," I retort, but his fingers tangle in my hair and tug, rendering me momentarily dazed. Fuck, I love it when he does that, and he knows it. "You're a pompous asshole."

His gaze ignites.

Unluckily for me, I'm naked. With a firm grip on my arm, he spins me around. "What was that? You want to say that again?"

His fingers are suddenly in my pussy, and he spreads my juices to my ass. My pulse spikes. I can't speak, can't open my mouth.

"Maybe you need a fucking reminder of who I am."

I lean over the sink, my cheeks flaming hot because I know exactly what he's going to do.

"Maybe I do." I lower my breath to a whisper. *"Asshole."*

He pushes on the ring of muscle, his mouth on my neck. "I'll train you yet, Harper Romanov. You'll learn to respect me."

"Make me."

My pulse spikes when he fingers my asshole. Pushes me against the sink. Opens the cabinet and retrieves a bottle of lube he just so happens to keep *right there*. Lubricant slides down my ass crack and over me. His clothes join mine.

"Call me that again and I'll spank your ass before I fuck it," he bites out, his eyes daring me, begging me, challenging me to defy him.

I stare at him in the mirror in front of me, his eyes meeting mine, and whisper in a singsong voice, "Have at it."

His hand crashes against my ass and I suck in a breath. "Stop fighting me. Stop taunting me," he orders with another hard slap. He peppers my ass with firm smacks of his palm until my skin's on fire and I'm dripping wet. He picks me up and carries me into the shower, facing me away from him when he sets me back on my feet.

"You'll respect me," he says with another hard spank.

I press my hands against the shower wall.

"This virgin ass is fucking mine," he growls in my ear. "I'll train you to take me, all of me, little by little."

The first push inside me makes me feel so full I lose the ability to speak or think or *breathe*. My whole body is consumed with Aleks, every cell vibrating with his energy and presence. My mind goes completely, blissfully blank, as if I've lost the ability to argue just by being filled by him.

The second thrust has arousal tingling in every corner of me.

I whimper with the third thrust and by the fourth, I'm unable to move or think and am completely incapable of anything even remotely resembling logical thought.

"You're fucking perfect."

"You are definitely not," I say, even as I'm grinning through the first flush of ecstasy.

But I still love you.

I don't say those last words out loud. I can't. He's so tortured and wrong and wants to do things to me no man should ever do. And yet... and yet...

"But are definitely hot as fuck," I concede with a teasing grin.

He spills in me as my body goes up in flames. I relish the feel of his warm breath on my back. The hot rivulets of water cascading between us. Our mutual bliss and ecstasy. The flaming heat of his marks on me, claiming me as his.

I'm boneless and tingling with arousal as he rinses me off and holds me to his chest.

"Don't ever get compliant," he says, bending down to kiss my cheek. I love the feel of his stubble on my sensitive skin. "I need a reason to fuck the brat out of you."

"I wouldn't even know where to begin, so we're good."

I stumble going back into the bedroom. "Good, it worked," he says, as he scoops me up and places me on the bed.

"Keep telling yourself that," I respond, even as I roll over to stare at the state-of-the-art monitor he's had installed that's a hundred times better than the one we used before. Ivy's peacefully sleeping.

He slides on a pair of boxers, then a pair of black sweats. I just got my brains fucked out of me, but I can still feel a rumble of awareness skate through me at the sight of his hardened abs, the dark hair that dips dangerously into the waistband of his sweats.

"Where are you going?"

Wordlessly, he pulls on a black tee and a black zippered hoodie. I suspect the bundle in his fist is a mask as well.

He doesn't answer me.

"You look like a ninja."

"Good. And you look like an angel." He kisses my cheek. "Go to Ivy and don't wait up for me."

Still, he follows me into Ivy's room. "I can handle this myself," I remind him, and he squeezes the back of my neck in that move that I love.

"I know, baby," he says gently. "But I want to see Ivy before I go."

Something in me melts just a little bit more when I see him bend and tuck the blanket around her carefully, so she's nice and secure.

Because that's what Aleks does — he makes sure the people he cares for are safe and secure. It's why he's going out tonight.

"Good night," he whispers. "*Sleep.*"

I curl up next to Ivy and close my eyes. In my dream I hear screams and see nothing but darkness. I wake, my heart pounding, somehow both secure in the knowledge that it was just a dream yet still craving reassurance.

"Aleks?" I whisper. There's no answer. I lie back on the pillow and remind myself that Aleks is gone.

CHAPTER TWENTY

Aleks

I HATE LEAVING Harper and Ivy, but it has to be done.

I've got shit to do.

Gleaming under the moonlight, engine purring, the pitch-black coupe nearly blends into the night. I check my weapons and slide into the driver's seat.

Viktor sits beside me, a silent testament of power. Our human weapon. Nikko's behind me. Lev next to him.

We're heading to Harper's family home.

"Tell us everything," Viktor says. He likes to know every sordid detail before we go on any kind of mission or hit. It fuels him. If he needs to beat the shit out of someone who owes us money, I'll make sure he knows the motherfucker beats his wife when he loses a bet.

So I tell them everything. "And the last time Harper found one of her father's guns, he beat her."

"To be fair," Lev says, "if I found one of my kids holding one of my guns, I wouldn't exactly be Mr. Nice Guy."

"That's beside the point," I growl. I don't disagree. "We all know there's a difference between parenting and beating the shit out of someone."

The worst of it is how Harper felt after having Ivy, though. How she had to hide her and how they shamed her. They've used her for years and it's time they pay the piper.

I remember when I first pulled up the drive to get to her family's home and left with my bride.

Adrenaline surges through me as we draw closer.

The forest around the estate where I chased her looks mysteriously vacant.

"Aleks..."

"What?" I'm still lost in the memory of the first time I touched her. Chased her. Captured her.

Now I can't be sure I'm not the one that's been captured.

"Are you sure this is the right place?" Viktor asks. "There's no signs of anyone living here."

He's right. As we pull further up the driveway, I note ours is the only car. The front porch is swept clean. There's no welcome mat, no wreath on the door. Not a light on inside. A buildup of collected mail sits on the ground below the overflowing mailbox.

Goddammit.

Did they go away after they visited us? That doesn't make sense...

"Strange." I cut the engine, mentally cursing because I came here tonight with a purpose.

We get out of the car in silence, stealthy and quiet, all of us dressed in black, masks pulled on.

I expect the front door to be locked, but when I turn the handle, it opens.

I push it inward.

I can at least leave them a warning. A message.

"Motherfucking son of a bitch," I grumble under my breath as my brothers fill the space behind me.

"They fucking played you, brother," Viktor mutters.

You'll see soon enough, she told me.

My parents have no money, she said.

The home is swept clean, not a single piece of evidence that anyone's living here. The fridge is empty. There's not even so much as a roll of toilet paper in the bathroom.

I go upstairs to where Harper's room was and know what to expect. I'm not surprised to find it also completely cleaned out. But when I open the closet, something catches my eye.

I tuck the little box into my pocket then walk back downstairs to where Lev's pointing to a sign. "Aleks? You see this?"

Right on the kitchen island is a little cardboard foldout with the words *AIR BNB. Thank you for visiting!*

I shake my head and pull out my phone.

Google the address.

The first hit pulls up a rental place.

How did Aria and I miss this? Harper's brother gave Mikhail an address and I got it directly from him. We never looked beyond that.

Harper knew this was a rental home. She knew her family had nothing.

You've been played.

A text comes in from Mikhail. I scowl at the phone and shake my head.

What else has she lied to me about?

CHAPTER TWENTY-ONE

Harper

I WAKE up in the middle of the night, Ivy's little body curled up to mine. Her lips are gently parted, and her hair is all wild around her. She reminds me of an angel. I still can't believe she's here. A part of me feels like I will never be able to thank Aleksandr enough for what he's done, for bringing her here. It's against everything in him to not take care of the people who belong to him. It's who he is, it's what he does. But still, after everything I've been through...

As I gently stroke my fingers through her soft hair, I wonder if I've made a mistake, allowing myself to be vulnerable with someone else. I still battle fears that may never go away. I still wonder if I am the kind of woman that's worthy of being loved by anyone, much less someone who's loyal and devoted.

My heart leaps in my throat when I realize that I'm not alone with her. Aleks stands near the window, still dressed all in black, his arms crossed on his chest.

"Aleks?" I whisper in a little voice. "Is everything alright?"

He responds in a whisper. "Come with me. I have our guards watching over Ivy. She doesn't wake at night, and they'll have the monitors. Now, Harper."

His voice is distant, detached. I feel a cold sweat breaking out across my brow. I don't know what's wrong, but this isn't good.

What did he do tonight?

I don't like leaving Ivy, but I know that he and I need to talk. In the next minute, he takes my hand and leads me down the hallway toward the doorway that takes us to the roof. I'm wearing a threadbare tee and a small pair of sleep shorts. Wordlessly, he slides out of his sweatshirt and drapes it over my shoulders, though the tight line of his jaw tells me he does it out of a sense of duty, not tenderness.

How strange.

A sudden realization hits me. Dread begins to claw at me, vicious and viral. If he wanted to get rid of me, taking me to the rooftop would make it easy.

Who am I kidding? If he wanted to get rid of me, it wouldn't matter where we were. He's practically untouchable.

I frantically wonder what I can use as a weapon.

Do I need one?

When we get to the rooftop, the wind bites through my clothing, though I'm not sure that's why I shiver. He flicks the remote, and the heaters come to life.

"Aleks. What happened?"

Without a word, he walks over to the small bar and pours two drinks. He hands one to me and takes his over to the lounge chairs. Moonlight escapes a cloud and illuminates his face. I draw in a sharp breath at the haunted look in his eyes. The utter sense of detachment. He's in a place I can't reach, and I don't understand why.

"I was sixteen years old when I fell in love," he begins, "for the first time."

I didn't think I wanted a drink at this hour, but I find myself taking a tentative sip.

"Who was she?" My voice sounds hoarse. I clear my throat.

"She was a girl on the street just like me. Orphaned, but unlike me, no one took her in. We started out as friends. I wanted to help her, but who was I kidding? My situation was barely stable."

He takes another sip of his drink, staring off into a place far beyond where we are now. Clears his throat. Continues.

"As you know, I was taken in by the Romanovs. Adopted. I became one of them and damn near convinced myself when I finally had power, money, and skill, that I was untouchable." He looks away. "She was not."

My nose tingles at the sound of the raw pain in his voice.

"There was a gang war, and we were at the epicenter of it all. One terrible night in the dead of winter, gunshots broke out in a street fight. She came out to look for me. She was supposed to be at a friend's house." He looks away, his voice distant. "She was shot. She died right there on the freezing pavement while I held her and screamed for help, tried to save her. But you can't stop someone from bleeding out when their carotid artery is hit."

I suddenly feel sick.

He's hinted at a loss like this, but I didn't know. How could I?

I give him a sympathetic look. "I'm so sorry."

He goes on as if I haven't spoken at all. "After that, I knew that eventually I was going to be married for my family's sake, not for mine. Not for love. I knew that wouldn't ever be an option."

He's staring into his drink, but finally, he looks up at me. The look in his eyes breaks my heart. My hands begin to shake, and all the reminders in the world don't help me to stop.

What happened tonight?

"And then I met you. And I thought you were someone completely different from who you actually are. I thought you were spoiled, selfish. I believed the lies that I was told. And I hated that I believed them, even for a minute."

I nod. I know this.

"But I got to know who you really are," he says on a sigh. My heart's beating too fast. I'm cold and hot and shaking, as I listen to him speak.

"You're someone who's endlessly devoted to your child. Selfless, even when it broke your heart. You did what you did because it was what was best for her. You did it because you had no choice."

He shakes his head. "To see you with her, anyone would know that you're not the person I thought you were." He swallows hard. "I believe you to be selfless, confident. Brilliant and talented." His voice drops. "And sexy as fuck."

I stare at him, confused. Bewildered. I don't know where this is –

"I went to your family's home tonight. I was going to exact justice. They have to answer for a lot of things, Harper. Your brother, especially."

I look at him sharply, this time more assessing.

There's not a trace of blood on him, nothing. And I don't think brutal violence is the only way he would deal with a situation, but I'm not sure I want to know either.

He pulls out something out of his pocket. My heart leaps into my throat.

The little box with a lock of hair, a folded picture, and a tiny charm.

"You found it," I whisper.

"I did. Is this why you were so adamant about going back and finding your possessions?"

I nod. "There was nothing else I cared about. Thank you." I clutch it to me, even though I don't need this as badly as I thought I did now that I have Ivy.

Aleks's voice hardens. "That was *all* that I found, Harper."

I look up at him curiously. "What do you mean?"

"They're gone. Every trace of them. Not a stitch of clothing, not so much as a tissue out of place. They vacated your home, Harper," he says, his voice hardening, a thread of mockery underlying his words.

"What?" What does this mean? Where did they go?

He stands, that same hardness in his eyes. Ice-cold blue pin me. "Don't lie to me. Tell me you didn't know that the home was a rental."

I'm confused. What does he think I had to do with this?

"Of course I knew that home was a rental. I knew my family's circumstances, Aleksandr."

"So you knew that they played me."

I stare, not sure how to respond.

"You won't even defend yourself? You lied to me."

I will myself to respond, because if this is what he thinks of me —

"Aleks. I don't know — how could you — I didn't know they were leaving. But why do you need them? Good riddance, I say. I don't care if I never see them again."

A muscle clenches in his jaw and he turns away from me. This is how he is, isn't it? His go-to. When things don't go the way he plans, he reverts to being his cold, hard self. Pushing anyone and everyone away. Walling up his heart so he's safe and no one can reach him.

"My family suffered an attack two hours ago at one of our establishments. What do you know about that?"

"What are you talking about? Jesus, Aleks. What is going on with you?"

"I trusted you."

"How interesting, I trusted you, too."

He searches my eyes. It breaks my heart to see a world of hurt reflected in his gaze.

I lift my chin and try to make him understand. "My family and I aren't the same. They barely told me any of their plans. I hardly know—"

"You knew that wasn't their home, didn't you?"

"Yes, I already said that."

He stands, towering over me. I'm reminded of how much bigger he is than me. How easily he could hurt me. We're alone on the roof, and if I screamed for help, *no one* would come and rescue me.

Would he harm me?

I was hurt by the very people who were meant to protect me and if there is anything I've learned, it's that *anyone* can inflict pain and suffering...including the people that should love you. Sometimes they're the ones that hurt you the most.

I learned to wall myself up, not to listen to what others said about me. But it was only when I was here, with him, that I silenced those voices in my head that called me worthless.

"What do you want, Aleksandr?" My voice wants to wobble, but I won't allow it. I stare him straight in the eye. When he reaches for me, I deflect him. If he touches me, I'll lose all sense of reason and my ability to think clearly. "No. Don't touch me right now. You look me in the eye and tell me what you really want to know."

"I want to know how far your lies go," he says, his voice hoarse and the blueness of his eyes piercing straight through me. "You knew you had a baby. You knew no one would marry you. So you and your family hid everything from me so you could trick me into marrying you."

Something in me...snaps.

The fragile thread of hope I held breaks like a string snapping under too much weight and a flood of vitriol storms into my thoughts.

Whore.

Slut.

Worthless.

"I told you the truth," I whisper. "I told you everything."

He reaches for the box of memories as I fight against the torrent of hatred rushing into my mind.

Slut.

Worthless.

Lying whore.

His thick fingers move through the memorabilia and pluck out a small piece of paper.

"Explain this."

Is he implying I lied to him?

My broken heart feels bruised. Ruined.

I stare at the paper in his hand but could recite the words from memory.

Though we're apart, I will always, always love you.

The note that *I* wrote for my baby.

I shove his hand away. He stumbles as I push past him. I don't want to talk to him. I don't want to talk to anyone right now.

"Don't you fucking walk away from me—"

"Watch me."

If he thinks he can hold me in the palm of his hand then crush me on a whim, he's woefully wrong. So, so fucking wrong. How could I have ever been vulnerable with a man like him? Never again.

I've always run when I was under pressure. But there's a reason for that.

This time, I have nowhere to go, but it doesn't matter.

I was foolish for thinking I could ever be vulnerable with a man like him. I storm down the stairs that will take me back to Ivy.

I have to see her. I have to hold her. Touch her. See with my own eyes that she's okay.

"Harper, if you walk away—"

I don't bother facing him and flip my middle finger off at him. "Fuck *off*."

So my family played him. They ran away and didn't give him his goddamn money. I'd feel bad about how they used him if I didn't know for a fact that it isn't money he needs but a wife and children. Puppets. Tokens.

His heavy footsteps follow me.

"Harper—"

I enter our bedroom and open the connecting door to Ivy's room, finding her sleeping peacefully. I release a breath I didn't know I was holding.

I turn and shut the door between us, locking it.

He could open it. He has the key. He could break it down if he wanted to be a dramatic douchebag. I listen for him but can only hear him cursing on the other side.

"This isn't fucking over," he growls in a low voice, likely so he doesn't wake Ivy.

Oh, it is, though, Aleks. It so fucking is.

I turn to face her.

Ivy's safe. For now.

I'm not, but I will be.

I fucking will be.

I don't need Aleksandr. I don't need his protection.

I climb into bed beside Ivy and make a mental inventory of the weapons I've secretly secured, due in no small part to Nikko's assistance and, unbeknownst to Aleks, his as well.

I lie down next to Ivy and brush my fingers through her hair. "Shh, baby," I whisper when she mumbles in her sleep. "Rest. Mama's gonna take good care of you."

CHAPTER TWENTY-TWO

Harper

WHEN I WAKE the next morning, the first thing I do is look at Ivy. I need to reassure myself that she's safe, that she's still here.

I watch the gentle slope of her shoulders rising and falling with her breaths. She's got a little twinge of precociousness to her when she's awake, a little silly look about her. But when she's asleep, she's nothing but a picture of innocent childhood.

My gaze sweeps to the door next.

Still locked.

I quietly tiptoe over and listen to see if he's still there, but I hear nothing. I grit my teeth and reaffirm the decision I made last night that I don't need him. Why would I? If this is how he's going to behave...

Still, I can't help but open the door.

At first, I think he's already up and made the bed, but then I realize after a closer look that he never went to bed. It's still perfectly made with no signs of having been ruffled at all.

I look at the side table where he always leaves his keys and his wallet.

Nothing's there.

What was the attack he said was on his family? What did he mean?

I call Polina but it only goes to voicemail.

Something strange is going on.

Or is that only in my mind?

I give myself one minute to wallow. One minute to curse the heavens that even though I'm no longer under my family's control, they can *still* wreck my life.

But I've learned a thing or two since I've come here and there's one thing I can say with confidence: I don't need anyone to help me protect my child.

I look over at Ivy's peaceful form and cross to the dresser as stealthily as I can so I don't wake her.

This world is dangerous, and I need to protect my baby. I don't know who or what would threaten us at this point, but I know that I can't trust Aleks.

There was a time when I ran away to protect myself. To run to my daughter to make sure she was alright.

Now, I'll run with her, to protect her.

I throw a few haphazard things into the princess backpack Polina bought Ivy, even as my heart aches. I don't want to leave her or Aria, the only sisters I've ever had.

I try calling her again and breathe a sigh of relief when she actually answers this time. "Hey," she says. "Can you help me with the gala prep today? Aleks says we need to move the date up and Mom and I are going to have to scramble to get things done. Normally, Aria would help us, but she's otherwise occupied at the moment!"

I don't want to abandon her. I want to help, but my daughter's safety...

I decide not to answer the question directly. "Did you get to see the baby yesterday?"

"I did! He's *sooo sweet,* darling little Sasha. I've never seen Mikhail so enamored. I hardly recognize him."

"Aw," I say, even as I'm folding some of Ivy's little things into the backpack.

I will not think of Aleks and how he is with Ivy. I won't!

Ivy walks around carrying this bag all the time, so no one will think twice about it the way they would if I walked out of here with a duffel bag over my shoulder.

I shove a few small items in the bag for me, too.

"I just need to decide what sort of appetizers we need. Hot? Cold? A variety?"

"Start with hot, because your brothers can *eat.* And if we're moving the date up, it's still a really cold time of year. Aleks can eat the hell out of a tray of canapes."

"Spoken like a true Italian," she says with approval. "I like how you think."

I turn away, grateful this is a phone call. It's easier to hide the fact that I'm crying.

"Did he say when he was moving it up to?"

"This weekend."

Why this weekend?

I don't need to know. I don't care. It doesn't matter.

I square my shoulders and nod. "Definitely hot apps, but you can also have a side table set up with standard things like cheese and crackers."

"Ollie's coming out. So we'll all be here. You haven't met everyone yet. And Aleks has hinted that he's finally going to induct the crossover members from the other Bratva group. He told you about that?"

In passing, sort of. I know there are a few men that came over from a rival organization and he was in charge of vetting them. That's all I know, though, and I doubt he's going to tell me anything more.

Ivy stirs, and I lower my voice. I watch her to make sure she stays asleep.

"Did he tell you why he's moving it up?"

"It's not out of the ordinary. He's not super patient and he said he had good reason. I tried to talk him out of it because my mother's going to have a heart attack, but I couldn't do it. He said it's essential."

Essential.

"I see," I tell her, though I see nothing at all. "Thank you. Where are you having it?"

"That's the strange thing. He asked that we move the venue to the waterfront this year."

"Which waterfront?"

"The East River, the one that separates Manhattan from Brooklyn and Queens. It's lovely there, with all the views of the bridges."

I nod. I'll miss The Cove, the only real home I've ever known.

This might be the easiest time for me to leave, with Aleksandr not here, and the house distracted with last-minute preparations for the gala.

"Ivy's still sleeping but I might come down when she wakes."

"Okay!"

I disconnect the call and know there's no way I'm going down to breakfast.

I can't stay here.

I open the door to the closet where my weapons are stored.

My primary obligation is to protect my daughter no matter the cost.

CHAPTER TWENTY-THREE

Aleks

"I'LL FUCKING KILL HIM."

"Of course you fucking will." Mario Rossi, an old-time friend, sits across from me nursing a drink. He tips his glass in my direction and smirks. "It's the Christian thing to do."

I snort and return the gesture, taking in the early morning blue in front of us. We're sitting on Mikhail and Aria's balcony, and we've just narrowed down the possibility of who attacked Harper to a small handful.

There's movement behind us and I turn to watch Mikhail hold the baby to his chest. Aria's passed out in the glider next to him, exhausted not just from baby care but because she tirelessly helped us with the research we needed.

Wordlessly, he rises and places a blanket over her before he nestles the baby into a bassinet and walks the length of the balcony to join us, looking disheveled and exhausted in his crumpled tee and sweats. But he's happier than I've ever seen him.

"How can babies sleep like that?" Mario says, shaking his head. "All tied up."

"It's called *swaddling*," Mikhail says, rolling his eyes. "Makes them feel safe and comfortable and mimics the feel of being in the mother's womb."

Mario and I snort. "Well look at Mr. Mom over here."

Mikhail flips him the bird then turns to me. "Who we killing?"

"Her brother for bringing his asshole friends around his sister and for failing to protect her. Then, whoever attacked her."

"Of course you're gonna fucking kill him," he mutters, crossing his arms on his chest. "But remember, that's her brother. She'll have feelings and shit."

"Her brother, who knew exactly who his friend was and what he was doing." Which friend? We have no idea, but based on Aria's findings, we've narrowed it down to only a handful.

"Fill me in," he says, running his fingers through his hair. Mikhail had held and rocked the baby while I worked with Aria and she did her hacker magic.

"Mario showed us video from the night she was assaulted. It was easy to do, it was the only party she attended because her parents were out of the country."

I reach for my laptop and show Mikhail the footage. In the uppermost corner of the screen, Harper turns to face the camera, her eyes wide and afraid. She's holding a cocktail with a shaky hand, but even though it was a couple of years ago and the footage is bad quality, it's still easy to see she's gorgeous. Stunning. So innocent-looking with her wide eyes and freckled nose, I want to jump into the screen and throw my arms around her to protect her. I wish I could get back some measure of her innocence for her. I'd beat the fucking shit out of anyone who took it away from her.

"So it was that night she was assaulted." I nod, trying to tamp down the need to break something. Red hot Lava surges in my veins. I breathe through my nose so I can see clearly again.

"We have a roster of who attended. Turns out that Volkov's men hosted the event. So I questioned Petrov and Kuznetsov."

Two men who came literally begging for us to take them in after the collapse of their Bratva group. Two men who have now proven themselves patient and loyal.

"And what did they tell you?"

"Almost all the guests were influential or wealthy, and often both. You know Volkov didn't even pretend to be anything more than who he was. There was no currying favors or playing Mr. Nice Guy. He invited who he could use and work with, no more, no less. And we were able to narrow down a few more points."

Mikhail nods.

"If she'd been assaulted by someone who had any stature or prestige, her family would've forced a marriage. But instead, they blamed her. So it had to have been someone who didn't bring them any value. Of all the people that went that night, only her brother's friends match."

Mikhail nods. "Makes sense. So what's your plan, then?"

"We're moving the date of our gala up. It's one place we could use to lure them in, and a venue we have total control over. I'll use personalized invitations to lure the suspects and make them feel compelled to attend. I'll leverage what Aria found out about who they are and what they're obligated to."

Mikhail nods.

"You know the gala is exclusive, not-to-be-missed. The whole exclusivity piece for people who are in the outer circle should appeal. Harper will go. It'll be risky, but I'll be right there."

Mario raises an eyebrow. "From what I've heard, she doesn't necessarily need any protection."

I growl low in my chest and clench my hands. He holds his own up. "I know, I know, I'm not saying you can't protect her, I know you fuckin' will. I'm just saying she can probably defend herself if she has the right weapons."

I turn away from him and face Mikhail. "Her presence should draw out whoever it was. We'll keep her under close surveillance. Make sure she's safe. But we'll lure them out. Our men will infiltrate the group as guests or staff, so we have an added layer of security."

Mikhail purses his lips, his jaw clenched. He looks out at the night sky and nods. "If someone hurt Aria, I would demand blood and a head served on a silver platter."

"Of course."

But...I know he's leading up to something.

"But the gala's our biggest event, Aleksandr. We can't cause mayhem and bloodshed, or no one will come again."

My nostrils flare. "You think our reputation is more important than my wife's honor? More important than retribution for what she's suffered?"

"Sit *down*, brother," Mikhail orders.

I look down. Didn't even realize I'd gotten to my feet.

Mario shakes his head and pulls something out of his pocket. "Mikhail, may I?"

Mikhail checks the wind direction and the distance between them, then finally grunts. A second later there's the sound of a lighter followed by a flare of orange and the sweet, heavy scent of weed.

"Take a hit, Aleks," Mario orders, holding the joint out to me.

I shake my head. "I'm good."

"You need to clear your head."

I draw in a deep breath of night air. "Your fucking secondary smoke's enough." He chuckles and takes another hit.

"Are you willing to listen now?" Mikhail asks with deceptive calm.

I refuse to back down. "We aren't kids anymore. You're the

pakhan, but I've stepped into your position in your absence. We won't settle this by beating the shit out of each other."

There was a time when our parents left all of us to Mikhail, and as the older brother he kept us in line. But that was then, and this is now.

I stare him down. "Someone raped my wife and fucking destroyed her as a result. When I find out who that was, wild horses won't keep me away from delivering the justice that's owed. But I've waited this long. I can be patient and not cause a scene. Fair enough?"

Mikhail holds my gaze, his lips pursed, before he finally nods. "That's all I'm asking. No slitting throats near the fondue."

Mario snorts and Mikhail thoughtfully strokes his chin. "Harper asked for nonlethal cases, Aleks. Are you going to involve her in any of this?"

I shrug. "That was only her first taste of her power. We'll see if that request still holds."

"So you're going to leave their final retribution in her hands?" Mario shakes his head. "What if she misses?"

Mikhail snorts. I smirk myself. "She never misses." I get to my feet. "I want to get back to her and Ivy. Fill her in. Make our plans. Today, Aria said she'll work with Mom and Polina to get the gala moving."

Mario blows out a breath of smoke. "Never a dull moment with you Romanovs." He drops his arm onto the armrest and inclines his head toward me. "You're in a unique position now, aren't you, Aleks? One child that came as a bonus wedding gift. Short of Aria having twins, you're more likely to pull ahead."

Mikhail grumbles but I can't help but grin.

Mario can't stop stirring the pot. "In my family, we fight over cannoli. In yours, you fight over the bambinos. Mama would be so fucking jealous, you have no idea."

Mikhail laughs but when he asks Mario to tally all the grandkids the Rossis actually have, it's no small number.

"Listen, I have to get back to Harper and Ivy," I say, stretching. "I'll be in touch later today."

I'm processing through every possible scenario in the car on the way home. It's the way my mind works, calculating possibilities and surprises, and the aftermath of the decisions we make.

I call Harper.

Her phone goes to voicemail.

It's early but that usually doesn't mean anything...

She's probably still sleeping, I tell myself, especially if she's next to Ivy and doesn't want to wake her up.

Settling into the drive, I remember my conversation with Harper.

I shake my head.

She was pissed at me. She shut and locked the door and climbed into bed with Ivy. I wanted to make her come out and hash it out with me, but the next minute I got the call from Mario that he had intel, so I left and went to Mikhail's. I needed space anyway.

Is she still pissed at me?

I call her again.

And again.

And again.

By the time I get home, I'm on the border of panicking. I screech into the driveway and whip the car into Park. Take the steps two at a time. "Harper!"

No response. My footsteps echo in the hall as I head toward our bedroom, only to find my bed still made and Ivy's, too.

Where's my security team?

"Harper!"

I call her again, and she doesn't answer.

When I heard about her, I was told Harper was a runner and the first day we met, she proved it to be true. When I found out why, I understood.

But now I wonder.

Has she run again? Have I been fooled?

My heart seizes at the thought of not seeing her again. Of being apart from her.

Did she go? Me and my stupid bullshit mouth, did I push her away?

I have to find her.

"Harper!"

She's gone. My actions have driven away the only person

I've ever opened up to. The only person I've ever loved. She's gone, and she took Ivy with her.

I'll find her.

I have to.

I burst into the hallway and finally see one of my men. "Where the fuck have you been?"

"Your brother called an emergency meeting, sir. We had to respond. He's putting plans in place for security at the gala."

Of course he fucking did.

"And you thought my brother's demands on your time superseded your need to protect my wife and child?"

I'll fucking *kill him.*

His eyes widen. "Never, sir. Harper and Ivy are right outside."

Heart pounding so hard my head's buzzing, I stumble my way out of the house and into the backyard. I don't see them. She fooled them. Told them she'd be outside and then when they were distracted by the emergency meeting, she left.

My knees give way and I sink to the bench outside the door. I bury my head in my hands. I've done it. I've driven them away.

I have to scrape my shit together so that I can —

The sound of a child's laughter brings my brain to a screeching halt.

The sound...it's Ivy's contagious little giggle.

I look around me. Where is she? Where are they?

The Manhattan skyline dims in the background behind her, the wind whipping her hair in a wild swirl about her face. Ivy is leaping up in the air trying to catch the bubbles Harper's blown, the bubble wand still to her lips. Harper sees me and waves a tentative hand. Seconds later, she and Ivy are heading my way.

Oh, God. My pulse is racing. My palms are sweaty.

"Look!" Ivy says. "Bubbles!"

I smile at her, my whole being flooded with relief. "Yeah, baby. Bubbles." My voice shakes. I look up at Harper. How is she doing?

"What's the matter?" she asks, her brow furrowed in concern. "Are you alright?"

I'm about to say no, when Ivy raises her arms to be lifted on my knee. "Bubbles, Daddy."

Daddy? Startled, I look at Harper. She heard it, too, I know she did because her eyes are misty.

"I thought you were gone," I say in a whisper because I don't trust my voice right now. "I tried to reach you and you weren't there. I came back and — and I—"

"I wanted to leave," she says, her head bowed. "I even packed a bag. But then we got to the door and Ivy pulled the bubbles out and I— I couldn't do it. I needed to see you. I needed to fight for this. For *us*. And I didn't want to take Ivy away again, not after everything she's been through."

I reach for her hand and squeeze it. "I'm sorry, Harper. I'm a fu— I'm a jerk," I say, censoring my words so Ivy doesn't hear me. "I've had decades of only caring for myself and that won't happen anymore. It *can't*."

"I know," she says with a deep sigh. "And I've had years of running. When you accused me, those thoughts in my head came up again and I—"

"'Those thoughts?'"

"Yeah," she whispers.

Ivy leans in and gives me a big hug before she slides down from my lap and runs after a particularly large bubble. I reach for Harper and drag her onto my knee. We watch Ivy chase the bubbles.

"I want to hear what they say, Harper. Tell me. What do you hear?"

She licks her lips and shakes her head. "I don't want to tell you."

I think about it before I speak. "I hear my own voice tell me shit that I shouldn't listen to," I say in a low voice. "Shit like *you'll never be loved. You won't have happiness. You've done too much. You don't deserve this.* And it takes effort for me to push those thoughts away."

"I think of the things my parents said to me," she says, in a voice only I can hear. *"Whore. Disgrace. Slut. Liar."*

She turns away and swipes at her eyes.

I hold her hand. "I wanted you to tell me yours, because it will help me replace them."

Ivy squeals when she pops a huge bubble with her index finger, and it bursts into little droplets. Harper blows a few more, her eyes fixed on Ivy. I watch the bubbles float her way.

"Replace them?" Harper says softly. "What do you mean?"

"When you go to bed at night, I want you to only have good thoughts. When you wake up in the morning to face the day, I want you to think again, *I am worthy.* I want you to think, *I am sexy.* But most of all, I want you to think, *I am loved.*"

"Loved?" she asks in a throaty whisper. I pull her closer to me and kiss the apple of her cheek.

"*Loved*, Harper. Because I love you."

Emotion overtakes her and she quickly closes her eyes. She draws in a breath. Whispers back, "I love you, too, Aleksandr Romanov."

"I was angry and I wanted answers, but I should always give you the benefit of the doubt. *Always.*" I kiss her forehead. "I promise to take care of you. I promise to protect you. I promise no matter what, your safety and wellbeing are my topmost priority. Yours, and Ivy's."

She nods. "Thank you."

"I'll make it up to you, Harper. I can't fall back into old patterns like that."

I hug her to me. Ivy's giggle makes us both smile.

"And it's for that reason that we need to talk about what I was doing last night. I have information and a plan."

CHAPTER TWENTY-FOUR

Harper

"MAMA. PRINCESS."

I look into the mirror to see Aleks holding Ivy, his eyes shining at me.

"Well done, Princess. You even managed to convince your daughter you're a princess."

"That's because I am," I tell him, tossing my head. It might have to do with the endless books about princesses and the tiaras we wear when playing, but I'll go with it.

He shakes his head. "Mama's not a princess, Ivy. Mama's a *queen.*"

My cheeks heat when I look in the mirror and finish putting my earring in. I slide the elegant pearl into place and fasten it, then turn to the side to admire the full effect.

I've opted for a look of timeless elegance, something sophisticated but seductive – yet perfectly designed for the plans I have tonight: a sleeveless floor-length gown with velvety accents. The bodice flares out from the waist into a gently sweeping skirt, but this outfit is a custom dress, borrowed from someone Polina knows. While it appears traditional, it's ingeniously tailored with a modern touch. The bodice is reinforced with seams that allow for maximum movement without sacrificing style, the high slit also facilitating movement. But most importantly, the design completely disguises the holster I have strapped to my inner thigh.

My long hair, usually down and wavy, is swept into an elegant up-do, a few curlicues around my face to make the look a bit more casual. My makeup consists of warm, earthy tones that accentuate my high cheekbones, brown eyes, and full lips. Even wearing low heels, though, Aleks still stands a head taller.

"You look gorgeous," he whispers in my ear. "And I know what you have underneath all that fabric."

I stick my tongue out at him, and he shakes his head.

"Are you two ready to go?" Polina stands in the doorway. Aleks has arranged for one of Polina's friends to babysit Ivy tonight because all of the Romanov family will need to attend the gala. Ekaterina and Polina have been hard at work, and in the past week, I've been helping them with the finishing touches as well.

"Ready!" I say, squaring my shoulders. Aleks puts Ivy down and takes her by the hand.

"Let's get you situated. Mama even said if you eat your dinner, you can have ice cream."

Ivy pouts, probably because she knows Aleks and I are going out. "Ice cream *for* dinner."

"No, Ivy," Aleks says with that blend of stern patience and love that makes my heart thump every time I hear it. "You'll do what Mama says and eat your regular food first. Go, now."

He sends Ivy out to Polina, and they walk down the hall.

"Don't listen to him," Polina says in a stage whisper. "Auntie Polina will give you ice cream for dinner."

"Polina!" he booms.

I shake my head. I'm pretty sure she only said that to needle him a little.

We're silent on the drive to the gala, the two of us lost in a world all our own.

"Let's go over this one more time," he says, clenching the wheel so tightly his knuckles whiten. I'm glad he said that because I'm honestly very much in the mood to go over this one more time.

"There are two potential guests tonight that could be the one who assaulted me. They've been invited to the gala as private guests of yours. Among the guests, the Romanov family has stacked allies. I'll be under surveillance, since I'll be used as bait because we're assuming that whoever assaulted me will at least want another look." I shiver because it makes me want to vomit.

If I could look into his ice-blue eyes right now, I'd bet my life they're murderous.

Good.

"You'll draw them out," he begins. "Then step aside to let me handle it from there."

I snort. "Nice try. We've been over this, Aleksandr."

We have, over, and over, and over again.

"I know that you would avenge me, but it doesn't mean that I'm alright with you taking that away from me. This is *my* revenge."

"You've never killed anyone," he says. "You don't know what it's like taking the life of another person. And yes, while vengeance definitely is behind this, and I wanted you to learn to shoot so that you could get your own revenge? I still don't want you to have the weight of the responsibility of knowing that you ended somebody's life, no matter how much they deserved it."

I look out the window. "And maybe that's how I want to learn. Maybe this is how I want to have that first kill, knowing it's justified. If I'm skilled at shooting, what's even the point of it all?"

I don't believe the words even as I'm saying them, but I don't want my autonomy stripped from me.

"Harper," he says in a harsh whisper. "You're so fucking stubborn."

"So are you!"

He clenches his jaw. "I swear to God, if we weren't on a timeline, I would pull this car over and put you over my knee just to remind you who the fuck I am."

"And then I would seduce you, lying down out there and

giving you a blowjob, then swallowing every fucking drop so that you know who *I* am."

My heart is beating at crazy tempo, but I'm not angry. Not at all. Neither is he, if the tent in his pants is an indication. He's fucking turned on. Because...this is who we are. We spar with each other, but in the end, we come back together. Because the two of us together are fire and neither of us ever wants to douse the other.

"Honestly, I have to say right now that I think it's good we don't have a specific plan. These are messy situations, and I've seen how it happens. We could have a perfectly orchestrated plan, but if we don't have a backup..."

"I'm going to let you have this, Harper. Because it isn't mine to take. And I want you to know that the only reason why I want to is because I love you. You're so fucking badass and a fucking genius with a gun. You've put up with so much. And I admire you for that, don't you know that?"

I widen my eyes. I will not cry. I will *not* cry. My eye makeup is fucking killer!

I swallow the lump in my throat and reach for his hand. His big, thick, warm hand in mine makes me feel reassured.

"That means a lot to me. Because you're fierce, too."

He snorts. "Of course I am. I could never handle a wallflower. Someone passive. I need someone to fight me." He gives me a sidelong glance, and the way his lips curl tells me he's thinking of doing wicked things to me. "I need someone who's gonna make me chase them."

"Of course," I say seductively. "Where's the fun with someone that just rolls over?"

I do a quick mental tally of what I have for shoes in the car.

Goddamn heels. I won't run for the hell of it, but a girl needs to be prepared.

There's time.

When we arrive, I'm a little stunned. The stars in the night sky twinkle, but they seem muted compared to the absolute glimmering elegance in front of us. Just because I helped Polina and Ekaterina put details down on paper doesn't mean that I would actually know what it would be like to see it all unfold. White fairy lights around every window and fixture. Staff dressed in crisp, white uniforms, standing at attention like soldiers. The cars that pull up are some of the most majestic luxury vehicles I've ever seen in my life. They glide, as if transported there by magic. And the *dresses*, it's like these guests stepped right off a runway.

Ten-year-old me would be in her utter glory right now — the click of heels, the swish of dresses, the deep voices mingling with higher-pitched ones, the diamonds and pearls. It's luxury at its finest on full display. As well it should be. Because I happen to know for a fact that this gala tonight is actually getting everyone together to spend money on some expensive artwork.

"Mikhail was the ostensible host of the last one," Aleks says, turning to me and lifting my fingers. He kisses the top of my hand. "And we are the hosts of this one, my lady."

My stomach plummets. "Is that right? So you take turns then? Why did nobody tell me this before?"

He shrugs and winks at me. "I was afraid if you knew there was this much pressure on you, you'd run."

"Okay so, wait a minute..."

"Yes?"

"Do you mean to tell me that I'm supposed to hunt down the person that assaulted me and one of us is going to – to end – on the night that we're actually hosting this thing?"

"Yes. Isn't it perfect? This is exactly how things should be. You, by my side. Mikhail and Aria have a baby now, and he's the *pakhan*, but with the three of us in our own nuclear family, do you know what that means?"

I lick my lips. "It means together, we rule."

"That's exactly right."

"And then it means that you're going to try to knock me up," I say in a whisper.

"Mhm. Preferably with twins."

I square my shoulders. "But that's for another place and time."

"Not too far off. But let's focus, Harper. Let's remember why we're here. Something was taken from you that never should've been. Someone stole from you. Assaulted you. It was an act of violence. And you have that beautiful girl as a result, our daughter. *Our. Daughter.* But that's only because of who you are – strong, selfless. You survived in spite of what they did to you. All of them. You are a survivor, and I'm honored to be by your side. "

Oh, God.

"Do not make me cry. I have the most beautiful damn

makeup on I've ever had in my life." But of course my voice wobbles, and I blink back tears. I nod. "Let's do this."

We walk in hand in hand, amidst murmured greetings and appraising smiles, but I know even now there isn't an ounce of friendliness from any of these people.

The first part of the night, Ekaterina and Polina are brilliant. They introduce me to their friends, and I remember nobody's names. I don't want to. I'm content just being part of this family. I don't need any more than that.

I check in with the babysitter multiple times, because of course I'm afraid for Ivy. But she's fine and the sitter even sends me little videos of Ivy being adorable and precious.

Nikko meets me at the bar, buys me a drink, and hands it to me.

I frown and shake my head.

"What?"

"I want to be alert."

He leans in and whispers in my ear, "It's lime and soda water."

I smile. "Bottoms up."

Nikko smiles back and says in a low voice only meant for my ears, "We have twenty men surrounding you, in every corner of this room. Trained. Nobody's gonna hurt you, Harper."

I take another sip and when I look up, he's gone, blending into the crowd. Camouflaged.

Viktor, however, is a lot harder to camouflage with his huge, hulking frame. He joins me at the bar. "You want a drink?"

"I'm fine, thank you. How are you?"

"Fantastic," he says, and for some reason, his eyes are trained in the corner of the room on someone I can't see.

I look over to see Nikko talking to a young woman who looks pretty out of place here. She wears glasses and has kind of wild light-brown hair. She's slender, her outfit appearing as if she's wearing her sister's dress-up clothes and shoes. She looks as if a brisk gust of wind would knock her over. As I watch, he bends toward her and says something in her ear. She stiffens her spine and marches away from him. I snort to myself. I know what that's like.

Aleks appears by my side, the warmth of his hand at my back.

"They've arrived. But I have news, Princess."

"Mmm?"

"Your brother came with them."

Jesus. "They were his friends, weren't they?"

"They were."

"At least that should make it easier, shouldn't it?"

"Yes, now we can narrow it down. I'll walk away now, so we can actually use you as bait." His voice is hoarse. This is killing him. He bends down and kisses my cheek. "You have no idea how hard it is to walk away from you," he whispers in my ear. "I love you, Harper. Don't forget that." He stands tall and blows out a breath. "I'm sorry I got called away. I'll see you later on." This was part of my plan, but it still feels terrible hearing him say that.

He kisses my cheek and vanishes.

And I'm alone, in a crowd of people. This is a feeling I am quite familiar with.

When my brother walks in, I hold my head up high. The two men by his side look vaguely familiar.

I know them. They were his friends. I've seen both of their faces a hundred times as they came back to my family home over the years.

The man who assaulted me, who ruined me wasn't hiding at all; he was under my nose the entire time.

I had no idea.

I don't even know which one it was.

Maybe they were both complicit.

I feel like I'm going to be sick.

Nikko is about an arm's length away. I give him a quiet little gesture, even as my brother and his friends head over to me.

"You alright?"

"I know them."

"Shit," he mutters. "You still don't want a drink?"

I shake my head. "Would love to change my mind, but no. I'm good."

"I can stay—"

"Go," I hiss. Draw in a deep breath and square my shoulders.

When Nikko heads to a side table holding some canapes, my brother reaches me. "There you are."

His two friends give me the once-over and nod. Marco Vittori has a shaved head and a ragged scar running down the right side of his face, along with coal-black eyes. His buddy Leonardo is not quite as tall and much leaner. He looks away when I look at him.

I give my brother a tight-lipped smile and nod. "Saul. How are you?"

"Oh cut the shit, Harper," he says in a low voice, as he scans the room. "You can dress up all you want, but I know who the fuck you are."

My smile broadens because I know who the fuck I am, too. "Where did you all go? Aleksandr went to pay you a visit and found the home vacant."

He can't hide the look of panic in his eyes. *Yeah, that's right, asshole, my scary-as-fuck husband came looking for you. Better be on the lookout.*

He covers up his fear with a shrug.

"I have no idea. I haven't been home in a month. I had shit to do. Think I want to hang around with Mommy and Daddy?" One of his buddies laughs, and a chill skates down my spine. I know that laugh. I know that fucking laugh. And when I look again at Leonardo, and he looks back at me... I see my daughter's eyes.

My blood runs cold. Against everything in me, I reach out a hand and lean in, lowering my voice. "Leonardo, isn't it? So glad you could come. Gentlemen, please excuse me."

I turn away and tamp down the nausea in my belly.

I text Aleksandr.

> "It's the one in the navy suit with a red tie to my brother's left. You don't have to test anything. I know it's him."

I don't think anybody else in that room would feel the difference in temperature. But I do.

Aleks's response is immediate and chilling.

> "Bait him. Isolate him. I'll do the rest."

No he fucking will not, but I'll let him have his fun.

CHAPTER TWENTY-FIVE

Harper

"YOU LOOK FAMILIAR," I say to Leonardo. "I know you came by the house when I was younger, but I can't shake the feeling we were out somewhere together once."

I tap the comm in my ear to make sure it's working.

"Good," Aleks says. "Keep going."

"I don't think so," Leonardo says, but the nervous twitch of his hands and the way his eyes flit over to my brother confirm his guilt.

Aleks talks in my ear again. "He was there the night of the party. You say there's no testing needed, but I've lined up a lab that will do a DNA test on the spot. Get a DNA sample and we're golden." There's a pause. "Eliminates any possible guilt, Harper."

He's thinking of my *feelings*.

And yet... Oh, sure, fine. *Get a DNA sample*, as simple as walking across the room.

"It's not that hard," Aleks whispers. "You just need some blood."

Alright, that didn't exactly alleviate my fears, Aleksandr. *God.*

I nod to myself, though, because I can do this.

"Bring him outside. There are fewer people there and it's a quieter setting. Fewer witnesses."

Okay, alright. I've got this. I can do this.

I raise my voice, thankful I've learned to speak when under pressure without showing any fear. "There's a bar outside, gentlemen. I'm going to get some fresh air and a drink." I give Saul a challenging look as if daring him to talk down to me again. "Join me?"

Saul looks around the room. "Where's your husband?" he asks, shifting nervously. I have to assure them he isn't outside. "He'll be coming into the ballroom shortly. He and his brothers went to secure the artwork we'll be auctioning tonight."

I walk ahead of them with confidence and grace, as if I assume they'll be following. *Who am I? Who is this woman?*

I catch Polina's eye from the bar. It appears she's leaning into the whole Elsa thing, because she looks as if she's about to set foot on the set for Disney on Ice in her ice-blue gown, her blonde hair hanging down her back. She gives me a wink, and it's all I need.

I belong to this family now. They love me. I can do this.

And if that isn't enough, I happen to see Ekaterina a few paces ahead. She's holding a flute of champagne, a gracious smile on her face. She pauses when she sees me. "If you'll excuse me, my new daughter-in-law is here." She turns to face me. "You and Aleksandr have done a truly amazing job, Harper." Her gaze fills with strength and warmth. "I am so proud."

I hear the undertone in her voice even before she leans in to whisper in my ear.

"You can do this. Hold your head high. One step at a time, darling."

She kisses my cheek and turns back to her friends.

Buoyed by Polina's and Ekaterina's presence and their confidence in me, I look over my shoulder to make sure the men are following me. Saul is right behind me, looking increasingly uneasy, and his two stupid friends follow right behind him.

I'll have to get rid of Marco.

I feel the eyes of the guests on me as I step outside, and I remember then that I'm not alone. I can feel the presence of Aleks's men, hiding in plain view. They're ready and able to fight.

"Saul, one of your best friends is here," I say with a fake laugh.

He narrows his eyes.

I continue innocently. "Mario Rossi. Down by the garden out back. He said he had something to talk to you about?"

That part's a lie, but I know Aleksandr heard every word and he'll follow through to make sure Saul goes where we're planning.

"Rossi? What the fuck is he doing here?"

I shrug one shoulder. "Who knows? I didn't invite him. I heard he had to talk to you though. Seems like a nice guy."

The last part was said only to needle him.

I hand him the drink and easily quell my shaking. No one needs to get the best of me.

"I'll go see Rossi." Saul leaves and fortunately Marco leaves with him.

I'm alone with the asshole.

"Your drink?" I ask him. "I really can't shake the feeling that you're so familiar."

He grunts. "Yeah, a drink. Beer. Something in a bottle."

Perfect. Glass cuts and blood will confirm DNA. Easy peasy. All in a day's work.

I take my drink and his and when I hand him his, I pretend it slips in my hand. It predictably shatters on the ground next to him.

"Oh, no, I'm so sorry." I clumsily fumble with the broken pieces of glass. I reach over to him. "Did it get you?" I slice the sharp glass against his palm.

He pulls back with a roar.

Pussy.

"You cut me!"

The look in his eyes makes me glad he's hurt. If Aleksandr Romanov wasn't my husband, I'd be dead meat.

Still, I don't know if I've ever been so happy to see blood.

"Oh no! Oh God, I'm so sorry," I lie, reaching for a tissue. "You're cut."

I dab at his hand with the tissue, but he yanks away and glares at me. "I'm fine. Jesus."

Nikko, dressed like a waiter, comes by with a tray and helps us gather the shards of glass and empties. He takes the bloodied tissue as well and whisks everything away.

"Let me get you another drink."

I ignore his scowl as I go back to the bartender and give her a nod, pointing to a particular glass bottle. She's been prepped ahead of time.

We considered giving him the same type of drug he gave me, but that would cause him to lose memory. I won't allow that.

He'll remember every damn minute.

She slips a drug in that will cause physical weakness and disorientation.

"Thanks," he mutters, taking the bottle and giving it a hard swig. "You said I was familiar?" He leers. "So are you."

Grossss.

I swallow back the bile in my throat. "Did we date?"

He keeps eyeing me. "In a manner of speaking, yes."

I pepper him with questions about himself, his job, his friends, his travels. He has three cats, sells used cars, and enjoys long trips to the beach in his free time. Liar. He tacked that on for good measure. I almost ask him if he likes piña coladas and getting caught in the rain, but I have too much self-respect.

I ask him questions until I have his full interest because this is why I'm here, this is what I came for. He's going fucking *down*.

His words are starting to slur. "This is a strong beer," he says with a grunt. "Do you remember that party we went to, Harper?"

"I don't in detail," I tell him, tipping my head to the sky and hoping he falls for the innocent woman trick. "Refresh my memory?"

He leans in closer, and I swear I can hear Aleks growl somewhere. "You were so young," he says. "So innocent. So beautiful."

I've completely lost the fear of shedding his blood. I will shoot this motherfucker and sleep *perfectly fine* at night.

"Oh?"

A voice sounds in my ear. Aria.

"DNA confirmed. And babe?" Holy shit that was fast. Did Aleksandr kidnap a DNA lab expert and chain them up in the basement?

Likely.

I clear my throat to let her know I'm listening.

"It wasn't just you,," she says in my ear. "I started digging shit up as soon as we got his name, and this son of a bitch has a record a mile long. He's been accused of sexual harassment, numerous accusations, and there's even evidence he's had a name and location change because of an allegation of sexual assault at work."

Oh God.

I take a small sip of my drink as he drones on and on about his stupid fucking cars, his words getting more slurred by the minute.

Aria continues. "Hurt him, Harper. Do it for all of us. Don't ever let this asshole assault another woman again."

I nod, ostensibly because I'm listening to his boring, self-serving stories, but I'm making a promise to Aria. To Polina.

To the whole female population.

Leonardo stumbles right into me. I frown and help him stand upright. I can't kill him if he's passed out.

"Found you."

Shit.

Saul and Marco come out of the dark. I look around me. The bar is vacant. Nikko's gone. Even the bartender isn't here anymore.

Did Saul do something?

I make a quick mental assessment of the sweet, loaded metal I have in the harness strapped to my leg.

"Shit, what happened to your hand?" Saul asks.

"Your clumsy sister broke a beer bottle and cut me," Leonardo the Douchebag says. I open my mouth to tell them off when a deeper, darker voice comes from the shadows.

"Now, now, Saul. Leonardo. You should know better than to come to my event and speak disrespectfully to my wife."

I breathe more freely when Aleksandr steps out of the shadows.

"Oh, hello, honey," I say brightly, raising my drink to him. It might be my heightened senses, but he looks twice their size and so damn sexy my heart does a little somersault in my chest. If I wasn't passionately in love with him, I'd be terrified.

"Your wife hurt my friend," Saul has the audacity to say, not backing down, his hand on my arm.

Oh you stupid, stupid man.

Aleks speaks calmly, but I am very familiar with that look in his eyes.

"Take your hand off my wife, Bianchi. Touch her again and you'll lose that fucking hand."

Aleks's hand is still in his pocket as if he's only having a casual conversation, but Saul releases me and steps back.

That's right, you jerk. Touch me and die. He'll kill you first, and if that doesn't work, I'll kill you second.

"I feel like shit," his friend says, shaking his head. Saul's eyes cut to him.

"Who gave you that drink?"

"Your sister."

"You put something in that drink?"

I shrug innocently.

Aleks is right there, and if Saul touches me he's dead, so I suppose it's time.

"Maybe I did, maybe I didn't. What would you know about roofies, Leonardo?"

"You motherfucking—"

Aleks moves so fast he's a blur and Leonardo's on the ground, covering his face.

"What did I tell you about disrespecting my wife?" he asks in a placid voice. "Get up, you fucking pussy, and face her. You owe her this."

Saul steps back and Marco only stares as Leonardo gets to his feet, shaking.

I glare at him. "I've confirmed your identity. I know who you are and what you've done. Your friend raped me at that party, Saul."

Saul's eyes widen. He didn't know. I don't know if that helps his situation or not.

My voice trembles, but it's the only part of me that does.

"Prove it," Leonardo says through bloodied fingers. Saul stares, his gaze furious, and Marco turns as if to run.

"Don't move," I say calmly. In one swift move, I take my gun out and cock it.

I go over my rules automatically.

Always act like your gun is loaded.

Check.

Never point at anything you aren't willing to destroy.

Check.

Be aware of what's behind the target.

Check.

No finger on the trigger until you're ready to shoot.

Last. Fucking. Check.

"If you try to run, I'll kill you," I say calmly. "I have perfect aim."

Marco has the nerve to make a derisive noise.

"Call them, Aleks," I say calmly.

"The left corner flag," he says, his own fixed gaze daring them to move.

"Red one or white one?"

The white one's no more than a speck.

"White, baby. Then take out the turret and hit the street-light at the outermost corner of the lot."

"Easy." I aim and shoot in rapid succession as Aleks pins them with his gaze. The flag turns to shreds, the turret and the light shatter.

"Holy shit," Saul mutters under his breath.

"All this time you had a fucking skilled markswoman under your own roof, but you and your father were male chauvinist pricks," Aleks says, shaking his head. "And you fucking wasted her skill."

I turn to Leonardo. "I had a child because of you. I believe you owe her some money."

Aleks nods. "Take out your bank information and send all the funds directly to the information I give you. It'll go into a high yield savings account," he says, likely more for my benefit than anyone else's.

It's satisfying to see Leonardo's trembling hands as he makes the transfer.

Saul is cursing under his breath. "You set us up."

Aleks takes a step toward him. "Remember your place, Bianchi."

"What do you want from me?" Leonardo whines.

"Retribution. Admit what you did." He nods to Saul. "You and your friend will leave your other friend with us."

Saul glares at me. *You don't look that way at me anymore, Saul.* "Careful, Saul," I say in a low voice. "My name is Harper Romanov now. The Harper you knew is gone."

He clenches his jaw and nods to Marco.

"Don't leave me," Leonardo says, trembling. "You can't leave me like—"

"Like the way you left me the night you raped me?" I ask, clenching my free fist.

"I'm sorry," he says, shaking as the medication fully hits. He falls to one knee. Soon he's going to pass out, but at the last minute, he stumbles back up onto his feet, takes one look at Aleks, and runs.

I cock my gun and shake my head.

Leonardo will never victimize anyone again.

No woman will ever suffer because of him again.

"Don't shoot to kill," Aleks says in my ear. "He deserves retribution before he dies."

I nod and pull the trigger. I know exactly where I'll hit him before he lands.

He falls heavily to the ground but is immediately swarmed on all sides by the people that came to take him.

Saul curses under his breath.

"Now get the fuck out of here, Bianchi," Aleks says, as he stalks toward him. "Don't ever contact my wife again. Tell your parents the same. If I need to interfere, you'll regret it." He grabs Saul by the front of his shirt. *"Capice?"* It's almost funny to hear him speak Italian in his Russian accent.

Saul and Marco flee.

I look back at the gala.

We did this quietly. Efficiently. No one's the wiser.

"Good girl," Aleks says softly, running his hand down the length of my back. "You deserve a reward for this. What can I do for you, baby?"

I put my gun away and delicately wipe my hands on a napkin Aleks hands me. "Can I go home? Did we do enough here tonight?"

"A few more basic formalities, and then yes, Harper, we can go home. Alright? That's what you want?"

I nod my head. "Take me home, please."

CHAPTER TWENTY-SIX

Aleks

I CALL my new men to come take Leonardo's sorry ass back to our house. He'll be immediately put into a lockdown room and Harper will be none the wiser.

We finally have a moment of peace.

"You alright?" I ask, drawing her closer to me, right before we head back into the main area. Behind us, the forest speaks in whispers and sighs, a reminder of where we met. Of the first time I chased her down. Of the night I caught her.

My men sweep away all remnants of a struggle, the quiet undercover crew melting back into the night as if swallowed whole.

"Yeah, I'm good," she says with a nod.

"How do you feel?"

"Relieved," she whispers, leaning against me. "You know, I could've shot to kill him."

"Of course you could have."

"But I wanted him to pay."

"I get that."

"I'm just saying I *could* have. Like if I really, truly knew someone deserved it, I could pull that trigger with no regrets."

I nod. "I'm proud of you. Jesus, woman, you've come so damn far. Look at you. Your hands don't shake anymore. You're confident. You know who you are."

"A lot more than that's changed," she says with a nod. "Thank you, Aleks."

I snort. "I brought you home and put a ring on your finger. *You* were the one that did the rest."

"You brought my daughter to me, and somehow having Ivy with me made me realize that I would do anything to keep her safe. *Anything.*"

"Finally," I breathe, shaking my head.

"What?"

"Finally we speak the same damn language, baby."

She grins as I open the door to the ballroom and she sweeps in with confidence in her step, all elegant grace. God, I love her.

At the formal dinner, she speaks with ease with my mother and sister, who introduce her to their friends. A live band plays, and as the hosts of the evening, we're the first people to take the dance floor. I walk onto the circular area with a swell of pride, with the knowledge that I'm here for the first time with my wife on my arm. A bold declaration, claiming her as my own.

She stands by my side during the auctions and raffles and other fundraising activities and in the end, we trump Mikhail and Aria's efforts last year, and I let him know it.

"You're not competitive at *all,* are you?" Harper asks with a laugh on our way out. "Speaking of which... should I just go ahead and take a pregnancy test?"

I freeze with my hand on the handle of the car door.

"Say that again."

"Oh, my period might be a bit late," she says with a teasing lilt in her voice.

"Is it? But Harper, you were drinking tonight."

"I only had sparkling water, I promise you," she says in a throaty whisper. "I didn't have any alcohol."

"Where do we get a test?" I ask. I don't know shit about these things.

"Any pharmacy," she says as I open the door for her and buckle her in. "We'd need to find a twenty-four hour one..."

"I'll fucking break into one and get one—"

"Aleks, for God's sake, save the heroics for when it's needed," she says, pulling up her phone. "Look, there's one right down on the corner." She grins. "Let's go."

CHAPTER TWENTY-SEVEN

Harper

WE COME OUT LATER with six different brands of pregnancy tests and a ridiculously huge family-sized bag of peanut butter cups because I just *happened* to say I love them, and he didn't know.

"I can't eat all these."

"You could be eating for two," he says seriously. "I'll help you. I love that shit."

At the stoplight, I lean over and kiss him. The moment his lips touch mine, I sigh, a flutter of lightness filling my lungs I haven't felt in so damn long.

At the next set of lights, *he* kisses *me*. While my kiss was tame and tentative, his is unfettered. Hands tangled in hair, fingers on my scalp, our tongues touching. I moan when the light turns green and we pull away.

"Go take the test," he says, when we park in the driveway.

I like to tease him a little. "They say early morning is the best time. Let's check on Ivy and then maybe just take it—"

"Don't try my patience, Harper," he growls. I stifle a giggle and do what he says.

"What does it say?" he asks through the door. I stand up and unlock it, letting him in. Ivy's fast asleep, her babysitter sent home for the night.

"Nothing yet. Takes a few minutes."

"*Minutes?* Are you fucking kidding me? I thought it was instant!"

I shake my head at him. "You do know that if it's positive, it takes nine months to have the baby, right?"

He slaps my ass, but not too hard, likely because he thinks I'm pregnant. I'm sure a good ass slap doesn't hurt a thing, but I don't tell him. Not yet. I'll distract him while we wait.

"So our...prisoner. What are your plans tonight?" I ask. "Are you keeping him in holding, or—"

"Do you really want to know what I have planned?" he asks. He's stripped out of his suit coat and tie but still wears his dress shirt and pants. He's sex personified with his tousled hair, burning blue eyes and chiseled looks.

I think about it. "No," I say honestly. "I really don't."

I reach over and unfasten the top button of his dress shirt. "Come back to me, though?"

He reaches for my fingers and kisses the tip of each one. "*Always,* baby. Always."

My phone beeps when the timer goes off. I blink and stare at the two pink lines on the test. He holds up the second with the word *pregnant* in bold letters and a moment later, gathers me in a hug so fierce it takes my breath away.

"Baby," he whispers, his voice all crackly.

"Ivy's gonna be a big sister," I say. "You need to call Mikhail."

"You sleep in our bed tonight," he says as he leaves. "Promise me, Harper."

"Of course, of course, I'll be there." I mean I'll check on Ivy of course but if she's sleeping well, I am more than happy to come back to our bed. I lean in and kiss his cheek. Close my eyes. Remember who I am and who he is before I tell him, "Make him pay, Aleksandr."

His voice sends shivers down my spine. "You know I will." He kisses my cheek. "When I come back, I expect you naked and waiting for me. No clothes, Harper. Nothing but you and me. *Nothing* between us."

I take a long, hot shower. I try not to think about where my husband is or what he's doing right now.

I peek in on Ivy and find her asleep. I sit beside her bed and watch her for a little while. It's almost therapeutic.

"I'll always protect you," I whisper. "No matter what you do. No matter who you are. I'll love you forever." I bend down and tuck the blanket around her. "Always."

Sometimes, it's having good parents that teaches you how to be a good parent yourself. And sometimes you have to find your own way... or beside someone else doing the same damn thing.

I love this sweet girl unconditionally. I know that in my soul. I'm going to pour love into her in a way my parents never did.

I climb into bed in the fluffiest pajamas I own and fall fast asleep.

I wake to the sound of a growl in my ear.

"What did I tell you?"

I yawn sleepily, though I'm immediately awake and my blood is pounding in my ears. Do pregnant women get turned on more easily? Because I am on *fire* at the feel of Aleks's hands on me, pinning me in place.

"You know what I told you, Harper."

I didn't hear Aleks come in, but he's obviously been here a while. His hair is damp from the shower, and he's only wearing a towel around his waist. I tentatively reach my hand out to his arm and stroke it.

"Is it done?"

A muscle clenches in his jaw and he nods curtly. "You don't ever have to worry about him again. Nobody does."

I swallow and lick my lips. "Thank you." I'm glad then that I gave over my need for vengeance. He wanted to seek retribution for me. He wanted to know for certain that I was safe.

"I love you, Harper." I close my eyes and let the words wash over me, a balm to my soul and exactly what I need to hear. "I love you."

He kisses my cheek and cages me in, his large, warm body braced over mine, one arm on the bed. "You've been through so much. And you deserve so much better." He kisses me again, this time dragging his fingers through my hair and pulling my head back before he captures my mouth.

I lose myself in the kiss. I feel lighter than I have in years, even as a pall of sadness hovers at the periphery. I'm not whole, not yet. I've seen monumental changes in the past few months, and I haven't even adapted to the new me.

But I will. *I will.*

When we pull apart, we stare into each other's eyes.

"I love you, Aleks. We've *both* been through so much. We need normal for a little while. Boring."

His piercing eyes hold mine and his lips twitch. "I can't give you either."

I blow out a breath and sigh. "Fine. I'll handle intense and high-stakes, then, as long as I get to partake in any shooting festivities."

He growls, shaking his head as he kneels and begins to strip my fluffy pjs off. "Under certain conditions."

"What's that?"

"I'll let you know when the situation comes up. I'll take it on a case-by-case scenario."

My top flops to the floor and I'm bare-chested in front of him, pouting. "What if I want to be the one that decides?"

That only gets me another narrowed-eyed look and a growl while he's tugging off the fluffy bottoms, so maybe my timing sucks.

"Sure. You get to decide when you hold a gun," he says in a voice that tells me he is totally giving me shit about this. "And *I* get to decide when you're over my lap and when you get to come."

I frown as he tugs the bottoms off my feet and tosses them to the side. I'm lying naked before him and he's only dressed in a towel. I don't think either one of us is getting any sleep any time soon.

"That's controlling," I say, as I reach for his towel and give it a yank, baring him to me as much as I am to him. "Come here."

I tug him down to me and frame his face with my hands. His piercing blue eyes stare into mine with a ferocity that would've made the old me quake. The new me eats it up with a spoon and feels energized. Excited.

Alive.

"Perhaps I'll get free rein with the weapons on condition of sexual favors," I say in a low purr. "Just don't tell my husband."

In one swift move, I push him off balance and straddle him. Pin his wrists beneath my hands and stifle the need to burst out laughing at the look of shock on his face. But it only lasts seconds, and the next thing I know I'm soaring through the air, gasping for breath, and somehow end up face-planted on the bed with my chest down and my ass in the air.

"Aleks!"

"You knew exactly what you were getting into. Don't you dare play that innocent game with me."

I brace just as the first smack of his palm cracks against my ass. Heat floods me and I'm momentarily thoughtless, my mind as free and empty as the big blue sky after a storm.

"You're my wife," he says in a growl that makes me instantly wet. "*My wife.* I don't ever expect you to roll over and be docile. I might as well ask the sun to stop shining or the tide to stop flowing." He palms my ass so hard I hiss in a breath, his rough hand gripping my ass without apology. I feel his mouth at my ear as he whispers, "But don't take this from me."

I think I get it then, at least a little. I can be powerful and strong and fight right alongside him. If he is the king and I am his queen... we rule together.

"Fine, then," I finally concede. "Then why am I like this? If we're equals..."

He slaps my ass again, hard.

"In bed, there are no equals, woman," he growls. "In bed, you're fucking *mine* to do with what I will."

Another hard slap makes me keen with the sting of pain before it morphs into something electric, pure fire.

I go right back to losing the ability to speak, barely coherent words coming out of my mouth as he spanks me again, and again. I push back against him just to feel the way his hand wraps around my waist to hold me in place. I push back against him just to feel him unyielding beside me.

"Open for me," he orders, gliding the head of his cock to my slick entrance. I part my legs and brace myself. The first thrust splits me in two and I fall to pieces beneath him. Pleasure ricochets through my nerves with electric fusion and awareness. I relish every touch, every thrust, every feel of his masculine strength and his perfection inside me. The sound of his own groans of pleasure makes me want to weep, for I know how much I mean to him now. I know how he much he loves me. How he cherishes me. I know who *we* are.

My thoughts are wiped to oblivion as the first wave of pleasure washes through me. I stifle a moan and writhe beneath the weight of his body. I want this so badly. I want *him*. I feel like we've scaled mountains together. I feel as if the two of us have walked through fire and emerged — maybe not unscathed, but stronger.

Victorious.

Being claimed by him like this makes me feel so much more than what I've ever felt before.

"You're mine," he growls in my ear before another savage thrust. "*Mine.*"

Fingers tangled in hair, breathing mingled. Dampened skin and the warm, sweet, seductive scent of our bodies connecting. The feel of his hands, rough and soft, hard and gentle. The utterly perfect *fullness* as he stretches me, enters me, makes sweet, savage love to me.

The palm of his hand wrapped around my throat spikes my pulse. I breathe into it. Savor his warm hum of approval. The flash of pain quickly becomes pleasure. Flirting with the edge of danger makes everything bloom in such vivid color.

I take in a deep breath. Brace myself, palms down on the bed. Throw my head back. Beg.

"Please, Aleskandr. Please let me come."

"Tell me you're mine," he growls.

I don't answer at first because I want to see what he'll do. In seconds, he pushes me down on the bed, his hand on the small of my back holding me down before he gives me a punishing swat. "Say it."

My eyes closed, swimming in a pool of bliss, I grin.

"I'm yours," I drawl. "All yours, Aleksandr Romanov. There was never anyone before you and there will never be another after you. You're mine as much as I'm yours, for all eternity."

"Fuck yes," he growls with another savage thrust of his hips. I shatter into brilliant perfection at the same time his hot seed spills into me. I'm vaguely aware of his groans of ecstasy and the slowing of his hips as we ride the waves of pleasure together. I've never come so hard, so long, or so quickly.

I grin, utterly blissed out.

He sinks down beside me and pulls out. I'm boneless and grinning as he rolls out of bed and returns with a warm cloth to wash us both off. We slide under the covers, spent and at peace.

"I love you," I say, my words blurry and hazy in my sleepy, sex-induced coma state.

"And I love you," he says back. He rolls over and checks the monitor to make sure our daughter's asleep.

Our daughter.

"Ivy's fine, too. So get some sleep, Harper."

Content in the knowledge that the only people I've ever cared about in the world are safe and happy, I fall into the deepest, most blissful sleep I've ever had.

CHAPTER TWENTY-EIGHT

Aleks

I WAKE the next morning to the sound of laughter. Harper's out of bed, and I don't have to look far to see where she's gone. I stretch my arms out above my head and sigh.

Last night was a long, long night and I'm so damn ready to be done with this shit. *So* ready.

I close my eyes and give myself a rare moment to appreciate the peace. I made damn certain that no one who hurt Harper is ever going to interfere in her life again. I gave her the level of protection she deserved long, long ago.

And while she can't live in a bubble, on my watch, she'll have everything she wants. I hear a beep on my phone. I don't want to work today. I don't want to give Mikhail the rundown, or find out what else happened after the gala last night. I don't want to do anything but enjoy this peaceful time with Ivy and Harper. Alone. Where no one can interfere. I love my family, but sometimes I need a little break.

After everything we've been through... I slip my phone in a drawer and close it. If it's Mikhail, he'll give me shit, but I don't fucking care right now.

"Let's go see if Daddy is up."

Daddy. I don't know if I'll ever get used to hearing that. I pretend I'm asleep by pulling the covers up over my head and snoring so loudly they both giggle when they enter the room.

I feel the blanket pulled off of my face and squeeze my eyes shut tight with another loud snore.

"That's too bad Daddy's asleep," Harper says in her distinctive voice. "We have the most delicious tea party set up, and it's a shame that he—"

My eyes fly open, and I leap out of bed. "Tea party? Why didn't you say so?"

Ivy giggles. "Come on," she says, reaching for my hand and tugging. I'm only wearing pajama pants, and Harper wears a T-shirt and a tank, but Ivy has a robe on over her pajamas and fluffy white bunny slippers on her feet, her adorable, blonde hair tousled. I go into her room to find a tea party set up for three with a plate of cookies and actual tea in the pot.

"How long have you been up? "

"About an hour, sleepyhead."

"I had hard work to do last night."

"Well then, have a cookie and some tea. Maybe it will help you to get some sustenance."

I sit at the little table, afraid that I'll break the chair, but Harper shakes her head.

"Don't worry, I read the reviews. I made sure that these chairs were sturdy enough for fully grown men to sit on."

Excellent. "You think of everything. But who said you could have cookies for breakfast?" I ask Ivy.

She points her finger at Harper. "Mama."

Harper shrugs. "Oatmeal raisin. It's practically like eating a bowl of oatmeal."

I pretend to be disapproving but take the largest one I can find, studded with raisins and cranberries and walnuts. I take a big bite. "Delicious. Where did these come from?"

"Polina said you have a friend here whose family owns a bakery or something? From Boston? She said something about them needing to talk with you, but I told her that you needed a little time to rest..."

The only friends I know that have bakeries in Boston are the Rossis.

"Mario?"

Harper shakes her head. "No, not a he, Aleks. She."

"She who?"

She shrugs. "I don't know."

Maybe I do need to check that phone.

There's a knock on the door. "You guys in there?" Mikhail.

"Come in."

He steps into the room, holding the baby over his shoulder and stops short when he sees me, bare chested, wearing pajama pants, holding a dinky cup of tea in one hand and an oatmeal cookie in the other.

"Sorry to interrupt," he says in a voice that tells me he's not at all sorry for interrupting. He smirks. "Brother, I am taking a picture of that and using it as blackmail."

I shrug. "Men have tea parties, a—" I stop myself from swearing, right in the middle of it. Harper gives me a look, and Mikhail's smirk deepens. "You'll get used to not swearing all the time."

"Baby sleeping?" Harper says, getting to her feet. We haven't told anybody that she's expecting, but we will. I will relish delivering the news.

"He is," Mikhail says. "Aria has been at work all night, which is why she's been texting you all morning, Aleksandr."

My full name. Hmm.

"She's resting now, so I took the baby for a bit. We take turns," he says to Harper as if to explain it. As if he wants her to understand that he isn't some kind of Neanderthal that expects that women's work is about childcare.

"Oh, he's precious," she coos. "Just wook at that wittle face."

"Thank you." He pats the baby's little diaper-clad bottom. I guess it's easy to look like a good dad when your baby weighs less than a sack of potatoes and can fit over your shoulder."

"Maybe it's time to tell him, Harper?"

"You really can't let him have his minute, can you?" she asks, her tone amused.

"Nope."

Mikhail looks at the two of us curiously, while Ivy pours more tea and promptly spills half of it onto the table. I go to the bathroom to get a towel to mop it all up, and when I come back, she has three cookies in her hand. Maybe this isn't the best breakfast idea, but she'll live.

"Are you going to tell me or what?"

"We're pulling ahead."

His eyes are flashing at me. "Do you mean to tell me – "

"Yep. Ivy's going to be a big sister."

"Congrats," he says with a grin. "This is a contest I don't mind losing."

I take a big bite of a cookie. I'm starving. "Now why is one of the Rossis here, and what was Aria doing all night?"

Mikhail looks thoughtful. "You guys should get dressed and come downstairs. Probably better for us all to talk at the same time."

Huh.

A few minutes later, we go downstairs. As soon as Polina sees Ivy, she sweeps her up in her arms and sits her on her lap and hands her a bottle of juice shaped like a Disney princess. They make the strangest things for kids.

"Alright, what's going on?" I pour a cup of coffee for Harper before I pour myself a cup. Wordlessly, I slide two sugars and two creams in it, then hand it to her. She smiles and nods her thanks.

"Impressive," Nikko says.

"What?"

"You know how she takes her coffee. You got hers first. Who are you?"

"A happily married man. Shut up. Are you going to tell me or what?"

The door to the kitchen opens and Mom comes out arm in arm with none other than Marialena Rossi. I haven't seen her in ages, not since we visited Boston years ago.

"Marialena! Harper, this is Mario's sister Marialena. Marialena, this is my wife, Harper." It'll never fail to make my chest swell with pride calling her that.

Harper smiles and extends her hand. "Nice to meet you."

"Oh, my God," Marialena says, staring at Harper with wide, beautiful, brown eyes. "Nikko showed me the footage of you shooting. You are amazing. I've never seen anything like it, even in the movies."

Harper blushes a little bit.

"She *is* amazing," I say. "What are you doing here?"

Aria enters next, holding a laptop. Her glasses are perched on her nose, and she looks like she just woke up, her clothes all rumpled. "Marialena happened to be in the area, she's going to a convention." She turns to Harper. "The Rossis own a little boutique in Boston, and sometimes they come here to New York to source their wares. She was here this weekend and I needed to talk with her. I needed to delve into family history."

Family history. What the fuck?

Aria purses her lips at me. "You should check your texts once in a while, Aleksandr."

I narrow my eyes at her.

"Can't I sleep in for once in my life?"

"No," they all say in unison. I throw my hands up in the air.

"Go on. What were you gonna tell me?"

"The Bianchi family has a long history with the Rossis. You know that the Bianchis don't like the Rossis, but the reason is because the Rossi family invested quite a sum of money in Harper's dad's business, and when it went up, they lost everything they invested." She turns to Harper. "What do you know about your dad's business ventures?"

She shakes her head. "Not much. My father is Italian mafia, he came up under the belief that women didn't have anything to do with business, so we were left ignorant about all of it."

Marialena laughs out loud. "Girl, you and I need to have a chat."

Harper smiles. "Maybe we do."

Aria goes on. "The reason why your parents were penniless was because your dad had a gambling problem. He has a long history of borrowing money he doesn't return, and recklessly borrowing his investors' money in hopes of doubling his profits or more, but it never worked out. Your family has basically vanished off the face of the earth," she says with a sad shake of her head. "From what I've heard, and what I've seen, that's probably not a bad thing."

Harper looks pained, but relieved. "Agreed."

"Harper, the reason why your father borrowed money from the Rossi family is because they were distant relatives. In short, what I'm telling you is that *you* are related to the most powerful Italian mob in all of America. You are not just from the Bianchis. The Rossi family disowned the Bianchis because of your father, but he's out of the picture now, so..."

Shit. Seriously? Harper's eyes widen.

"You're gonna like us," Marialena says. "I mean we're crazy Italians, so add mafia to the mix and forget it, but I'm telling you right now that we're gonna love you, Harper. We've already told you, but I'm gonna say it again, welcome to the family. I have five siblings and a whole bunch of cousins and they're all in Boston not far from here. You can come and visit anytime. We own restaurants and bakeries and all sorts of things."

Harper stares. "But if my father was on the outs..."

Marialena waves her hand. "Believe me, my brother Romeo is way more concerned with solidifying connections with the Romanovs than he is with worrying about your father."

My mother grins. "Good, it's about time that we had some connections with people who know how to make pastry." She winks at Harper.

"And I'll have you know, Harper," Marialena says, "my great-grandfather was an old, old man when I met him, and I was only a child, so I didn't know him well, but I've been told by many people that he was one of the most skilled marksmen in all of Italy. People would come from all over just to see him." She smiles. "It seems like your gift may have been inherited."

Harper smiles but her eyes water. "I'm sorry I'm so emotional." Ha, not many know the real reason yet. "I'm a little overwhelmed. I never had family like this before and I... I'm sorry, I don't know what to say. Thank you."

"Tell me you'll come shopping with me," Marialena says with a grin.

Harper grins back. "Consider it done."

CHAPTER TWENTY-NINE

Harper

I RUN, branches snapping beneath my feet, but no matter how hard I run, he's hot on my heels.

I look over my shoulder, and it's a calculated move that I shouldn't have taken. That quick look over my shoulder cost me precious seconds, and Aleksandr is closing in on me.

I squeal when I feel his fingers brush the back of my hair. I leap over a fallen log and quickly slide between a narrow opening in a gate he can't make it through. I laugh to myself when he curses and slams against it. Not that I want to hurt him, but I'm not ready to stop running yet.

When I run, he always gives chase. There's something beautifully primal and erotic about the way he chases me, and I love it.

I run into the clearing, picking up my pace, just as he grabs the fence and swings both legs over. It's so gorgeous, seeing such unbridled masculine strength, that I almost slow down just so he'll catch me. Instead, I turn on my heel and sprint even faster.

My foot catches on something in the field. I go tumbling, and thankfully fall into a bed of flowers. Now that I've fallen, he'll catch me in seconds. Game over.

"There you are, you little brat," he says in that growly voice that makes me hot.

He's heaving with the effort of breathing, his hands on his hips as if trying to catch his breath. He falls down beside me, captures my wrists in his big, strong hands, and pins them by my sides. "You know the rule."

"Maybe I do," I whisper, anticipation weaving its way through my limbs, in my arms, in my nerves.

"Strip."

If I provoke him, the rule is I get to run. If he catches me, the rule is he gets to fuck me.

"Right here in the middle of the field?" I say, just a little scandalized.

He slaps my ass. "Now, before I tear them off you and bring you back home naked."

"What kind of an example would that set for your daughter?"

"She wouldn't see you. I'd wrap you in my coat." He would, though my protruding belly might be visible.

I strip, keeping his eyes on me the entire time. He's already hard as fuck, and I'm wet. In seconds, we're rolling in the grass, my hands grasping for purchase around his shoulders, his around my waist. We lose ourselves in each other until we're sated, panting in the bed of flowers.

He lies beside me. "Remember that first day that I caught you?"

"IT'S A CORE MEMORY, etched into my brain for eternity. How could I forget?"

"I remember wondering how you were so damn fast. Now I know. You're a fucking prodigy."

"Why thank you."

We lie there in the flowers until the sun begins to set and a chill comes over us. I think I even fall asleep a little. These carefree days after the death of my enemy and my family's disappearance have been nothing but peaceful.

I went shopping with Marialena, and then we took a trip to Boston to meet the rest of her family. Well, actually, my family too now, I guess. I'm thankfully not nauseous at all, and my prenatal visits have gone perfectly. The whole family is so excited. Ekaterina has already had me picking up purchases, though she says it's against Russian tradition to buy anything for the baby ahead of time, because it could be bad luck. This is a little bit of a problem because Italians play very differently, but that's alright.

"We should go home," he finally says, leaning up on his elbow. With his hair tousled and his eyes twinkling, he almost looks boyish. Yet there's still an edge about Aleksandr Romanov that will always be there, something that tells me his innocence is long since passed, though there's a playfulness that marriage and having children have brought back.

"I'd like that."

"What do you think about taking a trip to Tuscany in the fall? You still have months before you have the baby. We can visit the Rossi's vineyard..."

"Oooh. Perfect."

As we walk back home hand in hand, I marvel to myself that I tried to run away from the only man that ever loved me.

I couldn't be happier that he finally, *finally* captured me.

EPILOGUE

Harper

"THERE. LIFT YOUR CHIN UP."

Aria lifts her chin up and stares at me, speaking through lips that barely move. "I cannot believe you do this every single day."

I smile. "I definitely do not do this every day, but on a day like today, we need to."

Aria's mentioned wanting me to do her make-up for a while, and since today is a family photo shoot, it's fitting. She's not a fan of the full make-up routine and really, who can blame her.

"Then how do you look so flawless?" She asks with a sigh. "That perfect skin. Those gorgeous beach waves. Not a single eyebrow out of place and yet if I so much as misplace my tweezers for like *one day,* and believe me that happens, I practically have a unibrow."

"Listen," Polina says, chomping on a carrot from the veggie tray Ekaterina's arranged next to the trays of sandwiches and cookies. "You just feel blah right now because you just had a baby. There's stretch marks and all sorts of things happening to you. And let's be honest, Harper's a natural beauty."

I blush and shake my head, but Polina holds up a hand. "Honey, you wake up in the morning and make morning breath smell nice. Just accept a compliment for what it is, okay? Italians have good genes."

I grin and Polina rolls her eyes. "Look at her *teeth*."

"Now those are due to my mother's insistence on braces and whitening strips," I admit.

"Hmmm." Aria scratches her chin.

"You're perfect," Mikhail says, shaking his head. "You look beautiful, Aria. Come on, it's time."

"You guys have it easy," she says, shaking her head at all of them. "Matching suits. Take a shower, fingers through the hair. Shave or touch up the beard, depending on who you are. You have no idea how easy you have it!"

Aleks's eyes twinkle at me as Mikhail brings her over to where the photographers waits for them to take their pictures.

"You really do steal the show, you know."

He kisses me full on the lips.

Polina rolls her eyes. "Go ahead, get all lovey. *Carbs* don't leave you on read or forget your birthday." She takes one of the sandwiches from the tray and a bag of chips and walks away, shaking her head.

Aleks gives me a quizzical look and I only shrug. I have no idea what that's all about, and I have to admit I'm a little curious what the rules are for Polina. Will she have to marry one day, too?

Lev comes in behind Nikko, both of them speaking in rapid Russian. Nikko looks at Aleks and says something I can't decipher. Aleks frowns and responds. I love it when he speaks his native tongue, but I get curious, too.

"What's going on? Why the Russian?"

"Not trying to keep you out of the loop. Sometimes it comes naturally to us and we lapse into it without thought." He shrugs. "Sometimes our mouths move quicker than our brains do." Leaning in, he kisses my cheek. "You ought to know that personally."

I bat him away, flushing at the subtle reminder of exactly how well he used that mouth this morning.

I gesture to where Ivy's happily coloring at a little side table with Ekaterina. Ekaterina's holding baby Sasha, asleep on her shoulder, dressed in the sweetest little baby tuxedo onesie. "Honestly, Aleks," I whisper. "Not in front of the children!"

My heart leaps at the sight of his wicked, crooked grin.

We take pictures, and the photographer shows us proofs before we even leave the studio. My eyes grow misty at the sight of the family surrounding me, my ample belly a sign of our own growing family.

After the pictures, we make our way over to the food.

Mikhail sits up straighter and nods to Aleks. "We need to talk."

Aleks's jaw tightens. "We do."

I sit beside Aria. "What's going on?"

She frowns. "We've found the identity of the men responsible for hurting Lev and suspect they have something to do with the attempt at poisoning you as well, but we aren't quite sure yet. We have a few more things we need to check out before we... act."

"Oh, no," I whisper. "Seriously?"

Based on my own family history, this could go many ways.

Aria nods. "The Romanov family is still relatively small, though they've been made stronger because of the two men they just initiated. But still, with fewer numbers, they'll have to plan another means of retribution."

Another means of retribution. What will that mean?

"Such as..."

"Could be anything. Financial demands. An insidious cyber-attack, which Aleks and I could easily orchestrate. They could take an eye for an eye. Or...something else."

I tap my chin thoughtfully. I'm one of them now. Someone hurt my brother-in-law, and that isn't something I'll allow to happen without serious recourse. "Perhaps they'll need someone who can *shoot*?"

Aria winks. "We'll make a good team, the two of us."

"Harper." Aleks gestures for me to come over. I stand, newly informed and ready to face whatever comes next. Life will never be boring beside Aleks and his family.

"So," I say, taking two sandwiches and nestling them onto a plate. "Time to tell Mikhail?"

Mikhail's sharp eyes meet mine. "Tell me what?"

Aleks begins to chuckle and I grin, taking the ultrasound picture out of my bag. "We have news, everyone. It appears...." I hold the picture up and point. "We're about to have *twins*."

THE END

BONUS EPILOGUE

Can't get enough of Aleksandr & Harper? Scan the QR Code below to get a FREE bonus epilogue to "Sanctum: A Dark Brava Arranged Marriage Romance"!

PREVIEW

SEDUCTION: A DARK BRATVA FAKE MARRIAGE ROMANCE

Chapter One

Nikko

My footsteps pound on the pavement like the relentless beating of a drum. My lungs feel like they're going to burst. My legs ache. I barely notice the rush of cherry blossoms past me or the pedestrians by the park, I'm so blinded by the sweat in my eyes. I push myself harder, faster, *longer*. It's a mind game, a mind fuck.

Everything is.

I turn the left corner between Maple and Tower street and see my destination in front of me. I'm so far away it's merely a blur, but as long as I can see what's in front of me clearly, I can keep going.

My mentor Kolya told me that training — *all* training — should be faced as if your life was on the line. Nothing's in vain. You're not running for the sake of a healthy heart or stronger lungs, you're running from an enemy who's going to slit your throat when he catches you.

So when I finally arrive at Mikhail and Aria's house, I come to a stop, elbows to knees, heaving with the effort of breathing. I barely feel the brush of wind past me, the promise of stagnant summer heat later. After a few moments of heavy breathing, I start to come to.

I notice cars outside — Aleks and Harper are here, likely with their small crew of kids. Mom's car's here, but no Polina. Viktor. Lev.

Frowning, I take out my phone and look down. I never miss a call or text, and today's no different. Nothing missed. Then why's everyone here?

I run my arm across my sweaty brow to clear my vision and trot up the stairs.

"There he is." Mikhail jerks his head in greeting at me as he walks past the doorway, his one-year-old son Sasha in his arms. It's fitting as *pakhan* to the Romanov family and older brother to all, Mikhail had the first child. It was time.

My brother Aleksandr holds his infant son beside his wife Harper who's holding the second twin. Both babies have their daddy's bright blue eyes and mama's honey-blonde hair. I turn to the sound of a child's laugh to see my mom walking toward the dining room hand-in-hand with Harper's toddler Ivy.

Our family's growing in leaps and bounds as Mikhail and Aria's baby just turned one, and Aleksandr and his wife just had baby twins. With Harper's toddler completing the ensemble, my mother is in her absolute glory with four grandchildren. I haven't seen her this happen in years.

It had to happen. If we're going to establish ourselves as the premier Bratva group in the Cove, the area of New York nestled between Coney Island and Manhattan, the stomping grounds we own and operate, we had to grow our numbers by recruiting and expanding.

"Where've you been?" Mikhail snaps.

I gesture down to the sleeveless workout tee clinging to body slicked with sweat, my running shorts, and my running shoes. "Thought I'd try out my suit for the gala. Prepare for the Paparazzi and all that."

"He's swimming in sweat from head to toe," Harper responds. "I can smell him from here. Either he's just come in from a run or no one's told us the zombie apocalypse is upon us."

Aleksandr chuckles from behind him, shaking his head. "Nikko *always* goes for a run on Sunday at noon, Mikhail. You know that. Monday through Friday you can set a clock by his five a.m. workouts but he takes a break on Sunday and only goes for a run."

"That's why I pay you to keep track of this sh—stuff," Mikhail says, scowling. The presence of children slows his roll. I'd bet he misses the days he could curse on a whim.

I walk past both of them and head to the kitchen. "Did I miss something? Why's everyone here?"

The two of them exchange a look as I grab a bottle of water. Mikhail nods. "Yeah. We have an urgent matter to discuss, but we wanted to wait until it was in person. Just us."

In other words, they waited for my mother to come so she could watch the kids, most likely. None of the nannies work Sundays.

Interesting.

I reach into the fridge and grab a pre-made protein shake. Twist the cap off, down half of it in a few gulps. "What is it?"

Mikhail frowns. "We've discovered a connection between the attempt at poisoning Harper and the attack on Lev."

I stand up straighter. Instantly alert. The type of retribution demanded by this type of situation will fall squarely on my shoulders.

When someone needs to die, you call me.

Seven minutes later, I'm freshly showered and dressed, sitting on Mikhail's balcony that overlooks the ocean. Aleks sits on my left and my younger brother Viktor to my right, nursing a cup of coffee. Mikhail's on his way because he had to consult with his wife Aria, our head hacker and cybersecurity pro.

"Aleks, what's going on?" I ask.

Aleksandr, who works alongside Aria, broods, looking over the Manhattan skyline visible from Mikhail's balcony.

He shakes his head. "Wait for Mikhail. We all need to be present."

Viktor, silent and hulking, sits brooding. Our group heavy, hulking, tattooed, and typically dressed in leather, sometimes his mere presence is enough to ward off enemies. And if it isn't, he's willing and able to get shit done.

Lev, however, gets to his feet and begins to pace. Our youngest brother by several years, Lev is a trained fighter and our team strategist. With his athletic build, he's the one we send in to maneuver through tricky situations and defend himself if needed. Confident, with a magnetic presence that women everywhere swoon over, Lev doesn't ever get romantically entangled. He's too occupied with other things.

"Ollie joining us?" Lev asks, his jaw tight.

"Remotely."

Jesus. It's been over a year since Mikhail and Aria had their son Sasha and our brother Ollie's been stationed in Moscow. He came home for Sasha's baptism, then went straight back to Moscow.

"When's he coming home?"

Aleks shakes his head, a muscle twitching in his jaw. "Don't know."

"We're stronger when we're together," I say, shaking my head.

"While that might be true," Mikhail says from the balcony doorway as he comes out to meet us, "In this case, it might not be."

What does that mean?

Mikhail slides the balcony door shut firmly behind him. I watch him curiously. The balcony at his home may be the easiest place to get to that blocks out all sound from any other floor or person. There's no interference. Whatever he needs to tell us is big.

"Aria and Aleks together unlocked some prime intel," Mikhail says, walking past the chairs and toward the edge of the balcony. He leans against the wrought iron fence and crosses his arm on his chest. Deep-set dark brown eyes beneath heavy brows, golden, tanned skin, and dark brown hair tinged with flecks of gold make him look almost godlike. He's a bit more civilized than the rest of us but they still call him the Siberian tiger.

"You know we've been on the trail of those who attacked us for some time now. You know we've narrowed it down to rival Bratva and a few subsidiary groups as well. In recent weeks, Aria's discovered that the subsidiaries weren't actually behind any attacks on us but funded by the larger groups." His tone grows sober when his eyes harden. Mikhail is known as the Siberian tiger for a reason.

"Brothers," he says, ensuring he has whatever residual attention he may not have fully had beforehand. "We have names."

Unlike a lot of other rival groups in New York, ours is one of the only not related by blood. Like other Russian factions before us, our father decided he would ensure allegiance by adopting all of us. But blood isn't what bonds us all together.

Loyalty. Honor. Trust. The ties of familial bonds run deep despite the way our family was born.

When Mikhail calls us by name, it's like a call to arms. A summoning. A flare that lights the night sky calling all of us to action. Any one of us would lay down his life for the other, a claim some of our rivals could never make.

"Names," Lev says, his jaw tightening. Recent years have hardened the softer features of his younger face. He was the one who suffered an all-out attack and a beating that left him hospitalized shortly after Mikhail was made *pakhan* in the wake of our father's death. He was the one outnumbered and left for dead outside a nightclub.

Mikhail straightens. While Lev was personally attacked, Mikhail's wife was nearly poisoned to death. "Ivanov. Petr Ivanov."

"Son of a bitch," Lev says under his breath, shaking his head. "After all we did for him."

"Right."

When my father was still here and we were a fledgling group, we ran surveillance for Ivanov at our own risk for what was a pittance in hindsight.

"He doesn't care. He knows we own The Cove and he wants in." Mikhail shakes his head, no further explanation needed. They all do.

After my father's death, we took down our greatest rival, Fyodor Volkov. But after his death, other groups vied for power and attention in the coveted Cove. Our location gives us prime access to several major ports and airports.

Ivanov.

A chill runs through me at the knowledge that we have a target. This is *my* area of expertise. I stand and straighten my shoulders. "Tell me everything."

Mikhail shakes his head.

"Problem with the Ivanov's is that Petr is untouchable. He's invested more time and money in his own protection than most invest in their entire family. Classic, textbook narcissist. So he's surrounded by an army of monsters who will stop at nothing to keep him safe."

I snort. "Like I fucking care. Give me a sniper rifle and a sight and I'll take him down no matter the protection he's put around him. I don't care if he lives in a fucking protection so impervious he's practically in another dimension. You know I will."

Mikhail nods. "I know you will, but it isn't worth the risk and Kolya and I have been consulted. We have what we believe to be a better plan."

"Mikhail. Better plan? Better than sending me to take him out once and for all?"

"Sit down, Nikko," Mikhail says calmly. "I'd bet my fucking life on you exacting revenge. But then what? It's more complicated than that. What if his was only the beginning of a much larger plan to take us down? What if he acts as the lackey for another man in a position of power? What if the assassination of Petr Ivanov is the first domino we strike down, only to start something too big for us to handle? We do need to take Ivanov out, but we have to have a crystal clear strategy before we do." "

He has a point. I cross my arms on my chest and listen and finally give a reluctant nod. "Go on."

"And I have more details that will help us form our plan." Kolya's voice comes from behind me. I turn to see him entering the balcony. Ten years our senior, he was one of my father's best friends in the military. He became an older brother to us, a mentor, trained us in hand to hand combat and so much more. While Mikhail has become the patriarch of our family, Kolya will forever be our advisor.

We're all ears.

"Ivanov has two daughters. One is engaged to be married to a high-ranking captain of the *Ledyanoye Bratstvo*."

A shadow passes over Lev'e features but it passes so quickly I wonder if I've imagined it. Does he know more about them than he's letting on?

"But his younger daughter, Vera Ivanov, is single. Brilliant. And stunning."

Mikhail's eyes are fixed on me as he continues where Kolya left off.

"Vera Ivanov's been selected to join a prestigious graduate student program for gifted medical students in Moscow. Thanks to my wife's impeccable research, I have it on good authority that he cares more about his reputation than he does his actual family. He hasn't shared a bed with his wife in twenty years and has a different mistress in every major city in Russia. He has nothing to do with his daughters, but treats his son as if he were the next coming of Christ."

Classic. I roll my eyes but nod.

"His wife, Zofia Ivanova, has insisted her daughter bring a bodyguard to Moscow. His wife also despises her husband's homeland and disallowed her daughter to learn the language, which puts her at a disadvantage."

"Ahh," Viktor says, his deep rumble of a voice getting all our attention since he rarely speaks during meetings. Or, honestly, at all. "I see where you're going with this."

I think I see, too, but I want to hear Mikhail explicitly state what he's thinking. I'm slow to make decisions, and I don't ever jump to conclusions.

Mihail nods. "No one's ever met this new bodyguard. Vera has no idea what he looks like, and Vera's father won't be anywhere near her...at least at first. And we only need a few weeks."

"I could go," Viktor says. "I could pretend to be her bodyguard—"

Mikhail nods. "You will go, Viktor. You'll take out the current bodyguard." Mikhail's eyes ice over. "We happen to know for a fact that the man her father's hired as bodyguard was only hired as a favor to his Moscow Mistress. He's been convicted on charges of child abuse and ownership of child pornography, and only released because of his connection to Ivanov." Mikhail scowls. "I want you to know who you're dealing with before you end him, Viktor." He leans forward. "Be silent. Be decided. We'll due away with his body so there's no evidence. But for the love of Christ, make it fucking hurt."

Viktor is someone we easily rely on but he does better work when he has a clear motive. He has no qualms about taking the life of an enemy but considers it an act of justice to do away with someone whose actions he considers heinous and reprehensible.

Fuck. He's chosen Viktor instead of me, for whatever reason. If he—

Mikhail turns to me. "Nikko. You'll go with him."

It takes me a second to register what he just said. "Me?"

Mikhail nods. "You most closely match the profile of the man hired to protect her. With a few small tweaks, you'd pass for him at a distance. The others would stand out too much." Mikhail holds my gaze. "Listen carefully. Your job is to pretend to be her bodyguard. Get close to her, Nikko. Find out everything you can about her father and his operation. And only when the time is right," he pauses, his words weighing heavily as he lays out my job. "You'll end him."

I nod. I'll accept this responsibility. It's the only choice I have, and even if I had another, this is the one that I'd choose. I'm dedicated to protecting the life of my family, no matter the cost.

"You said she speaks no Russian," I say thoughtfully, tapping my chin. "Should make things interesting since *I* don't speak any English."

Lev snorts, Aleks grins at me, and even Kolya cracks a reluctant smile. "That will absolutely make it easier for you to gather intel," Kolya admits, with a shrug. "To a degree."

"When do I leave?"

Aleks pulls out an iPad and pulls out what looks like an itinerary. "This is Vera Ivanov's schedule. Aria's set a drone in place to map her for a few days so you can get an idea of her habits, how she operates, where she goes and what she does. I've tapped into her mobile and online browsing as well." He shakes his head. "I'm telling you, Mikhail, the fact that Aria and I run cybersecurity for you guys puts you head and shoulders above everyone. They don't even have biometric sensors or quantum encryption GPS trackers in place." He shakes his head and curses in Russian, obviously disgusted.

I have no idea what the fuck a quantum encryption GPS tracker is, and only the vaguest idea that the biometric sensors monitor our health and location remotely, but I take his word for it that it's important and maybe even necessary.

"Her father's set it up so that her new bodyguard will accompany her from America to Moscow. They're scheduled to meet in three days at the airport. She'll fly from there to Moscow. And you, Vera's bodyguard, will go with her. It doesn't matter if anyone else sees you since no one else has met the real bodyguard. The only person who can't see you is her father's mistress, but those chances are slim and none." He jerks his chin at Viktor. "And thanks to Viktor, no one will notice he's gone. He'll be given a burner phone to communicate with the rest of the Ivanov team as well."

I've never had such a mammoth task before me. An assassination is a clear instruction, something easy to accomplish with the right tools. This is something entirely different — an assassination with a twist, one might say.

"Perfect." I love a challenge.

"Here," Aleks says, taking a file out of his laptop bag and handing it to me. "This is everything we've complied for Vera Ivanov for you to familiarize yourself with her before you go in."

I open the file and school my features so I don't give away my shock at seeing her. Delicate features framed by long, chestnut hair cascades in loose waves around her shoulders.

Emerald-green eyes highlighted with long, thick lashes display intelligence and curiosity, but the slight upturn of her little nose hints at mischief. A smattering of freckles across her nose adds to her wholesome appeal. Despite her slender frame, there's a quiet strength in her posture and movements, hinting at hidden reserves of determination.

I stare at the portrait of the most beautiful woman I've ever laid eyes on and can't have.

Kolya looks over my shoulder as I continue to read the specs. "You've been trained for this, Nikko. Pretend she's poison. Tell yourself that if you touch her you turn to stone."

Mikhail grows cold. "Tell yourself that if you touch her you'll die."

Or, stay completely detached. Made of stone. Impermeable.

Stay focused on my job, because I have an obligation to kill her father.

Order your copy of 'Seduction: A Dark Bratva Fake Marriage Romance" by scanning the QR code below:

Fueled by dark chocolate and even darker coffee, USA Today bestselling author Jane Henry writes what she loves to read – character-driven, unputdownable romance featuring dominant alpha males and the powerful heroines who bring them to their knees. She's believed in the power of love and romance since Belle won over the beast, and finally decided to write love stories of her own.

Scan the QR Code below to receive Jane's Newsletter & be notified of upcoming new releases & special offers!

Be sure to visit me at www.janehenryromance.com, too!